For Arthur,

RUNNING DEEP

G. B. Strong

E L F
Books Ltd

RUNNING DEEP

ISBN 978-1-9993297-0-9

First Edition (Revised)

Published in Great Britain 2019 by
Elf Books Ltd,

International House, 12 Constance Street, Silvertown, London E16 2DQ

Printed in Great Britain by
CPI Group (UK) Ltd,
Croydon, CR0 4YY

www.elfbooksltd.com

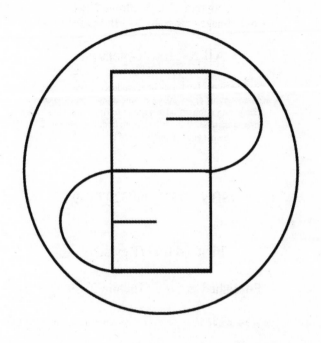

SIMUL AUTEM SOLUS

To the family,

For those that have been and will become,
And for its life now.

CHAPTER 1

AN INTRUSIVE SIGHT

Flashes of light sliced through Eddie's squinting eyes as he lay there on his back, in pain and feeling hazy. He lifted his head slowly and queasily up from under the leafy low branches of a large oak tree. The flickering sun was messing with his senses and the fresh grass trimmings decorating his freckled face weren't helping either. Eddie blew out his cheeks, trying to get a grip of himself.

The tall, athletic figure of Eddie's best mate approaching was enough to send the two boys standing over Eddie sniggering away.

'Aren't new kids supposed to be on the receiving end of this sort of thing? They act like they own the place,' Simon moaned.

'Tell me about it,' grumbled Eddie as he accepted Simon's hand up, 'they only started a few weeks ago and they've already wound up half the school.'

It was a warm, early summer lunchtime at Mildham School and the field was awash, as usual, with an army of tomorrow's footballing legends, all playing in small battalions with *Major* attitude and *General* fooling around. Eddie Freeman had just been pranked by a devious set of twins who had only joined the school a few weeks ago. The irritatingly cocksure Stratton brothers were, once again, taking joy in others' suffering. The slightly smaller of the two, Sam, had distracted Eddie from his kickabout with a line about some made up party invitation while the other twin, Ben, had crept up unseen and crouched

1

on all fours right behind. Sam's whispered punchline plea to Eddie, *'don't tell Ben 'cos it's a…'* was followed by a loud yell of *'…SURPRISE!'* and a double-handed shove through the chest. Eddie had been launched off his feet and helplessly watched his smaller than average legs fly over his head, high into the air above him.

His fall seemed to last forever. It ended with a sickening sensation as the back of his head met the ground with a heavy thud. He lay there, under the thick swaying limbs of Puff, a well-loved but solitary and oddly placed oak tree. Simon had jogged over from his nearby goalmouth and pulled Eddie up off the ground.

'If only they stuck to showing off their talents on the pitch, they might stand a chance of being remotely likable,' Simon sighed.

'You know what Simon…' Eddie said, beginning to hear and see straight again, 'You're right. We could be on for a great season with our players next year.'

'Yeah, they might act like idiots…' replied Simon, eyeing the twins as they circled round their next victim, '…but Sam and Ben are annoyingly *good* when it comes to footy!'

Eddie, still rubbing the back of his head, begrudgingly agreed.

'If Mr. Wernham puts us in the district tournament this year we could finally be the tough team in the competition,' Simon continued.

'Instead of the cannon fodder,' chuckled Eddie.

'Are you going to actually stay switched on for a whole game this season mate?' Simon teased his shabby haired friend.

'Your daydreaming is gonna get you dropped, or drop-kicked, one of these days.'

Simon had a point. Eddie was regularly detaching from reality into a world of his own. As if to make the point, Simon's harmless joke had already triggered him off. The

2

football on the field transformed into the dying moments of an end of season final, complete with commentary.

'Eddie Freeman has Mildham's fate in the palm of his hand... There're just seconds remaining here in the regional schools' cup final and the young striking sensation is lining up for one of his trademark free kicks. He runs up…and shoots! It swings high around the wall…it's dipping…it's dipping…!'

As his thrilling thoughts entertained him, every other students' head turned, in domino effect, towards an unexpected distraction down at the far end of the school field. The breaktime bustle had been frozen by the appearance of an unnerving and rapidly accelerating intruder, blazing a fast and frightening trail up the field…

--

With Eddie, missing great chunks of reality was nothing new; his daydreaming had started young. He remembered being four and hearing a pack of hounds howling out of a backstreet, chasing towards him while on a family holiday. In reality, it was just the one wolf, well, more of an over-excited retriever really. Nevertheless, Eddie felt forced to talk it out of attacking him by adopting the language of woof. He would adopt this simple dog language whenever he needed to befriend stray or wild canine. Eddie thought it weird though and could not work out how he'd ended safely up on his dad's shoulders when the commotion settled.

--

… This lunchtime, the disturbance unseen by Eddie was a striking and curious man, looking well out of place amongst

3

the students of Mildham. Dressed in a dark and well-tailored suit, he appeared daringly scaling the school's rail-wired fence before springing, cat-like and charging towards the main building. Naturally, this had drawn a large audience, including some of the staff.

'Excuse me!' shrieked "Pencil" Andrews, reacting to the disturbance. Mildham's headmistress was so-called because of her amazingly tiny frame and her famous decree; that *"all children should not touch a pen until their handwriting is faultless"*.

'Where do you think you're going?' she demanded.

The man sped fiercely on, silent and unwavering. With a mixture of intrigue and mild panic, everyone's eyes tracked the high-speed trespasser. Everyone's that is, except Eddie's...

--

Looking back, Eddie always thought his daydreaming was partly a by-product of the dull and uneventful world of Mildham School. For example, at six, in his first year, Eddie sat with the rest of his school in the main hall. They were watching an educational show featuring the bulls, matadors and unique culture of Madrid, Spain.

Suddenly, the action burst out of the screen and rows of onlookers watched in horror as a raging, black beast bounded out from the screen and onto the stage. It hurtled past Mrs. Andrews, thumping her chair and sending it skywards. The old girl always seemed like a bird on a perch, wherever she sat, as if she was constantly expecting some bizarre kind of incident to happen. She flew half way up one of the red curtains that hung either side of the old wooden stage. Despite her minute weight, the old worn felt started to rip, lowering her agonizingly down into the gaze of the rampant bull. While the hall held its breath as the bull's roar rang out, Eddie answered the call.

He bravely leaped forward from the front row and grabbed the torn cloth from Mrs. Andrews' quivering hand. Waving the red rag, Eddie lured the angry animal and raced for the fire exit. With the bull charging, a befuddled matador got caught up in the middle, adding to the fast-moving mayhem. Three blurred shapes crashed through the doors, all at full gallop. Eddie scrambled clear and slid to a halt on his back. Above him, he saw the image of the mighty bull leaping away in rage with the puny matador back to front and face down on the bull's hindquarters. With each bounding stride, he yelped as his face juddered against the pounding beast's rear end.

They tore off together away from the school, bursting through hedges and smashing into a line of bins along the street, spraying a trail of destruction in their wake.

Back inside, as more parts of the school crumbled, the debris raining down on Eddie had forced his full and bulging eyes to clamp shut.

When the noise of screaming children and shattered glass faded, Eddie slowly squinted out. The scene of carnage that he expected had become instead, a silent sea of students, all staring at him. He lay confused and helpless on his back. Eddie noticed Simon who was looking down at him from the bench he had fallen off, shrugging his shoulders in puzzlement. 'What was it this time?' he asked, in a sort of laughing yet understanding voice. Simon was the only person at Mildham School who could keep pace and interest with Eddie's wonderful, funderful, utterly wild world.

--

…'You're not permitted on school property!' shrieked Mrs. Andrews, with concerned authority.

The man showed no interest in her words and accelerated to an incredible speed. Instead of getting help and to everyone's surprise, Mrs. Andrews stiffened her petite and delicate frame and took off after the uninvited guest. Her pace and power were even more exhilarating to watch than the intruder's!

The football playing out in Eddie's head had reached its happy ending. He left the fantasy, looked at the scene in front of him and immediately fell into another; his happy eyes glazed over. He pictured a sleek and agile black panther being efficiently tracked by an elegant and lightning-footed antelope. Andrews and the man, in their weirdly reversed roles, chased through the open double doors of the school's main building and out of view...

--

Around his eighth birthday, Eddie's creative imagination took on a new dimension. Far more powerful and stirring sensations took over his whole being. For the first time, he was propelled into the air by a force beyond his imagination. He had dreamt about flying many times, making run after run over his school, controlling each turn and classroom fly-by but this was different.

His mind felt out of control and unpredictable. He felt vulnerable, rapidly shooting up, then back down. Eddie was lurching all over the place; spiralling and looping like some kind of stunt kite. Not being in command of his thoughts was unnerving and unlike the daydreams he was used to. Worse still was that the sensation became an ever more familiar, though never welcomed, occurrence.

--

Recently, he had also started to notice the behaviour of the people around him. Perhaps it was his age, or maybe he had just never thought about it. Either way, the actions of those he'd known for years had suddenly become completely bizarre.

Mrs. Andrews, for example, had a caring face and slight features that gave her the appearance of someone who wasn't naturally suited to being in charge. Now however, she was strung like a tightly coiled spring. She seemed to have become more like a sentry guard on lookout duty. It was hard to tell what she was expecting or why, but something had changed in her.

Then there was Mr. Wernham. Although he was a rather over-confident PE teacher (some would say delusional), he always had the students' interests at heart. Not any longer. He had become unreasonable and seemed to dislike the concept of teaching sports at all, other than to compete and win at almost any cost. No one dared argue with the barrel-built lump.

Anyway, things were about to get far more abnormal for Eddie. His out of control visions and sensations were about to transform into something altogether more significant.

The onlookers on the field had lost sight of the man and Mrs. Andrews but Eddie was about to experience the chase, first hand. His view had inexplicably changed as he stood fixated under the tree. Without explanation, he was now using, or at least seeing through, Mrs. Andrews' very eyes! His own eyes gave a distant glaze and stared emptily across the field.

Simon had noticed that Eddie was not joining the stampede towards the school building. Instead, he remained on the field, casting a bizarre shadowy figure under the span of

Puff's canopy. Simon ran over to snap his short and vacant friend out of his daze.

'What's up with you mate? Come on, something's going on up there,' he yelled, with his face almost pressed up against Eddie's.

'Why are you just standing there?' he questioned, disbelievingly.

Eddie remained motionless in his trance. He was gripped by his inner sight which had left his face and body looking like an upright corpse. Simon's concern grew.

'Eddie?' he begged.

Eddie's stillness was made more distressing by the way his eyes were shifting. They pulsed and twitched all over the place.

Inside, out of the view of the rest of the school, Eddie witnessed Mrs. Andrews' version of the chase. Through the twists and turns of the school hallways, it became obvious that the man knew his way around. He flashed past the school office and down a corridor, but Eddie's view suddenly became dark, then was lost, just at the entrance of his own classroom door.

The blackness lasted for a second then was attacked by a bright blinding flash. Eddie fought to regain his supernatural sight and as he did, he found the suited man had now completely lost it; screaming in all directions and throwing himself wildly around in a strange and windowless room. The faint image of panicked people, thrashing around at unhuman speed, made it impossible for Eddie to work out where he was or what he was looking at.

A large screen and many smaller screens displayed around the room were cutting off from their covert transmissions. With the room in chaos, the intruder turned and charged towards Mrs. Andrews. His face grew large and clear in Eddie's sight. Then, blackness again.

Outside, the school field emptied and began converging on the door that the man and Mrs. Andrews had run through. The other staff blocked off the entrance and called an emergency fire drill to restore order.

'Eddie, snap out of it!' exclaimed Simon, in growing desperation.

Eddie remained unmoved, except for his eyes still chasing around in their sockets. Then at last, with a great gasp, he came round.

'What's going on? What happened?' Eddie babbled.

'Oh good, you're back. Fleas in flippers, Eddie! You had me worried there!' said Simon.

It took Eddie quite a while to regain his bearings, this had been no ordinary daydream. His surroundings returned to normality and though his traumatic expression remained, he at least convinced Simon he was ok, blearily nodding whilst rubbing his eyes.

Everyone seemed to be in a manic state of fear and excitement. Eddie, recalling the event, leapt into life and followed Simon, back towards the school.

'I saw it!' exclaimed Eddie.

'Saw what?' asked Simon.

'Mrs. Andrews! She was after that bloke,' replied Eddie. 'I could see this room, it was like a secret bunker, underground…like some kind of observatory with workers. It's all under the school somewhere.'

'What?' Simon froze with nervous curiosity but Eddie was too caught up to notice his panicked reaction.

'It was so weird, like a bunch of flashing images. It was hard to work out what was happening.' Eddie thought that he'd probably already said too much.

Although Simon was a trusted friend, there's only so much he would believe. Eddie couldn't be certain what or how much he'd seen. One thing was for sure though; this hadn't been imagined. This was real...very real.

He wondered how he'd seen the chase in the school so vividly. What power had transported his vision?

He wanted to help but didn't know who or what he was dealing with. There must be a reason he had seen the event and decided, one way or another, to find out more about Mrs. Andrews and this mysterious underground room.

CHAPTER 2

AN AIR OF CHANGE

The staff seemed to sweep the event quickly away and the regular dull routine of school soon returned. But in the grey and boring hallways, fantastic fabrications about what happened *that* day were fanning their way around. Spreading through the stifling and sticky classrooms of Mildham, from a jail breaker to the new janitor, the rumours over the intruder's identity burned wild.

The punchy engine of a busy tractor mower tugged Eddie's focus from his lesson as he sat slumped over his desk in the afternoon heat. The boiling red faces around him sat in their sweltering classroom, with sleeves rolled up and ties dropped low, struggling to stay alert enough to learn.

The scent from the grass-spraying mower blades wafting in through half-opened windows beckoned his attention and a new story played out in his mind. The tractor swung sharply round and returned towards the school building, Eddie spotted the driver standing up on the seat with one leg forward like someone about to leap from the back of a horse.

Mrs. Andrews, in full cowgirl gear, circled her lasso high around her head. She was rounding up a herd of fully dressed cows! The cattle, comically clothed in suits complete with shirt and ties (identical to the intruder's), were driven through an open gate into their paddock.

Mrs. Andrews gave a 'yippee ki-ay!' and jumped from her steed onto the back of a steel-barred gate. Her agile landing helped swing the gate shut with a clonk. The coolly dressed cattle shuffled and mooed with dissatisfaction at being crammed in their corral.

Waltzing up towards the school, Andrews' image blurred behind the kicked-up dust from the moaning bovine. Eddie strained to see and leant forward against the window. His daydream ended abruptly with a horrible sick feeling; a result of his overly inquisitive nose smashing hard on the window.

With Noddy the groundsman now in his rightful position, whistling cheerfully as he peeled away onboard the tractor, Eddie detected Andrews staring right at him through the window; a little too close and curiously for his liking. Her pointed finger and forceful gaze told Eddie to get back to his work.

Along with her nervy and odd ways, the headmistress had started to develop an unhealthy interest in Eddie's whereabouts. He had wanted to get closer to her but she strangely seemed to be doing the job for him, though not in a way that made her at all approachable. She looked stiff, almost confronting. Her gentle face scowled whenever Eddie caught her looking his way, as if she was aware, somehow, that he had seen things he shouldn't have.

Eddie also noticed that Andrews spent a lot of time lingering in the cove behind his classroom door. She hid where the coats were usually hung, right by where she had flashed into that dark and mysterious room.

Watching slyly, Eddie wondered how he had never noticed her coming down the corridor behind those coat hooks. Where else could she have come from? She was stalking him in the school's hallways too, making a poor attempt to disguise it by pretending to look at the old curled and crumbling displays on the wall. Why didn't she just stay in her office, with her strange shelves packed with models of flying objects and animals?

Her quick and sharp movements and her strange behaviour caused Eddie's mind to wander. She was following him constantly and when she did, she wasn't subtle. She'd march through a congested passage, cutting through the students, in Eddie's mind like a martial arts fighter on fast forward. Children's bags, books and belongings were sent flying, some sliced, some chopped but all sent skywards in a frenzy of fist and foot power.

Eddie wondered more and more about what was going on and why. And there was something else bugging him too. As far as he could remember, Mrs. Andrews had been on the scene of almost every imaginative episode he'd ever had in school. Certainly, any that had involved flying; those that had taken him into an uncontrolled and unnerving world.

Come to think of it, Simon was different now as well, protective and parent-like.

Eddie being the shortest kid in his year meant he had fallen on the wrong side of much of the banter in school. His bizarre performances while daydreaming, added to their comedy. But where Simon had used to laugh or even join in with the jokes, he would rip into anyone who became *too* interested with him, especially those who tried to befriend him. He would quietly talk to Eddie, giving all kinds of bogus reasons why they wouldn't be good as friends. It was as if Simon was trying to keep him apart from the others at school.

Eddie's head pictured Simon as a human helicopter, hovering and intercepting would-be friends, buzzing them threateningly as they approached. He was lots taller than Eddie and the shock of inherited, pale blond hair made him stand out. Eddie and he had shared so much over the years. Simon's misty blue eyes would sharpen and glaze every time Eddie waxed about the goings-on in the far-off world inside

13

his head. Why now, had he appeared so possessive of him? He was a little eccentric at times, spending hours away in his room, developing robotic toys and gadgets, but there wasn't a jealous bone in his body. So, the last few days of summer term passed with Eddie still waiting for answers.

The boys always made their way to and from school together. They'd been friends since Eddie had moved to the area and he would wait at the end of his road before school for Simon to come. He never needed to wait long. On their walks to and from school, Eddie and Simon found they could ponder life, out of the earshot of others.

They played a type of catching game called *Crow* with Simon's trusty old black rubber ball. Conditions were set by the thrower for how the ball should be caught. Different parts of the body had to be used as well as sounds. It was all the more fun, or embarrassing, when passing others on the pavement.

They walked now, *crowing* the ball off garden walls a few days from the end of term still wondering about *that day*…

'It's been weeks now, Eddie. Have you seen anything else?' quizzed Simon.

The question came up a lot.

'I've told you enough times Simon, no! It's not like I can control it,' replied Eddie, abruptly.

'Like a reared-up raccoon!' he shouted, throwing the ball hard at his friend.

With his arms outstretched and voice yelping, the ball stung into Simon's legs. Still, he managed to cleverly wedge it between them. 'Bears in bandanas, Eddie, I only asked!'

'Sorry, mate. It's just that the final part of it was so strange. I wish I could have seen more.'

'Me too,' tailed off Simon.

Eddie decided to change the subject.

'How about I come 'round yours after school? We can check out your dad's machines, plus I bet your mum misses her chief taste tester.'

Simon knew exactly what he meant. Eddie had computers and devices of his own, but his love of Simon's dad's tech gear and his mum's baking meant Eddie had sort of made a habit of inviting himself round. 'OK but first, how about a whimpering wolf?' he demanded. Eddie pathetically obliged.

The Bird's home always carried a smell of warm and delicious treats. Stealing a snack from Simon's lunch box had been a breaktime tradition for years. In fact, it was partly how they had made friends.

The Bird Cage sat squeezed in the middle of a terrace of three cottages, on the edge of town. It backed on to woods and wide-open fields. Although the walk from Eddie's to Simon's was not far, it was a charming change of scenery, often in more ways than one. Simon's mum and dad had always been pretty predictable. His mum was always getting on at home working and his dad was always working on getting home.

A chirpy little girl excitedly greeted them as they entered through a back gate that swung open with a piercing screech. Simon's outgoing little sister, Sarah, had been sitting on the stone wall at the back of the house. Behind her, in the back garden, the swing set was still swaying. Her skipping rope and hula hoop were resting on her lap. Sarah enjoyed her own company but her brother and especially his friend were always fun to be around.

'Hey, mums got one for you too,' she called as she waved the stick of a large, half-eaten ice-lolly. It had left her lips and whole mouth intensely red.

'There's only one, so you'll have to share,' she said, trying to be funny.

Simon dismissed her with an unimpressed look. Eddie said nothing. He had immediately lost himself, imagining Sarah, with her comically coloured lips, as a circus performer; the type that dresses as a clown but has the skills of an acrobat. With a bright oversized smile, she performed outrageous tricks all over the garden. Looping 360 degrees on her swing like it was a trapeze and flipping through the air onto her trampoline where the show continued with acrobatic twists and tumbles. Eddie watched in amazement. Sarah performed an astounding routine; balancing along the fence, vaulting over a hedge and somersaulting through the air before sticking her landing inches from the boys.

'Aren't you going to say hello?' she chirped.

'Hello, Sarah,' Simon muttered, brushing by.

Eddie, staring through her with a distant grin, whispered a musical 'Ta-da!' and trailed in after his mate. Sarah shook her head though not to be put off, cracked a satisfied smile of her own and went happily back to her lolly.

Inside, Eddie's senses lit up at the aroma in the kitchen.

'Ah, my mum never makes that anymore!' he exclaimed, his eyes fixed on the jam roly-poly cooling on a rack by the oven.

'And hello to you too Eddie,' Mrs. Bird responded.

'It's bad enough that I have to beg Simon and Sarah to save any for their father… anyway, how was school?' The boys glanced at each other knowingly. They had pledged to keep the events of *that day* to themselves.

'Same old thing mum,' Simon said as he quickly walked down to the hallway, towards the cellar door, trying to avoid a deeper conversation.

'Save me some, Mrs. B,' pleaded Eddie, craning his neck at the steaming dessert, as he followed Simon out of the kitchen. 'Oh, alright. I'll wrap you a slice to take home, Eddie,' obliged Mrs. Bird. She made her way around the red brick tiled floor of the kitchen like she was dancing a foxtrot, gliding through each task. The room was the Bird's mothership, Mrs. Bird was the helm. Everything in it functioned seamlessly.

The boys tapped down the old concrete steps that lead to the only room in the house that really mattered. Mr. Bird, a self-confessed technology freak, owned all kinds of hi-tech hardware. He worked, although Eddie wasn't sure for whom, developing bits and pieces designed to make human life more convenient. The cellar was a squeeze of shelves, drawers and boxes spilled over with all kinds of techno clobber. From a robot's switchable arm to projector bulbs the size of a pinhead, Mr. Bird had an accessory for any gadget. What the boys loved most though, was stuff that could fly. From a young age, Simon had been taught about the ways and workings of drones and had seen them evolve from a hobbyist's plaything, to being part of everyday life. Although robots had transformed the home in many ways, large commercial drones had utterly revolutionized transportation.

'Woah dad, that's the *Acculander*!'

'The very same,' Mr. Bird replied, smiling smugly in the boys' direction.

'Crows in coats, how did you get it?' interrogated Simon, his voice elevating with pulsating delight.

'What's an *Acculander*?' asked Eddie, confused over Simon's overreaction to what looked like an ordinary, though sleekly designed drone.

'It's *the* drone Eddie, you daft wally!' retorted Simon. 'It's one of the quickest long-range drones you can get. It can reach destinations hundreds of miles away by remote coordinate entry. They land within six inches of any target.'

'Great if you've forgotten your shorts for the beach,' joked Mr. Bird. 'Not only that, Simon,' he added, 'along with the lightweight power cell, this one is being fitted with my W*ingreacher*. Look, it slots underneath and works to harness wind power.'

Mr. Bird showed them the blade fitted underneath the machine, then with a click it deployed, shooting down like vertical wing. The self-adjusting foils twitched; searching for a gust to latch onto.

'If I've designed it right, the wind should maximise this unit's flight speed and range.'

'It must be worth thousands,' declared Simon.

'Yes, I'm not sure your savings will stretch for one yet, son,' laughed his dad.

Eddie lost himself in a slow-motion world of money and self-propelling drones. The sound of soft flowing music echoed as he walked through his estate. Passing overhead on his way, the coolest craft were being raced at high speeds around his own impressively built course. He casually sauntered over towards his huge swimming pool, where hundreds of jam roly-polys were cascading down a curving slide and into a warm pool of creamy custard. Money rained down in its thousands, having been dropped from a flashing, jewel-encrusted squadron of *Acculanders*.

'Don't get too carried away,' interrupted Mr. Bird, almost instinctively knowing where Eddie had been. 'I'm developing it for a client.'

'Who is it?' asked the boys at the same time.

'Ah, that is one question too many, lads,' responded Mr. Bird, killing the moment. 'Now haven't you got a home to untidy Eddie? Go and help mum lay the table now, son.'

The boys split at the top of the cellar stairs, Eddie grabbed the foiled dish waiting for him in the kitchen, thanking Mrs. Bird on his way out. Simon shouted his goodbyes as he laid the table for tea. Both were buzzing with the sights and sounds of the room they'd just left. As Eddie looked back and up through the window of the room with all the incredible gear, he pondered on what Mr. Bird's world was like.

Simon's dad was always tinkering with things, especially drones. Of all forms of technology, this was his speciality. They had advanced in size and power over the last few years and were being used for everything imaginable. The sky would sometimes appear alive with these blade-spinning birds, whirring quietly on their way or hovering, awaiting their next order.

Drones were now one of life's essentials. Enthusiasts raced them in all kinds of tournaments and both indoor and outdoor leagues had become popular. Then there were the big boys; professional pilots toured the world's most exotic locations, making big money in the process. It was the perfect sport for a generation driven by media and the newest technology. Minute detail was captured and magnified for the viewing audience. The tiny racing drones that hummed around circuits in the sky at absurd speeds were painted clearly for spectators and camera angles seemed limitless.

The drones that populated city skies served many purposes. Airports and train depots used them for surveillance and safety inspections while businesses were saving on their costs, using them for deliveries of everything from food to footwear. Emergency services used them to make raft or food drops for flood rescue or to carry vital organs, blood, vaccinations and lifesaving gear. The police maintained them as a vital form of overhead observation as well as a way of combatting the growing criminal use of drones.

Conservationists, coastguards and cattle farmers had all found a use for them. Even homeowners had S.H.A.D.E. (**S**ecure **H**ome **A**irborne **D**efence **E**nactor) drones installed. They were as common as yesterday's satellite dishes. When triggered, the unit would lift from its secured case and using motion sensors, its camera would train its spotlight and lens on any movement below. Their hum had been dubbed "*the robber's moan*" and were perfect around the perimeter of all kinds of properties. Supremely powerful and efficient, drones were known more by their nicknames:

Simple delivery drones got called box droppers and emergency service drones had become known as the H.U.M.M.E.R. (**H**igh-speed **U**nmanned **M**obile **E**mergency **R**esponder). The **H**ydra **a**nd **L**and **O**bserver (H.A.L.O.) surveillance drone had a huge range. It could hover with precision over land or miles out at sea for hours and was equipped with exceptional recording and transmitting technology. It was even able to function underwater.

The Civil Aviation Authority (CAA) had set up flight paths called Standard Navigational Lines (SNL) along which all commercial drone travel was regulated. This included specific lanes at precise altitudes for all forms of air traffic. Safety features of the mass-produced units included motion and range sensors to prevent mid-air collisions. '*Flailfall*' was also seen as an important safety innovation. Its use ensured that in an emergency, falling drones would descend at a slower rate with chutes and airbags deploying to offer safety and protection for the craft and those below.

To deal with transport problems, special drone bays had been prepared across the country for crafts interrupted by technical fault, bad weather or physical damage. These bays were preprogramed into many drones G.P.S. settings and were secured by a national drone support service. Drones were also being thought of now as a quick and safer means of communication. High security drones flew on protected routes across cities, enabling a confidentiality that the hacked and ransomed world of emails and the internet could no longer reliably offer.

Control centres were set up in all major cities and drone travel was now considered indispensable. Even the interactive walls of coffee shops and the huge screens above downtown bars carried remarkable live footage of everything a drone could find. From the basking seals of Blakeney to a scout troop's foggy scramble up Ben Nevis, versatile and pioneering technology had transformed the concept of visual information gathering.

Around secure areas, such as stadiums, prisons and airports, invisible defence systems, such as geofencing, had been set up to deactivate illegally flying drones. Unmanned aerial vehicles (UAVs) without registration were known as *Dark Drones* or *Sky Bugs* and despite the technology designed to hinder them, some of these units could get around the most sophisticated digital or physical barriers. Simple jamming and disabling systems were often not enough and this brought trouble for those required to hold up the law. New steps were needed to respond to their ever-growing threat. New steps and a new force.

Eddie arrived home and was eager to demolish his dinner, so he could polish off Mrs. Bird's pudding with his favourite ice cream. As he stretched out his arm to unlock the front door with his watch, he was surprised to see it already opening. There, standing as cheerfully and upbeat as he could remember seeing her, was his mum. She clearly had something to tell Eddie. However, the news that followed was not as joyously received by their son.

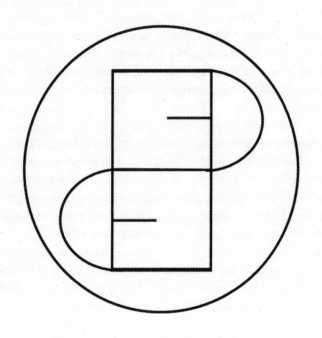

CHAPTER 3

AN
ATROCIOUS
IDEA

'Darling!' chirped Ally, Eddie's mother, 'we've got some news for you.' It was already good news as far as her keen-eyed son was concerned. Eddie had just noticed dad's car in the drive (a rare site before bedtime during the week, let alone dinner).

The statuesque and powerful figure of his father was crouched weakly attempting to disguise itself behind Ally.

'Oi!... What's that you're trying to sneak in?' came the playful boom.

'Dad!' shrieked Eddie, speeding through the doorway and smashing into his father's arms. The roly-poly shot up like a rocket and whacked against the hallway ceiling.

'Got it!' Mrs. Freeman calmly announced, saving the now misshaped sponge from a messy crash landing. Eddie and his glasses-knocked-off-his-face dad obliviously continued with the over-animated fight scene. It was their customary greeting.

'I'll be in the kitchen when you've quite finished,' sighed Mrs. Freeman, despairingly.

'What are you doing home?' interrogated Eddie, trapping his dad in a headlock.

'Thought you could use some real training,' he replied, crushing Eddie's ribs with his hard, coiling arms.

'Urghh…' Eddie's voice fast faded.

'Aghhh!' screamed his dad, feeling the burn of his son's grip ripping around his neck.

They both eased off, laughing.

'Hey, I've got some good news…for both of us. Come on, let's see your mum.' And with a final sweep kick, Peter Freeman whipped Eddie over his shoulder and bundled him through.

Ally was waiting with an anxious smile at the end of an old shabby wooden table in the middle of the kitchen. Though it was rare for all of them to be there at the same time, it had been the place for all the Freeman's "big talks" as well many of Eddie's daydreams starring his absent dad. Mr. Freeman's work took him away for days sometimes. Eddie always had eager questions when he finally came home but the replies would never live up to Eddie's imagination.

He saw his dad by the open door of a luxury jet liner on a remote airstrip. Like a state official arriving as a hero of a far-off country, the thronging masses below cheered and chanted "Freeman, Freeman!" Then he watched, as his dad stood at the site of a new and iconic building, casting an architectural eye over the work in progress while those around him looked on in awe. The truth was that Peter Freeman said very little about what he did for a living, or where he did it for that matter.

'Well?' Eddie's face was alive with anticipation. It pulled the rest of his body to the edge of a chair now tipped on its two front legs.

'Well, all that time dad has had to spend away from us has been worth it Eddie,' Ally began, 'he's got an amazing promotion which means we can make some exciting changes as a family.'

'What kind of changes?' Eddie questioned, dreaming himself, chauffer driven along a leafy private lane that wound

24

into a sports car-loaded driveway, backdropped by a huge mansion with his mum and dad standing at its regal doorway. Mr. Freeman's voice, focused and stern, brought Eddie back.

'It's an important year for you next year and we think a change of school might help you develop a few of your strengths.'

Eddie felt the unnatural and hollow words echoing all through him; they left sickening thumps beating in Eddie's chest and slumped him into the pit of his seat. He hadn't excelled in his work lately but moving schools wasn't going to put the brakes on his lesson-wrecking daydreams, he thought. He gazed down. It was it too hard to look back into the expectant eyes of his parents.

'Westlake is a fantastic school and there's so many good reasons why you'll love it.' His mum continued with a fake, unconvincing enthusiasm.

Mr. Freeman continued with the sweet-talking.
'Just think about your football, son. Westlake has tours on top of the school league and tournament you already have at Mildham. They even play in your favourite colour!'

The words helped a little and Eddie decided to leave his complaints unspoken. Deep down, he wondered if it was his drifting fantasies and strange encounters that had brought all this on anyway.

He picked through his dinner, numb, sharing his roly-poly with his dad as a token. He could tell that his parents were hoping for a decent reaction from him and didn't want to see them upset, especially as their new plan seemed so great to them. But he was struggling with his own feelings.

'I need time to work it out in my head,' he finally and honestly admitted.

The fear that he wouldn't be able to ever discover more about Mrs. Andrews and the secret room was almost unbearable. The overwhelming ache that twisted and wrenched his stomach must have been written all over Eddie's face because his mum and dad's happy expressions faded. The last flame of hope flickered in Peter and Ally's eyes as they searched for something to say.

'There's something else that might make it easier for you Eddie,' Peter suddenly sparked.

'What?' replied Eddie.

'Simon has got a place at Westlake too!'

Eddie's expression instantly transformed, much to his parents' relief, bolting upright and howling;

'Simon! I can't believe I had forgotten about him.'

The thoughts about the weird stuff at Mildham had been so powerful in Eddie's mind, that he had not been able to think naturally. Having his best mate with him might at least ease the strain of things.

As he got up and left for his bedroom, Eddie murmured down the hallway, 'I suppose, at least with Simon, I can suffer it.'

It was good enough for his mum and dad and Eddie was left to his own company for the rest of the evening. He spent it lying on his bed, drifting between the dread of starting a new school and the anxiety of not knowing enough about his soon to be old one.

The feeling ran long into the summer holidays. It was pushed to one side by camps and new term preparations, but it never went far. Simon's family were away in France for a good chunk of time and the two friends only managed to catch up for a few days of fun at the *Bird Cage*. They loved any time together and the innocent mischief they got up to. Lifting the grumpy neighbour's laundry from his washing line and dropping it on the roof of his potting shed with a crafty drone was endlessly amusing. They made it up to Mr. Denison by protecting his bird feeders from the local cat with their "Aerial Feline Surveillance Service".

There was always fun to be had. If they did get caught, Mr. Bird would put them through dull lectures about the correct use of technology. The impact was largely lost on the boys though, mainly due to Mr. Bird's constant smirks rather than frowns. As the holidays became replaced by school shopping and catch up homework, Eddie started to realise that those dreaded and volatile flying sensations hadn't returned for weeks. In fact, it was only on a packed field, during a football camp, he'd remembered one happening at all.

CHAPTER 4

AN
AWKWARD
ENCOUNTER

'Eddie, you've got an invite to pre-season training at Westlake!' called Mrs. Freeman looking up from her fridge door's interactive screen. 'Simon's mum messaged to say he has too! It starts this morning!'

Eddie's heart flooded with adrenalin.

'She's picking you up in an hour, so you better get ready.'

He raced around his bedroom so excited to get ready that he lost his balance pulling a sock on and clattered straight into the trophies and toys on his wall shelf. Eddie fell hard but the shelf fell harder, dumping its contents with a mighty crash.

'You ok?' came the call from downstairs.

'Yeah…fine,' slurred Eddie, shaking his head and blinking hard.

With one thumping headache and even more bruises, Eddie stood waiting at the end of his driveway for what seemed like an age before Mrs. Bird's car finally came into view.

The boys chattered frantically, their hearts and nerves jangling, as they strapped into the back seat of the Bird's battered and beaten family Ford. Most cars were almost completely automated, with onboard displays showing everything from the price of houses in the streets you passed to carpool opportunities for those who cared to share their journeys. The Bird's, however, was of a dying vintage breed that still left the driver in full control.

'I hope they have a few decent players, so we can smash old Mildham and those Stratton idiots,' Eddie cracked.

'Not too decent mate, we need to make the team yet!' Simon joked.

Eddie's face flattened. He had never had to think about being selected before. Sensing the change in Eddie's mood, Simon fired some quick reassurance.

'You'll be fine Eddie, just do your thing.'

It wasn't just his playing position that was bothering Eddie. There, in the back of his mind, were the questions that only his old school could answer. He had seen that room over and over again. It would reappear in tormenting glimpses that flashed and were gone. It had gotten to the point of Eddie wanting to almost rid himself of that day. Deep down though, he knew the underground vision would never leave him. Simon could not see the full picture in Eddie's mind but could sense he was suffering. He tried to help and found ways to side-track and distract Eddie whenever he saw that distant pain in Eddie's eyes.

'We played them last year, didn't we? In some local tournament. One of their forwards was like lightning!' Simon remembered.

'Oh yeah. She turned our defence inside out!' recalled Eddie.

'But not the keeper of course,' reminded Simon.

'And she knew not to challenge Mr. Skills here either!'

They both laughed and for a moment felt better. But the moment quickly evaporated at the sight of the old steel gates of Westlake. The schoolhouse was ancient and eerie though a little smaller than the boys anticipated. Simon was a mixture of dread and disbelief.

'Frogs in frocks Eddie, it's spooky. I bet the tech room is like a haunted antique store!'

They wandered on with Eddie imagining students lining up impatiently to sit at the only computer in the place; a cobwebbed old contraption that took an age to operate. A dusty cap and gown were draped over the skeletal features of the teacher whose voice was a vacant moan with no meaning. Rounding the corner of the school building, laughter, loud voices and the crashing sun broke Eddie from his spell. The boys' stomachs then churned harder than ever as they took in the sight of a half-assembled football team staring back at them.

'Good morning lads,' greeted a greying yet burly gentleman. He had a rugged, wrinkled face and lips thinner than the edge of a coin, though a warm smile and kind eyes softened his harsh exterior.

'Hello sir,' replied Eddie.

'I'm Mr. Jacobs, the headmaster here at Westlake, as I'm sure you already know.'

'Yes sir, I'm…..'

'Eddie Freeman, right?' Mr. Jacobs reached forward and shook Eddie's hand. Eddie had a sudden sense of intrusion, as if Mr. Jacobs could see right through him. He couldn't be sure if it was just the nerves, but it seemed something oddly familiar. Yes, he thought, it was just like that day with the intruder and Mrs. Andrews. With his hand still tight in Jacobs' grip, he looked up, forced a smile and nodded.

'Don't be shy,' Jacobs said, shaking Simon's hand with his eyes still trained on Eddie, 'we're all expecting you.'

As they walked to join the team, the headmaster forced his attentions away from Eddie and back onto football.

'I have to say,' he remarked, eyeing Simon from the ground up, 'your height is something we've needed in goal for quite a while.'

It made Simon wonder just how much he really knew about him and Eddie. They'd only ever met before while on opposite sides of a football field, yet this affable headmaster seemed to know more.

'You'll get to know this lot in no time, once we start training. Let's get on, eh?' With that, Mr. Jacobs struck up his traditional warm-up of a circuit of the school field.

Training itself was more of the same. The exhausting long runs, and short rests were taking their toll, especially on Simon who wasn't given any slack just because he wasn't an outfield player.

'If he keeps this up, I've had it, Eddie,' Simon panted, doubled up after finishing yet another shuttle sprint. He was drenched in sweat and struggling in the late summer heat. From his pulsating head, down to his blistered and throbbing feet, his whole body was screaming.

'He's just testing us out, don't give in, he'll ease off in a minute,' replied Eddie.

'OK, let's finish with one last sprint!' bellowed Mr. Jacobs. 'Down to the bottom of the field and back.'

The whistle blew, and the players took off, all desperate to finish strong, or at least not last.

'He'd be better off in the army,' shouted Robert Moore. Westlake's athletic, smart, short-haired-side-parted captain and defensive giant was first to turn. He headed back through the group, wincing into the sun's full glare.

'Your lace Bobby!' gasped Joe Mackenzie, the beefy-legged goofball of the team, trying to slow his skipper down as he lumbered at the back of the chasing pack.

'Nice try Macca but he's not seven,' laughed Max Willis, the school's sporting analyst, psychologist and morale lifter. They all heaved back up the hill as one hot and sticky horde.

'Good effort lads!' enthused Jacobs, who was quietly impressed. 'Once you've got your lungs back take in some water and sit for a bit.'

As the team rested, one of them came over to where Eddie and Simon had collapsed.

'Hey, you guys look whacked!' the girl said. 'Don't worry, the rest of us have got used to Mr. J's pre-season drills. We're a good lot really.' She turned and rolled her eyes despairingly at some of the boys who were messing about just out of earshot. 'Well, most of the time.'

'I'll take your word for it,' Simon replied. Eddie said nothing, but his face gave away his surprise at the girl's bold self-assurance.

'Truth be told, they're a little intimidated by you. You see, they remember you Eddie… from last season… when you scored those two goals that knocked us out of the cup. And I am still annoyed at some of your saves from that day, Simon.' She spoke, reluctantly impressed by their previous exploits.

'You… they, remember that…? I mean me?' puzzled Eddie.

'I wouldn't flatter yourself too much, football is the only language they speak,' she said cuttingly.

Eddie stared forward and glazed over while the girl and Simon carried on chatting. 'Don't mind him, he's always off with the fairies,' Simon said, dismissing Eddie's vague trance.

'Well that's weird… but whatever,' remarked the girl.

As both she and Simon discussed football, the team and *General Jacobs,* Eddie sat, aware enough to listen. He was amazed at how knowledgeable the girl was. Not because she knew the boys' names and personalities but more that she spoke about playing styles, positions and tactics too. It was obvious football was like a second nature to her. Eddie had never been around anyone like this before, yet there was a familiar feeling to the way she spoke and moved. He put it down to the tiredness from training and just sat, soaking up the conversation. Casually walking back to the group, she swung her head back towards them. The sun caught her waving hair as she did. 'Oh, I'm Avery by the way… but they all call me Howie.'

'Course they do,' said Simon under his breath, rather bewildered by the whole encounter.

Eddie remained silent and held himself together as best he could, feebly attempting to hide his obvious fascination for her.

She needn't have said anything about the players. During match practice, they spoke for themselves. Jonny Wilson, who had as much arrogance as he did skill, took no time in starting on Eddie.

'I'm gonna tie you in knots, Freeman,' he bragged, as the ball fell between them.

Eddie drifted and imagined being strung up by his arms and legs around the goalpost. Hearing the sound of Jonny's cackle, he snapped back and found the mouse-haired mouth of the team taking off towards him, at lightning speed. Eddie slipped over Jonny's lunging two feet and swiftly spun away with the ball leaving Jonny slumped in a heap behind. More opponents game to challenge Eddie, all in a rather menacing and over-competitive way. He rolled and turned each one with an agility that seemed beyond his natural talent. Eddie felt between worlds, joyfully untouchable as a footballer but terrifyingly unnerved by the power that was gripping him. As Mr. Jacobs awarded a corner for his team, Eddie tried to shake off the force that seemed to be in control of his body. He crouched down and closed his eyes, desperately flooding his mind with all the distracting thoughts he could muster. It was of no use. As the ball swung in, he sensed the dreaded uplift. He quickly opened his eyes to find himself airborne, feet above the ground. Despite his height, despite his huge lack of inches, he had managed to outjump the team's towering talisman, Robert 'Bobby' Moore. With the ball sailing towards him, Eddie instinctively took his opportunity, heading it forcefully goalward. It cracked the back of the net and rippled down. Simon let out a joyful scream at the other end of the pitch, punching the air. The whole team, Howie and all, stood motionless.

'What was that...?' called out Bobby Moore, in disbelief. 'I mean, how did he…?'

Eddie, recognizing the surreal situation tried to turn the attention from him. 'Hey, they weren't joking about the goalkeeping around here, were they!' he quickly spluttered. Thankfully, it worked a treat. Embarrassed at losing the aerial battle, Bobby turned to blame his keeper. 'You should have got to that one, Joe,' he complained.

'I thought you were good in the air, mate. How was I to expect that?' the stout and upset keeper replied. The spat descended into a heated squabble and noticing the fast-approaching headmaster, Eddie ducked away to escape the fallout. Mr. Jacobs was not one to tolerate indiscipline. Making an example of them, the skipper and hapless goalie were given a punishing run around the school field.

The practice came to an end and the players headed off with their families, each as tired and still rather shocked as the other.

'Well how was it, boys?' asked Eddie's mum, as they both climbed into the car. 'Pretty good fun,' Eddie said, 'but don't bother expecting him to say anything. He's out of it!'

Simon had to be shoved across the backseat of the car and was barely able to get his belt buckled. The relentless drills had left his long limbs looking, to Eddie, like strands of cooked spaghetti.

Later that night, Eddie's mind flicked between the flashbacks of *the room* and his freakish skills during training. Eddie, staring up across his bedroom ceiling, tried to think how things were before. His posters of planes, drones and footballers, once the subject of his happy imaginations, seemed distant; almost irrelevant now. With that question, *"what was down in that room?"* still rolling over in his restless mind, the day's training took its toll. Eddie's eyes closed, and sleep defeated his thoughts; if only for a few hours.

The squad trained hard all week and during practice matches Eddie continued to enjoy some happy accidents. He appeared to bravely put himself in the way of a bullet from Jonny Wilson, standing firm as the rest of the defensive wall flinched and twisted away from the blast. If only those who admired his courage had known that Eddie was in another world when the ball welted him in the face, he may not have won them over so easily. His mind was constantly hijacked by the idea of getting back to that *room*.

Simon, on the other hand, had settled in without so much as a murmur of complaint. The team were in desperate need of a good goalie and Joe Mackenzie, Westlake's current shot-stopper, did not seem bothered about Simon taking over the job. In fact, if the truth be known, he was actually quite relieved. He was not going to miss the constant wrath dished out by his defence for his *weighty* mistakes.

'Do you think I've done enough to make the starting line-up, Simon?' asked Eddie after the session.

'Well if you haven't, I don't know what else you're supposed to do. Some of your moves were borderline out of this world,' he answered. Eddie looked awkward, so Simon changed the subject.

'What d'ya think of Howie?'

'How do you mean?' Eddie replied.

'The GIRL! Eddie,' Simon jeered. 'She's so…unbelievably fast.'

'Fast…yeah, she's pretty quick!' added Eddie, trying to disguise his own emotions.

It seemed now there was something, or rather someone, that could compete with *the room* for the control of his subconscious.

His infatuation only grew during the long last few days before term started. Simon was of no use. He had gone to Scotland, visiting relatives and only caught back up with Eddie on the first morning of school. They could still walk and did so, far less anxiously than either expected. Westlake was a smaller school and seemed friendly. Their only concern appeared to be getting some parent-pleasing grades.

After registration, as he left his home room and headed across the grounds for his first class, he noticed Simon was walking with Howie. Feeling green-eyed, Eddie tried to ignore them and walked on quickly through the school, looking down at his planner without really reading it.

In escaping his friend's company, he'd also got away from his whole class and found himself, after a bit of hallway wandering, alone in a small out of the way corridor. By some stroke of luck, it seemed he'd conveniently found his English room.

'It says 13, but where is everyone?' Eddie muttered to himself, checking his planner properly this time.

The door had no window and the number was barely visible. Stranger still, was a circular kind of emblem that had been scratched into it. The tiny symbol triggered a powerful flashback from Mildham. Had he seen this sign before? With anxious curiosity, Eddie knocked then waited. He suddenly craved the company of Simon and the rest of his class.

'Where were they?'

Starting to feel edgy, he knocked again. Perhaps they were already inside but somehow could not hear him. Eddie panicked and whacked hard on the dilapidated door. The next sound was of heavy footsteps, clomping on the tiled floor behind him. Mrs. Crandall, Westlake's deputy head, was stomping ominously towards him. This was not good. She had a reputation for being as mean as she was massive.

Despite her larger-than-life appearance, Eddie had not seen her before. In fact, his only contact had been noticing her shadowy frame through a window of her office. He had been looking for the piercingly loud, pretty coloured parrot that she was famed for keeping caged behind her desk. Perry was the only reason anyone ever went near that room.

Crandall arrived and bent down sternly to meet Eddie's face.

'And what exactly, are you doing down here?!'

'Er, er…..' Eddie fought his imagination from taking over.

'What are you bumbling about, boy? This corridor is for the school caretaker only!' she barked aggressively. 'Tell me your name!'

'Sorry miss, I thought this was my English room. I'm Eddie Freeman,' he quickly blurted.

'You may be new, Edward Freeman but I know skulking around when I see it. You have been told to stay with your class when walking to lessons!' she chided.

Eddie regretted not having done just that and nodded in agreement whilst trying to shuffle inoffensively past the heavy-set and brutal looking woman. He was unsure where to go but knew where he didn't want to be.

'Wait one moment Freeman….what are these scratches on the door?' cried Crandall, accusingly pointing at the part of the door that had sent Eddie's mind back to *the room*.

'I d-don't know Miss; they were already there.'

'LIES!!' screamed Crandall.

Eddie instantly understood why she was nicknamed "Cranky Crandall".

'These marks are fresh,' she added.

As hard as it was to accept, the scrapes on the door did look as if they had just been made, particularly the scratches across the older mark of that haunting motif. Mrs. Crandall continued with her manic and melodramatic outburst.

'Defacing school property isn't tolerated at Westlake. You shall come to my office after lessons today and explain yourself.'

'Yes miss,' he agreed and hastily left.

Despite the injustice, Eddie thought it a waste of time to defend himself. He could see that this tyrant wasn't going to listen to anything he said.

Mrs. Crandall was indeed a vicious and vindictive woman. She looked for any opportunity to land Eddie in trouble during his first few weeks at school. This made Eddie's start at Westlake much more of a struggle than he had hoped. A stray lace, talking in the lunch hall too loudly, not holding bannister rails and especially his "mop of overgrown hair" were all subjects of the nit-picking contempt she seemed to have for him. The beginning of the regional schools' football season was only a couple weeks away. It was a welcome distraction and a means of escape that Eddie couldn't wait for.

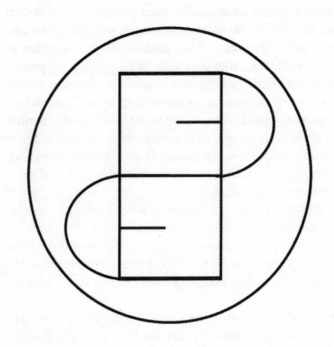

CHAPTER 5

AN UNDERGROUND EDUCATION

Autumn brought an unusually deep and colourful fall with it. Leaves like endless invitations to winter, were delivered on the stiff and chilly breeze. They circled into enticing piles in playground corners; ripe for a kick from any passing pupil. There was a bright vivid air that carried the clear and familiar smell of the colder season to come. Familiar still to Eddie, were the continual visions of the room he had left behind at Mildham. They were distracting enough for him to not notice how much his dad had been away from home lately and so overbearing that he had decided it was time to try and do something about finding it.

Every morning, the car journey to school became more and more unbearable as Simon and Eddie spent the minutes speaking only about random vlogs, video games and football scores. Sworn to secrecy around others, neither uttered a hint of the ever-deepening details of their plan to sneak back in to Mildham.

The boys found themselves alone before school most days. Mrs. Bird dropped them off early so that she could fly off with Sarah to finish the family school run. Now, standing together on a quiet part of the playground, their scheming was near its end. The plan was set.

'So, it's still Friday then?' Simon asked, hunching into his jacket. The gusty autumn air flicked and tangled the fringe of what had become brown more than sun-bleached hair.

41

'You're quite sure you wanna do this?' he continued. Dishonest actions were as hard for Simon to deal with as dishonest words.

'It's a good time to do it…It's the only time to do it,' replied Eddie, 'we've got the day off and they haven't. We'll wear our old uniforms and slip into the crowd during lunch break.'

'Have you told your mum and dad what we're doing?' questioned Simon.

'You're kidding, right?' choked Eddie.

'Camels in clogs Eddie! not what we're actually getting up to! I mean what is our cover story going to be?' Simon countered.

'It's the day after the Dellview match, most of the team are getting together at Bobby's house. Apparently, it's tradition for the captain to invite the team after the first game of the season…to build team spirit,' explained Eddie.

'So, shouldn't *we* be there?' questioned Simon, though he was quietly pleased with the idea of having Eddie miss out on the whole thing.

'Yeah, we should,' Eddie said enthusiastically, 'and that's why it's the perfect alibi. We'll just get to his house a little later.'

'Whose house?' asked a light and inquisitive voice. Neither Eddie nor Simon had noticed Avery Howard's arrival. Her interruption made them both jump out of their skin.

'Woah, where did you come from, Howie?' Simon cried, his face flushing with guilt.

'What are you, some sort of undercover spy?' added Eddie, desperately trying not to look equally as uncomfortable.

'Never mind all that, what were you boys plotting?' she asked with a playful interest.

'We're just talking about going to Bobby's on Friday,' blurted Simon.

'Oh, that,' said Howie, 'it's just a bit of a laugh really, we always end up playing football video games and making fun of Jonny. He takes it so seriously but he's really terrible with a controller and nothing like as skillful as he is on the pitch. He swings his hands all over the place and kicks about like a monkey that's lost its marbles!'

The boys laughed, trying to stay natural but Simon's overacting got the better of him. He let out a squeaky kind of giggle which made him feel like a wide-mouthed muppet. The squeal made Howie lurch and swing her head back in shock. Eddie was lost. The look of Howie's hair, shimmering in the morning breeze, her confident playful personality had all made mush of his insides. The two boys, both now with dim-witted expressions, stood and stared. Howie continued, trying to make sense of their overheard words.

'So why aren't you going to be there until later then?

No sooner had she asked, and the morning registration bell started ringing. It was impeccable timing and it woke Eddie from the spell Howie's golden locks had put him under. Seeing Simon staring expectantly at him, he knew he had to move the moment on and put this sneaky beak off the scent.

'Er… alright inspector, that's enough interrogation for one day!' he chirped. 'My mum asks less questions than you.'

Eddie squirmed away, hating himself for mocking Howie's curiosity and leaving Simon standing alone with her. With a shrug of his square shoulders and shaking his head despairingly, Simon tried to offer a bit of cheer as he shuffled quickly after Eddie.

'He's always a bit touchy before his morning muffin.' Howie frowned and threw an unimpressed look of annoyance towards them both.

'That was awkward,' Simon said to Eddie with a low voice as he caught up with him. 'Do you think she suspects anything?'

'You worry too much, Simon,' said Eddie, 'as if she has the first idea of what we're going to do. Remember, the only way we'll get found out is if we keep acting this weird.'

They were hunched together and their sneaky whispers weren't going unnoticed. Simon's awkwardness was down to more than the unwelcome eyes on him, however. He had been keeping much too much to himself lately; things he knew Eddie would eventually have to find out. But how he would handle it worried Simon.

'Anyway,' Eddie said, noticing a pained expression on Simon's face, 'I feel like Howie's on our side, she's been pretty good to us. You know girls, they just like to know what's going on, don't they?' Simon agreed with half a smile and headed with Eddie to class.

The build-up to the match against Dellview could not have gone better for Westlake's newest additions. Simon had been picked for the goalie spot and Eddie had done enough to start up front. In the changing room, Joe appeared quite happy to be on the bench instead of stuck between the posts. Callum, who Eddie was in for, had also been sporting; resigning himself to the fact that a worthy teammate was getting his chance. That, together with the navy blue number 7 shirt he was handed in the changing room, took Eddie to brimming point with excitement.

'Ok lads, this is our first game and things may not click straight away. Let's keep it simple and just remember to work hard for each other. You all know the Westlake way by now.'

Mr. Jacobs had a way of making it seem like he didn't expect much from you but you would never want to let him down.

'Let's get the ball forward quickly and get at them with our speed and skill. And don't get caught in possession!' He aimed his voice at Jonny though he would have had to scream in his face for him to realise it. Jonny had great feet and his street skills were slick but he would often breeze around players just so he could take on more.

The game got underway. It was a mild day, but Westlake started cold. Throughout the first half Dellview, wearing red and white stripes, forced save after save from Simon as they threw all their energy into attacking. But this left gaps in their defence and against the run of play, Howie picked up Max's clearance and took off on the break. Her speed was as bewildering as it was breathtaking as she pulled away from the nearest opponent with the ball deftly under control. The Dellview keeper left his line and rushed forward. Howie took one final touch, pushing the ball onto her favoured left foot and then cracked her shot off. It was past the keeper before he was even set and the ball chinked against the underside of the crossbar before crashing into the net.

'Great shot Howie, you didn't give him a chance,' approved Eddie as he high-fived her in celebration.

'Oh, you're talking to me now are you?' she marvelled sarcastically.

After half time, Westlake took over and scored three more as their opponents wilted from their early exertions. Howie got another and George 'Digger' Gardner, the team's selfless and composed wide man, also picked up a brace; one from a header from a well-worked corner and the other sliding in at the back post to finish off a great passing move that involved both the "engine room" midfielder, David White and Howie. Everyone returned to the changing rooms in high spirits.

"If we keep this up, we'll be on for a cracking season, lads,' Bobby exclaimed.

'Keep what up?' said Max, 'we could have taken a nap all afternoon and still not lost. Bird, you're something else!'

Simon took the compliment with a confident nod and the laughing and joking carried on. The match seemed to carry the promise of a great season ahead and everyone could feel it. Everyone but Eddie that is. He'd been plagued throughout the game with thoughts about the following day. Apart from a lucky deflected pass that set up Howie's second, it was an afternoon of suffering. His mind had been consumed by coincidental moments, taking him back to the day the intruder charged through the school. The sunshine, Simon's hero goalkeeping and playing on a freshly mowed field were all reminders that took him back to that day. That day with no reason or answers. The day when Eddie's view of the world took on a whole new dimension and changed forever. He wished that he could daydream himself out of his slump but it had gripped his every thought. His was the only Westlake face that didn't have a victory smile plastered all over it.

Mr. Jacobs pulled the team together on the pitch, after the customary handshakes with the Dellview team.

'Well played, lads.' Howie was well-used to the reference and felt more a part of the team for it.

'You all stuck to your jobs and made it a great game to watch. The passing was excellent all over the pitch, plus you all got back; defending together like a real team and that is what will make you so tough to play against this season.'

He was careful not to praise anyone individually and instead sent them off to the changing rooms with a pat on the back and a reminder of how important the upcoming captain's day was.

'It's a school tradition so make sure you all make the best use of the time you have together.'

As he said it, some of the boys looked knowingly at each other. They were likely to get the most out of the day but not necessarily in the way the Headmaster would approve of. Jacobs' words tugged at Eddie and Simon's conscience. They shared the ride home without speaking, both feeling even more anxious about explaining away their lateness or even their absence should things not go to plan back at Mildham.

As Simon was dropped at his house by Mrs. Freeman, the boys briefly maintained the smokescreen.

'See you on the corner in the morning, we'll walk from there,' Eddie called out of the window as Simon made his way up the craggy, gravel drive in front of his house.

Bobby's house was a decent walk from both of their homes but they daren't ask for a ride; that could mess up the entire operation. Instead they had planned to stay on foot and meet at their local park. It was close to Mildham and had plenty of places where they could change and hide their backpacks.

That night, Eddie and Simon slept restlessly. Eddie thrashed in his bed as he imagined the extremes of what tomorrow's adventure might bring. Simon lay awake, his eyes alert. Though he knew a hidden secret, he had been trusted by his father to say nothing to Eddie. This was only marginally easier for him than carrying the weight of so many vague stories and half-truths. He craved the chance to come clean.

Though he had timed his arrival to the second, Eddie waited alone at the rendezvous. The meeting time had come and gone minutes ago, yet the long stride and wide gait of Simon's characteristic saunter was nowhere. Just as his hopes were fading, Eddie finally caught sight of Simon, carrying what seemed like a lot more than necessary.

Eddie sighed then ran towards him. 'You had me worried there, mate,' he exclaimed, 'what happened?'

Simon had arrived at the park over ten minutes late wheezing and out of breath. 'Sorry Ed, mum wanted to make snacks for the team and I had to wait,' he gasped. 'It was agony just waiting there watching her fussing about for so long.'

'Well at least we'll have a peace offering for the lads, eh?' Eddie said, easing Simon's stress level. His breathless panting was replaced by choking laughter. They both were past caring about anything now and had just one thought in their mind; the plan.

They changed quickly and checked each other over.

'Freeman, where's your homework? Get that shirt inside your trousers!' Simon croaked, in the voice of his form teacher at Mildham. It was a surreal moment that they both enjoyed, standing there in old uniforms, ready for action. It felt an easy disguise to pull off and Eddie was encouraged by the news that Mrs. Andrews had resigned from her post over the summer. Another bizarre encounter with her was the last thing he wanted today. Leaving their bags hidden and walking out of the park, they turned towards their old school.

'We'll walk along the path by the side of the school, the hedges will give us some cover. Then we'll time our run in with the lunch bell. There should be loads of 'em coming out.' Eddie recapped the plan even though they both had had nothing in their minds but that, for days. 'Then, it's straight down to the classrooms by the playground. We'll get in through our old back door. It was always open at breaktimes.'

Checking their watches, they started down the path from the park.

They paused a little distance from the school entrance and crouched behind the hedges. Simon lifted his head and with his icy blue eyes frozen and wide open, turned to Eddie 'You hear that?' he quizzed.

'It's the bell!' yelped Eddie, in horror.

"It's early!' gasped Simon, muddled in confusion.

'Go!' Eddie yanked Simon up with him and they burst forward from their cover. The boys dashed out expecting to mingle through a steady stream of students heading out of the gate but there was not a soul in sight.

'It's not the lunch bell, Eddie,' Simon said, recognizing the steady tone…

They stopped dead in their tracks and for a split second, just stared at each other as they suddenly realised where their reckless running had taken them.

'...It's the fire alarm!' they both shouted.

Completely exposed in front of the main entrance, they had to do something.

'Come on, we've got to go now!' declared Eddie, looking at the school's main gate like it was a castle portcullis dropping fast in front of him. He bolted for it with Simon haring madly after him.

As they flew into the school ground, pupils were gathering in their masses in the car park on one side of the school as well as on the playground on the other. Their planned route now cut off, Eddie took a huge gamble and made for the main doors. Pulling hard on one, he was relieved to find it unlocked, no doubt as part of the drill's safety code; they flew in.

Inside, the school was conveniently deserted. Handy for the panicked duo who dived out of sight and caught their breath.

'We've put the chimp up the chimney now, Eddie.' Simon gasped hysterically.

'Shh, let's get going,' Eddie said, not wanting to waste a moment. The boys headed down the old familiar corridor that led to their classroom. The fear of being caught was now replaced by the fear of the unknown. Eddie's heart juddered as he reached the point where Mrs. Andrew's eyes had failed him. There were coats and bags hanging on the wall but some had spilled into the small entry way ahead of the classroom door. In the tight area, Eddie worked his way around in search of any clue. But before he could get a good look, he felt a hand resting on his shoulder. It calmly eased him to one side.

'I'll take it from here.' Simon's voice was as sure and unruffled as Eddie had ever heard. A far cry from his distressed screams of only moments ago.

'What?' gaped Eddie, as he witnessed his truest friend moving slowly towards the wall behind the door.

'This is what we're looking for,' Simon proclaimed, 'and I suppose you'll want an explanation to go with it.'

Eddie was aghast.

'Let's get in before we're rumbled.' As Simon finished speaking, he lifted a section of coats away, revealing a hairline crack that ran from the hooks down to just below the floor.

Immediately, Eddie could see the outline of some sort of entrance. Not only that but the same type of crude marks on the door that he'd been accused of making at Westlake, outside Room 13, were scratched over part of the cracked outline. Simon pressed firmly in two separate areas on the wall, one by a hook at head height and another lower down towards the base of the wall.

He paused, double-checking his position before stretching his foot along the very bottom of the wall and kicking against a section of the skirting board. A small hatch on huge hinges dropped into the wall with a tiny puff of air and a smell of cold acrid stone. A narrow set of ladders fixed to a hidden wall inside, led down into the darkness.

'We've got a little bit to talk about,' Simon said apologetically and turned towards the hatch 'It's ok....... after you.'

He gestured to Eddie to go first. Silent and unable to think, a stupefied Eddie climbed in. He reached for the first rung and started to step down the ladder. The hatch above him firmly sealed closed. He was left with no light but a faint red glow below.

'You there, Simon?' called Eddie up into the black above him.

'Keep going, mate,' Simon called down.

'I thought you'd left me for a minute.'

'Not a chance,' replied Simon, 'I'm not missing you seeing this…'

Eddie stepped quickly down to avoid Simon's rapidly descending feet and lowered himself onto the hard, concrete floor. The journey down completed what was missing from his memory. What was waiting for him would give meaning to everything.

Low level lights flickered and glowed dimly from the shallow ceiling. Eddie could just identify some of the room's features. It had a deserted feel, as if people had left in a hurry. Spreading to his left were a series of booths, all containing identical high-backed and streamlined seats, resting on sprung-loaded posts. Eddie walked mystified, towards one of the chairs. He was burning with ideas of who had used it and what for. As he sat and mimicked some manoeuvres, he looked up saw a deep hollow carved in the wall.

'What used to be there?' he thought. Attached to each chair arm was a type of casing for a control panel. Amongst the severed wires and debris on the floor lay a container, still half-filled with food. It had been festering for some time.

'They call them action bays,' Simon informed Eddie. 'That's where they fly them from.' Before Eddie could even respond, his attention was then seized by something. There, imprinted on a wall on the other side of the room, *the symbol* from the door of Room 13 at Westlake!

Eddie had seen so many reoccurring visions of the place he struggled to believe that he was not still looking at a picture from his own imagination. His mind shuddered, sensing that the sign must be part of a much bigger and highly secret organisation. The shape appeared much more imposing compared to the etched versions he'd seen at both schools. As he looked further, he could make an even bigger holed-out part of the wall. The same symbol was displayed symmetrically on either side of the now abandoned space.

'Once the intruder got close, they had to shut this place down. They only took the technology…they won't risk returning for this now,' Simon announced.

'You knew about this…all along?' Eddie turned, marched at Simon, wrapped his hand around Simon's tie and fisted it up under his chin. 'Why didn't you tell me?!' he exploded.

'You don't understand Eddie, I didn't have a choice,' Simon replied with a tone of despair whilst trying to ease Eddie's grip. 'You've no idea…' he gasped, 'the way you saw this place… it wasn't supposed to have happened like that.'

'Happened like what?' demanded Eddie.

'You, having consight so young. Please! We'll talk about this when we get to a safer place. It's too risky staying here,' Simon begged.

'Consight? What's that?' Eddie demanded, his eyes distantly twitching around in desperate confusion.

'I've said too much already!' replied Simon. As Eddie stared back, trying to get his head round what was going on, they were both disturbed by a heavy thud from above.

'Please Eddie, let's go! It's not safe here,' implored Simon, his face paling.

'Ok,' Eddie agreed and released his grip. 'But you better have some good answers,' he demanded.

Simon gave a nod of reassurance before fleeing towards the steps. Eddie took one final glance over his shoulder of the room to try and fix the picture in his mind. As he did, he caught some old metal casing with his foot and stumbled to the ground. In the dim light, Eddie hit the ground hard. The impact threw up a murky cloud of dust which settled to reveal something strange shining from the floor right in front of him. A thin, straight piece of silver metal. The flashing glint in the filth caught Eddie's attention; he picked it up. As he did, his already overfed thoughts took another bite of astonishment. It couldn't be… it was. The inscription on the back could not be mistaken: "*simul autem solus.*" Although he had never really taken the time to discover its meaning, he'd recognise his dad's tiepin anywhere.

'Eddie!' barked Simon from the base of the steps, 'Come on!' Eddie slipped the clip into his pocket and followed Simon back up the ladder and out.

In the corridor, to the boys' relief, the coast was still clear. By the distant sound of marauding youngsters, it was obvious that the fire drill was over and lunchtime appeared to have started.

'Which way now?' asked Simon as he secured the hatch.

'Keep to the plan and head for the fire exit at the back of the classroom, we're not getting caught now!' exclaimed Eddie.

The two boys hurriedly zig-zagged through the chairs and desks, keeping low to avoid detection. It seemed strange that so much had changed, yet their old room appeared no different.

'Look, they're heading around to the main entrance,' Simon noticed, hunkering down by the door. The boys waited for the playground to empty then bundled out and charged like mad towards the gate. Once clear and out of sight, they stopped briefly to look back; it was obvious that their plan had worked. With the help of the strangely well-timed fire drill, the boys had got in and out without being seen. They both quickly lost their jumpers and ties and jogged back to Grove Park. Simon tried to keep the plan in effect.

'We should try and keep our cover and get to Bobby's, fast.'

Eddie ran along silently beside him, staring forward. An anger had replaced the adrenalin-filled excitement from the break-in and he wanted Simon to know it.

'Eddie?' Simon repeated.

'Let's just get back and changed…this isn't over,' he replied.

Retrieving their bags from the craggy undergrowth in the park, Eddie decided he would stay quiet about the tiepin. It may serve to help with Simon's *whole* confession, he thought. He slipped it deep into the pocket of his spare trousers and folded them carefully into the top of his bag. As he crouched and zipped the bag tightly, he took a moment. How was his dad even involved in this? What the heck was consight? That sign stood for something... but what? His friend was about to get the grilling of a lifetime.

CHAPTER 6

AN
ABUSE
OF
TRUST

The sense of accomplishment they both savoured was immense. Simon was glad that a secret that had burdened him for months had now been lifted and he could climb out of the shackles that had caused him to act so possessively. Eddie felt proud that his plan had worked but now was more interested in what else his best friend was keeping from him. How were Simon and his dad so involved in the whole saga? Eddie stuck with the silent treatment as he thought where to start.

They headed to Bobby's house to join the rest of the team. 'Here, you want one?' Simon handed Eddie one of his mum's sausage rolls to try and ease the tension. Eddie's instincts were faster than his emotions and he took it.

They both pecked at their snacks like watched sparrows, constantly checking around, in a state of shock, for who knows what. Finally, as Mrs. Bird's kindly cooking replenished empty stomachs and lost energy, Simon took the courage to speak.

'Don't you want to say anything, mate?' he asked. Without caring for a reply, desperate to get things off his chest, he started blurting all he knew. Eddie eagerly feasted not only on the food but on Simon's spouting too...

'So, my dad explained a lot of things about you. He's only heard rumours from the people he works for. They seem to know everything about you, especially your daydreaming.'

'What do you mean?' said Eddie, instantly forgetting the silent treatment he had been giving Simon.

'Well, dad's developed these crazy drones for this agency. They seem like a secret service group and he says they're there to keep us safe from people like that intruder,' Simon began...

'He spent a lot of time in that room, helping these runners learn to fly them.' Eddie slowed down and turned to Simon.

'Runners?' he questioned.

'A runner is the name for the pilot that sits in one of those booths and flies drones remotely,' Simon revealed.

'There's loads of people who do that. It's nothing new,' responded Eddie, unimpressed.

'Yeah, but these are different... These machines are quick, really quick, with incredible handling. They're designed for pursuits and getting out of tight spots. Dad said they're the best there is, you know, even beyond military stuff.'

'So, what was it down there and why did they use a school as a base?' Eddie asked.

'Can't help you there, mate. All I know is it was a small unit...they had to be shut down. I don't know why exactly, but it's got something to do with you, Mrs. Andrews and that man in the suit,' he added.

'When did you find all this out?' badgered Eddie, keen to hear exactly what Simon knew.

'A few days before that guy in the suit broke in. You see, dad knew something was going to happen. He wouldn't tell me more, just enough to keep me, *and especially you,* safe. Don't forget, he just plays with stuff and tweaks these things...you've seen him.' Simon ended with a tone that reassured his best friend that his dad's involvement was limited. Not much else could be known.

Eddie's mind was fizzing with questions but he barely knew where to start. Was he in danger? Is this the real reason why he had changed schools? How was his dad involved? Most importantly, how much more did Simon and his dad know about him and this…*gift*?

As they walked on, nearing the Moore's home, Eddie squeezed Simon for more information.

'What's my imagination got to do with all this?'

'Consight…or Connective Sight to give it its real name,' Simon responded, 'Dad reckons it's like a different dimension that somehow connects people together.' Eddie could feel the truth coming but the mystery was still heavier than Simon's frustratingly light explanation.

'To tell you the truth, I think he heard too much and just shut down. It must be a family thing,' he continued with a nervous chuckle, 'it's been agony for me, these last few months. They still didn't want you to know but I knew I wasn't going to stop you going back to Mildham.'

Their walk eased Simon's conscience and fixed their friendship. On they went, working on an excuse for being so late to Westlake football team's D*evelopment Day*.

They approached Bobby's outskirts-of-town, stately farmhouse, Eddie slowed and asked the question he wished he'd started with.

'So why have you waited 'til now to tell me?' Simon stopped by the old wooden gate entrance and turned to Eddie pleadingly.

'If I'd have told you before, you'd have had us down there before things were safe. My dad couldn't tell me what dangers there were, he just insisted that I wait for him to tell me when it was ok…for your own good, he said. It's been hard work to get anything out of him…You should try talking to him!'

'Oh, I'll be doing that alright,' replied Eddie with a look of intent and giving Simon a friendly 'dead-arm' punch. They strode wearily up the gravel stone drive towards the house. The place looked old but grand and dignified. Neither of the boys had noticed the walls covered in trailing ivy, the lead-

framed windows or the ornate stonework let alone the array
of hidden security features. Instead, they walked straight up to
the arched and imposing, oak-wood door.

Unbeknown to the boys, the guests inside were already
aware of their arrival through the cameras and sensors
scanning the front of the house.

Eddie, not seeing any bell or doorknocker, pulled on an old
rope that dangled to one side of the door. The echoing clang
he expected was replaced by the soft sound of something
slimy, splurging out from the large bell that had been resting,
upturned above them. A mass of ruby red jelly swung out
from the bell, like paint pouring out of a giant brass bucket.
The wobbling muck splattered off Eddie and sprayed
everything nearby. Simon tried but wasn't quick enough to
avoid the sticky slop cascading down the side of his arm and
leaving an embarrassing mess all over the front of his jeans.

A huge chorus of laughter went up as the rest of the team
burst open the door in hysterics. Many doubled over laughing
uncontrollably as Simon's attempts to scrub away the smear
only made things worse.

'That'll teach you to roll up late, fellas!' barked Jonny with a
mocking beam on his face.

'I'm afraid the *Jellybell* is the customary prank for any late
guests here, lads,' added Bobby in consolation of the boys'
humiliation.

Eddie and Simon stared haplessly at each other whilst the
rest of the team jostled round them, delivering a frenzy of
friendly gags and wisecracks. It was a singular moment of
sudden and unexpected diversion. The dismay on the boys'
faces slowly transformed into a smile before giving in to the
barrels of laughter. The jelly had fittingly bonded the team, in
more ways than one. Eddie and Simon answered the shoulder
patting and head rubbing with nods of acknowledgement and
respect for a clever joke. Surrounded by glistening eyes and

teary fits of giggling, the scene suggested that Eddie and
Simon were now members of a very tight company. The
moment needed no words; acceptance rarely does. And that,
for the two boys, made it all the more real.

The merriment was finally broken off by a gentle whirring
overhead. As Howie handed the two sweet-smelling victims
some kitchen towel, the other lads turned their attention to a
drone, efficiently landing in a marked bay by the side of the
driveway.

'Pizza!' they all drooled and sped off towards their lunchtime
delivery. Howie was clearly glad of new company.

'Where have you been?' she demanded. The boys stopped
mopping themselves for a second and stared at each other.
They responded as one.

'It's a long story!' Howie rolled her eyes at the two smirking
faces but before she could say anything more, Simon pulled
out an opened box of tepid and misshaped sausage rolls.

'Care for one? They're a Bird specialty,' he offered with a
put-on poshness and stuck-up expression.

'What are they? They look like something from the dinner
hall muck bucket,' replied Howie much to the amusement of
the boys. After suffering the guilty pangs of an unwilling
cover-up for months, Simon was now beginning to return to
his old self.

'Harsh but fair, I suppose,' he said, staring down into the
grotty mess left in the container.

Sliding their bags under an old bench in the porch, they
entered into the hallway, behind the jubilant pizza precession
going on through to the kitchen. Bobby's house was palatial.
Every room seemed to have the latest gadget and this was
enough to hold Eddie and Simon in a state of wonderment
for most of the afternoon. The kitchen was a blend of
scientific sleekness and rustic country living. A crystal-clear
screen fronted a large refrigerator which was synched to the

Moore's home network. From the panel, you could connect to stores, stream whatever you pleased, put the domestic robots to task or simply adjust the home's heating, lighting and security. The torn apart pizza, bottles of drink and various snacks strewn around the work surfaces did nothing for the kitchen's sophisticated look, however.

The lounge was marvellous for the team. Voice activation stopped the bossy members taking control. Bobby closed the blinds with a simple command. Lights were dimmed and sofas and seats reclined in the same way. With an expectant atmosphere, he directed his voice towards a small illuminated device and summoned the type of game required. Wireless control decks were set out in front of each competitor. Eddie and Simon joined the team at the restart of a hotly contested football tournament. Although it was certainly competitive, it now became more of a comedy as Jonny Wilson started playing. Having heckled and maliciously mocked his mates, he struggled in every way to get to grips with the controls.

'It's this useless control deck, it doesn't work properly,' he whined. Unfortunately, his erratic and clumsy approach together with his overactive body movements gave him away.

'Really?' countered Bobby, indignantly. 'You're questioning my equipment?'

Everyone in the room knew this was a bad move. Their groans of mocking sympathy acted like fuel on Jonny's shortening fuse. Jonny was a slick and skilful footballer but the reams of sarcastic scorn and scathing criticism he would dish out to those teammates who fell below his expectations were now coming back to boil his insides. Still, there he was, with a seething and bitter scowl, denying his own obvious shortcomings.

Eddie pictured Jonny, in his desperate state, like a stick of dynamite, his fuse burning more fiercely and feverishly the more he grew angry with his own awful play and even worse excuses. Sure enough the fuse ran its course. 'Aghhh! You're all idiots!' Jonny finally detonated. His face overcome with rage and humiliation *"the selfish one"* kicked his foot attachments across the room and sent his control deck flying.

Jonny made for the door, hoping to avoid the retribution Bobby was about to deliver but still managed to throw insults at anyone within earshot as he scarpered. The atmosphere in the room immediately improved after the classless, though mercurial Jonny Wilson had made his getaway.

'Typical Jonny, stirring up trouble then off home to wallop the cat,' joked David in a tone that revealed his team's long-suffering but enduring friendship with the troubled soul of the team.

'He'll be fine, it's just that he was hoping that Eddie or Simon was more dreadful than him…' remarked Max, '…turns out, that's not possible.'

'Even Macca was too much for him,' reflected Max wistfully, 'it must have all just pushed him over the edge.'

Losing to the cursed coordination of Joe Mackenzie indeed, took some doing. Still, Jonny had managed even that en route to his massive meltdown and now, despite Max's endless positivity, the team was down one. Howie re-entered the room with the echoing thud of the front door still rolling around the house.

'What happened to Jonny now?' she asked

'Goats in golf shoes, Howie, you must know what he's like!' laughed Simon.

'I think he's looking at Olympic qualification by the speed he left,' added Max.

'Well, he didn't seem to be that much of a hurry when I saw him. He was messing around in the porch, kicking and pushing stuff around. When I tried to speak with him it felt like I disturbed him, actually.'

The rest of the team blew it off as Jonny being Jonny and with Bobby calling an end to the gaming, the day then took a more serious tone. 'Let's go into the other room to get this season underway properly. It's time we reminded ourselves what's at stake.'

The boys then made their way into the spacious dining room and sat round a large, immaculately polished old mahogany table. Trying to create a boardroom feeling, each player was given time to speak, rouse or motivate the team in any way they liked.

'Beating Brockton remains our top priority,' announced Bobby during his stirring opening. The room, however, had become like a Colonel's office in an army barracks in the drifting lunacy of Eddie's mind. Bobby, in full dress including shiny shoulder epaulettes and a banded peaked cap was clearly in control.

'Skill is useful but we need to play as a team that outworks our opponents,' added David White who stood resolute and focused too during his delivery. Eddie manufactured David's dark hair and red hoody into a bearskin hat and tunic. The intently disciplined midfielder stood tall in front of the large cabinet behind him. Eddie saw only an expressionless guard in the archway of his sentry box.

Simon and George were crouched either side of military radio equipment, in combat gear, taking everything in on their army issue headsets. Composed and alert, they absorbed every word, without judgment or question, ready to relay the mission across the battlefield. Through the sound of static and high-pitched feedback came the voice of one of the Stratton twins.

'Hey lads, you're welcome to tweety pie and his little runt tag-along,' Sam mocked, 'you'll need more than those two jokes to get near us!'

'Yeah, they're only gonna get flattened again!' scoffed Ben.

The Colonel, with a fierce grip on his chalk and head steaming with rage, instantly took down the name of Mildham and added it to the list of foes to be overcome for the honour of his regiment and its new members. The painful screech of chalk clawing along the board snapped Eddie from his special forces fantasy.

The rest of the boys' time at Bobby's was spent eating, joking and enjoying more football out in the garden.

As the day came to an end, parents arrived with wondering questions about the red floored front steps. Bobby's teenage brother, Theo, also strolled in. Though he agreed to be at home to look after things, he had decided that he wasn't going to waste his day "looking after that bunch of *hypers*." He helped himself to some of the left-overs, oblivious to the disapproving looks of the parents around him.

As they made their way to leave, Eddie and Simon chatted to Bobby along the hallway.

'If you keep doing your jobs at each end of the pitch fellas, we'll be in great shape,' complimented Bobby as the boys picked up their bags to leave. Eddie didn't notice that his bag had been left unzipped as he collected it, still talking as he was with his captain.

'Got any more of those headers in your locker Eddie? I still don't know where you got those wings from,' Bobby called down the pathway as the boys strolled away.

'Don't ask me, guess there's more than one *bird* on the team eh!' replied Eddie, waving his arms out and making a comical face.

Walking home, with the fast-setting sun giving off more glare than warmth, Eddie's thoughts reflected on the day and the experiences at Mildham. Ignoring the temptation to overreact with more wild plans along the way home, he and Simon chose to keep the conversation light, both reliving the fun they had shared at Bobby's. They parted at the top of

Eddie's road, with faces that seemed older. The events of the day had created a new and profound responsibility. Perhaps that was why their expressions carried the maturity and purpose.

Great friends though they were, Eddie did not mention what he had found in *the room*. It remained stashed, or so he thought, in his bag. Keeping the bag out of sight as he got to his front door, Eddie flung it high onto the flat garage roof knowing that once inside, he could get to it from the landing window at the top of the stairs. As usual, his dad had not returned from work. The work that Eddie now guessed probably was not that of the everyday travelling businessman.

Leaning out of the landing window, Eddie hoisted his bag from the black-tarred garage roof. It was the last secret of a day that had provided more questions than answers. 'Surely he would have told me,' Eddie thought as he lay in bed that night, wondering if Simon knew about his dad's involvement. He certainly could have no idea what Eddie had picked up off that grime covered floor. The tiepin!

Eddie shot up with his face burning in panic. He grabbed his backpack and unzipped each compartment frantically. Preoccupied with hiding the evidence from the Mildham raid away from his mum, he had forgotten to check for his dad's pin. The clothes were as he left them but as he reached into the pocket of his old school trousers, he felt nothing but cotton and stitching. Anxiously, Eddie pulled each garment out one by one and frenziedly turned the creases; still nothing. The main section was clear and only some crumbs and a couple of pencils remained lying at the bottom. Eddie's eyes did that mad flickering from side to side again, trying and failing to explain its disappearance. He instinctively lifted the bag up to gauge its weight and the contents of its other sections. There was a clink of coins in a side pocket. Opening it as wide as the zip would allow, he delved in and pulled out the contents. Throwing his head up and with a huge breath, he released the emotion of rediscovering the flat-sided silver clip.

No sooner as he did, his thoughts whirred. 'Who found it? How did they find it? Why did they move it and not take it?' The questions streamed like blood from a wound leaving Eddie feeling pained and exposed. The only consolation was the fact that in his hand lay the evidence of his dad's connection with *the room*.

For the rest of the night, he clasped the tiepin close to his chest, waiting for the front door to click open and make its familiar scratching sound on the bristled mat that would mark his dad's return. Despite wanting, more than anything, to remain awake and confront his dad, Eddie's energy and alertness betrayed him again. His eyes faded as he succumbed to the tiredness brought on by the craziness of the day.

CHAPTER 7

AN UNRAVELLING JOURNEY

'Hey buddy boy, shake a leg!' barked Peter Freeman, Eddie's dad, waking his son abruptly. Before Eddie knew where he was, the sun had crashed through the window and his nose had been belted by the smell of freshly fried bacon.

'Here, get your fangs into this!' he insisted, holding a heavily sauced bacon butty in front of his wincing and startled son. Mr. Freeman always spent what little time he had with Eddie acting like a hyperactive little brother.

'Guess what you're doing today, Elf?' his dad enthused. E, L and F were Eddie's initials and a tightly guarded secret for obvious reasons. Mr. Freeman had always used this name in affection and only out the earshot of others. Thanks to his dad's shrewd, tongue-in-cheek remarks, Eddie actually enjoyed the irony of being short by name as well as nature.

'What…What's happening?' replied Eddie, now sharper and diving into his breakfast treat.

'We're going flying,' his dad exclaimed, his eyes gripping Eddie's, waiting for a reaction. His face closed in and bit the back of Eddie's sandwich.

'Hey, stop!' cried Eddie then continued, 'Flying? When? Where? Who wi….' He was dazed in amazement.

'Never mind all that, Elf my boy, you've got ten minutes before we're off,' said dad, cutting him off. 'Finish that sarney and whack some jeans on. Meet you downstairs.' After his orders, Mr. Freeman left the room with the speed he had entered it.

Eddie gleefully grabbed the stray clothes nearby, flew round the bathroom before leaping loudly down every other step and clouting his whole body into the wall waiting at the bottom of the stairs. Then, without slowing and clutching the remains of his breakfast, he spilled out through the front door which had been left conveniently open. To his surprise, there was a car waiting on the road outside. To his even greater surprise he saw the faces of both Mr. Jacobs and Mr. Bird sitting inside it. They were chin-wagging like old friends, in casual clothes and relaxed in the front seats of Mr. J's estate. Eddie's eyes widened with crazed mystification.

'You ready then?' called his dad, noticing Eddie's charge out of the house suddenly freeze as rigidly as early morning frost.

He was so entranced, the S.I.D.D. (Secure Independent Domestic Drone), went completely unnoticed as it dutifully melted the ice from his mum's car with its heat emitting fan blades. The sight of the men together was utterly bewildering to him.

'Don't worry Eddie, they won't bite us,' quipped his dad, gesturing to join him as if this were some sort of everyday occurrence. Walking towards the car, trying to hold his nerve, Eddie's head invented all manner of reasons to explain what was going on. But try as he might to stay in the moment, his thoughts wandered and he now watching the rear door open with his mind emptying everyone from his subconscious onto the back seat.

First a man, suited like the intruder and wearing an oversized sharply flashing tiepin appeared, followed by Howie wearing trendy clothes and a fun smile. After that, a human-sized version of Mrs. Crandall's excitable parrot, Perry. He leapt out flapping and hopping madly around the driveway. Jonny Wilson then suddenly came charging and began ferociously chasing the huge bird with an oversized butterfly net on the end of a long wobbly pole. Finally, there was Simon, leant up against the car, shrugging with confusion whilst sitting happily behind him, his doting sister, dreamily gazing in Eddie's direction.

A loud clonk of the door handle snapped Eddie from his wigging out. Up 'til now, the tinted rear windows had obscured his view of the back of the car. Now, climbing in, he found himself alone and underwhelmed. Worse still, the mysterious partnership of the two in front made an odd atmosphere inside the car.

'Morning Eddie,' said Mr. Bird from the passenger seat.

'Morning,' replied Eddie in a quiet and reserved voice.

'Yes, good morning young man!' resounded Mr. Jacobs. Eddie cringed, raised his hand and chewed on the remains of his bacon roll.

'Ah, yes I suppose it is a little early for you,' Mr. J consoled.

'Right chaps, let's get going,' urged Eddie's father.

Mr. Jacobs sped away from the house with a confident squeaking of tyres. As Eddie recoiled, he was surprised that only Simon's dad reacted in the same way. The others seemed unmoved by the car's forceful thrust.

'Get going where?' asked Eddie.

'You'll see son…You're in for quite a day,' came the reply.

The dew of the morning lifted with Eddie staring out of his window. The spider that had carefully spun its web in the car's wing mirror was now making a frantic escape along one of its threads and back behind the mirror casing. Eddie wondered if he might be better off back there too. He was pleased to be with his dad but the trip seemed very, very weird… almost ominous. It was as if normality had vanished, just as it did during his strange and overwhelming daydreams.

As they travelled, Eddie felt, or at least hoped, there would be an explanation before they reached… well, wherever they were going. The car appeared to be heading towards London, about half an hour away but he still had no idea why they were going there, let alone why they were all together. Had his dad and Mr. Bird always known Mr. Jacobs? What type of flying could you do in a congested capital city? One thing was for sure, Eddie's mind seemed less and less his own in the crowded silence which was broken only by Mr. Bird's rustling through a paper bag. He retrieved another one of his wife's baked treats and reduced it to crumbs, in one satisfying bite. At a similar speed, Eddie felt flashes from his other wild unrealities start to confront him in relentless waves. From his earliest days to the recent events on the football pitch, the visions had developed with an airborne theme a lot of the time. His mind connected these pictures to his dad's promise of flying today.

It seemed a moment later when a jolt of the car and the sound of tyres riding over a hard surface interrupted all thought. Eddie refocused his eyes. He found himself with his head gently pressing against the window and instantly recognized the view of Canary Wharf as they crossed the Thames.

From the flat and low Connaught Bridge, that seemed just feet from the water of Royal Victoria Dock, he squinted at the intensity what stared back at him. The river passing to his side, shimmered in front of him and reflected the crisp, morning skyline behind.

Driving on, the windows of every skyscraper appeared as minute panels on a disco mirror ball and the lines of each building and their towering emblems created a pearlescence that danced into the flawless blue sky above. Eddie was just getting in his right mind again when his dad leant calmly over.

'Eddie, I'm just going to put this on you. You see, we're taking you on a bit of a mystery tour.' With that, some sort of oversized, thick hood was pulled down over Eddie's head and eyes. If he hadn't before, he felt utterly in the dark now. The runway of the London City Airport, out of the opposite window, was the last thing Eddie noticed.

'Don't worry Eddie, it won't be long now,' reassured his dad, in a tone mixed with soft comfort and excitement. He sat in the continuing silence only for a while longer. The three men were talking quietly, using words sparingly, with Mr. Freeman directing Mr.Jacobs' manoeuvres.

'Yeah, just there,' confirmed his dad shortly before another jolt and the feeling of the car dropping down a steep slope.

'Why didn't Mr. Jacobs just use the car's navigation system?' wondered Eddie. As they descended, something heavy and metal seemed to cause the ground to vibrate in time. Eddie couldn't tell if something was opening or turning but either way, the mechanism was affecting some massive structure. The car had come to a stop and the sounds around now echoed. It was clear that they were underground.

'You ok, Eddie?' asked his dad. He had left his hand on Eddie's head for the last stage of the journey, perhaps partly to offer Eddie comfort or more likely to ensure Eddie couldn't attempt to remove the hat that concealed the last ten minutes of the ride.

'Yeah, I'm alright,' Eddie replied, 'can I take this thing off now?'

'One more minute son, I'll get you out of the car first,' replied his dad.

A smell like a museum, as if ancient and aging materials were surrounding him struck Eddie as he was lifted out from the idling car which peeled off with a drifting whine. Eddie's dad took him through a face scanning, military grade clearance area, though Eddie was none the wiser. He heard a door shut behind him and through the quiet that remained, a faint humming noise beckoned them. The concrete walling and heavy-tiled floor had given way to a metal-framed corridor leading to a final heavily protected door. As it opened Mr. Freeman took his hands away from his son.

'There you go,' he said.

Eddie took the prompt and slid the hat slowly up and away from his face. For the first time he witnessed, towering before him, an expanse full of bewildering excitement; a view which would soon become all too familiar to Eddie. For today, Eddie had been brought to the D.E.E.P.

'You're in my world now my lad,' said an eager voice behind him.

Mr. Bird had got out of the car at the same time as Eddie and his dad and followed them in.

'After your little *find* yesterday, I thought you might like a tour as somewhat of an explanation,' he added, out of Mr. Freeman's earshot.

The building more resembled a vast, dome-shaped hangar. From the entrance that Eddie had arrived through, he could see drones being prepared in service areas. Action bays, above on a balcony, curved the arena. Higher still, in the lofted extents, crafts that looked far more agile and developed than anything Eddie had seen before were manoeuvring at incredible speeds; navigating with power and precision. The ceiling of the place seemed to stretch almost out of sight. It was hard to make out any of the structural detail apart from the huge vents that forced air across the spans of emptiness up there. Eddie guessed they were wind gust simulators and tried to work it all out. However, he could have no idea what he was involved in.

Wrapping high around the side of the hangar at the far end was a horseshoe-shaped balcony. On it were what looked like pilots, controlling the airborne drones. Each operator's seat swayed in time with the movements of their machines in mid-air. The link between the two was astonishing; fluid and instantaneous.

Eddie stood, utterly mesmerized, feeling like he needed hours just to see, let alone understand, the magnitude of his surroundings. This was no ordinary test site. The drones here looked larger and more sophisticated than any he'd seen in the daily traffic. Every individual was occupied and purposefully working together in harmony. Like an engineering army preparing their forces, drones were stationed in fleets, creating a perfect pattern across the hangar floor.

'Jonathan, this is very kind of you,' remarked Eddie's dad before looking down to his son.

'Eddie, this is what Mr. Bird gets up to for a living and today, you're getting a bit of the action!'

'What action?'

'Well, Jonathan here is really the one to ask,' his dad quickly deflected.

Eddie's dad playing innocent was understandable. After all, he didn't know what Eddie had found in *that* room but here was a great opportunity to explain before Eddie was forced to ask.

'What could be so difficult about telling me?' Eddie asked himself, beginning to feel twangs of resentment and suspicion. For a moment he doubted whether his father had even been down in *the room*. Perhaps somehow Mr. Bird or someone else had got hold of the tiepin without his dad knowing. Anyway, at this point, Eddie's thoughts about it were all but dissolved by the sights and sounds around him.

Mr. Bird had a rather satisfied smile on his face. There was only one question Eddie had for him.

'What is thi...' Before he could finish, a deep-throated horn drowned his voice. It bellowed majestically around the hangar and seemed like the whole of London. Then, a bright light separated a pair of massive metal sliding doors at the farthest end of this secret sunken retreat.

Eddie hadn't noticed that the people previously working in the bays and service areas had vanished from view. His eyes magnetised to what could only be described as a mind-bendingly futuristic looking craft. A meticulously engineered drone slowly entered the hangar, shimmering on its steel carrying frame. Its streamlined, tear-shaped body gave it the sleekest of appearances. The curves of the machine were elegant and seamless. The lights that lit up the hangar faded to just one bright, shining beam that centred on the rumbling beast. Eddie's skin was swept by a breeze of electricity caused by the sheer power preparing inside the ducts of the barely turning blades; pulsing anticipation overtook his body.

'This should be fun,' announced Mr. Bird, knowingly.

Eddie looked up into his warm, bulbous eyes. He momentarily thought about Simon but before he could say anything, felt the ground roll beneath his feet. What he had thought were vents, opened like giant trap doors and solid steel structures extended out and up into the empty heights. As the sections connected, Eddie saw that some sort of test course was taking shape. Parts were suspended like aerial gates, tunnel openings had appeared and transparent tubes, like a rollercoaster's curves filled the arena. It all seemed set up for speed and danger. Light projections and lasers created a neon roadway in the air. As the final pieces secured themselves in place, the drone wound into action.

A rapid rush of air spilled from the four fan blades. They wound, almost silently, to an incredible speed. It unnervingly replaced the expected explosion of noise as the craft came to life, lifting with intent from the hangar floor.

'I can take credit for much of this Eddie,' said Mr. Bird as he crouched behind Eddie's stunned, silent frame.

'But the way it sounds? Well, none of us seem to understand how that came about.'

It was a sound that was both unreal and unerring, almost ghostly. Such a powerful machine should have shaken the walls of the hangar but its only tone was a great gust of the airstream being thrust from the blade ducts. The drone lifted from the dark floor, accelerated and blasted around the course.

In awe, Eddie scoured the balcony for a glimpse of its pilot. From what he could make out, in the darkened arena, there was no sign of anyone up there. He figured that it must be operating remotely. Turning back, he marvelled at how the craft barely slowed throughout the entire course. Somehow, it navigated through the tight tunnels and along the long, clear tubular piping, immaculately timing each curve, corner and corkscrew with such precision and speed Eddie had to believe he was imagining it. As it powered out of the final turn and completed the course, its gusty draft blew up fiercely around Eddie, reassuring him that he wasn't.

The majesty of this machine was breathtaking. Its creation; revolutionary. The drone took its place, high in the hangar and hovered with an air of invincibility.

'What is that? I mean, how can a drone do those things?' Eddie pleaded, his head turning to Mr. Bird though not his eyes.

'It hasn't really been given a name yet, Eddie. That was its first proper test,' replied Mr. Bird.

The engineers reappeared, gave a dignified applause at the successful voyage and returned to their work and testing stations. The drone landed and shut down back on its platform.

'Just look at it,' Eddie cooed in amazement.

'Yes, it'll do the job,' said Mr. Bird modestly.

The unit was just as fascinating to behold when powered down. Eddie held his gaze as it was wheeled to the back of the arena behind the doors. Just as they were closing, however, Eddie thought he caught sight of a crack, widening on one side of the drone's rounded shell. A small hatch was opening. He deepened his stare and made out the faint movement of a silhouetted shape, part in, part out of the capsule. Surely nothing was inside it he thought. The very idea caused Eddie's imagination to swell. He couldn't be sure if it was something alive or robotic but it was clearly intended not to be part of the demonstration. Judging by the actions and conversations of those around him, Eddie was sure that no one else had noticed what he had seen. Either way, the machine and whatever else was with it, had now completely disappeared.

Mr. Freeman and Mr. Bird had been talking quietly together but noticing Eddie advancing, their conversation broke off.

'What did you think, Elf?' asked his dad quickly, adjusting himself and smiling as if trying to avoid suspicion.

'Dad, was that a…?' Eddie had started to think out loud.

'Yes Eddie, a pretty crazy demonstration, don't you reckon?' his dad not seeming even remotely aware of Eddie's line of conversation.

'Oh…..oh yeah, but…'

'But what, Eddie?' Peter said quizzically.

'Er, nothing dad…I'm just a bit in shock I guess,' Eddie rethought his words; no awkward questions yet he decided. Instead, he added another to the growing line of unanswered mysteries coming from his fast-changing and unpredictable world. His dad ruffled his shaggy tufted locks.

'Come on Elf, your trip's not over yet.'

They turned together and Mr. Freeman took Eddie around the side of the arena away from the action bays and work areas. The bare wall was interspersed with vents, lighting and finally, through the murky light, the faint outline of a small door. It had no handle, just the four outlined seams of its frame. Eddie suddenly realised that his dad wasn't walking with him. He span round, puzzled.

'This is your trip Eddie; I'll see you later ok? Mr. Bird will take you where you need to go.' Mr. Freeman spoke abruptly, then left. Eddie was confused.

'Where is he going?' he asked as Mr. Bird opened the door in the same way Simon did that hatch at Mildham.

'Good question, Eddie. There is more than one reason we brought you here today,' he chirped and led Eddie through the narrow entry into a passage beyond.

'You see; I'm pretty involved with these machines but Mr. Jacobs may have more answers for you about this room you found. He's very knowledgeable about school buildings and their history.'

Eddie couldn't help feel like Mr. Bird was shielding something or at least, was enjoying playing dumb.
Eddie was led by Mr. Bird through another door. On the other side, after a short walk, they entered a small holding room. There was a rugged carpet on the floor and a single black chair like those in the *action bays*, filling one corner. This small symmetrical chamber, with an opaque glass door at each end and blackened walls whispered a sense of separation from reality. Happy daydreams, the recent moments of marvel and carefree thoughts of his friends left Eddie. He felt hollow.

Then, just as it did when he followed Mrs. Andrews after the intruder, his sight was no longer his own. His eyes met with the door he was facing, only now he was viewing it from the other side. Eddie struggled with whoever was steering his senses and tried to retrieve control. Failing, feeling powerless, filled with fear but intrigued, he gave up his resistance, hoping to discover the answers he craved by allowing his mind to follow, into the unknown.

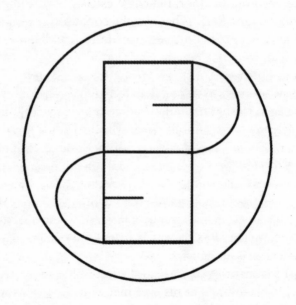

AN
ALTERNATIVE
VIEW

Eddie, or at least his view, freakishly approached the very room he and Mr. Bird were standing in! There was *the symbol* again, etched on the door. First at Westlake, then with Simon at Mildham, now here. What was the connection? Simon would have been welcome company but Eddie had to settle for his dad, who incidentally, was merrily rocking on his heels; calm and oblivious.

Without sound or warning, the steel-framed door they were facing began to shimmer and become translucent. Eddie could actually make himself out at Mr. Bird's side, inside the chamber. Eddie's vision ended with the sudden snap of the door. Although it was like glass, the door still held *the symbol* somehow inside. Coming out of his trance, Eddie found Mr. Bird exchanging some sort of coded hand signal with Mr. Jacobs. He stood blank-faced as Mr. Jacobs, now wearing a navy blue, military looking set of overalls, looked down to give a stern reassuring nod.

'I trust that demonstration was a success?' he chirped.

'What?' Eddie blurted as his eyes met with *the symbol* stitched on Jacobs' chest.

'Our new drone,' Mr. Jacobs chuckled, 'don't tell me you've forgotten it already?'

'No….no I just wasn't sure if you meant….'

'Yes!' Eddie was cut off abruptly. 'It's all this place has been living and breathing for over the past few months.'

Mr. Jacobs had picked up Eddie's thoughts and seemed eager to pre-empt and avoid further conversation in the company of Mr. Bird.

'I'm glad you had the chance to see the demonstration. Thanks Jonathan, I'm sure you'd like to get back to the hangar. I can take the boy on from here.'

Mr. Bird dropped his head, winked down and gave a kind squeeze with his plump fingers on Eddie's shoulder. The expression on his face, however, gave away the fact that he didn't know what lay ahead for the young visitor.

'See you later Eddie, and enjoy the tour,' he called, shuffling back through the holding room door to leave Eddie on his own with Mr. Jacobs. Eddie's stomach churned with a heavy expectancy.

'Let's go Eddie, the sooner we get started the better.' Mr. Jacobs was always brisk and to the point but he carried an extra verve and vigour as he paced on.

Eddie's anxious steps took him to a split in the corridor and two more of the emblem-etched doors. Mr. Jacobs' hand, once again, triggered its opening. They made their way along a darker passage from the door on the left.

'Where does the other door go?' asked Eddie

'Deeper,' came an evasive response before a change of subject.

'Eddie, you were looking through my eyes earlier. You know what it's called but you haven't been told how it works…It is only possible between those who are looking and those who can see.'

Eddie didn't appreciate the riddle.

'You have, as you well know, a great appetite for looking at things differently. You may think you have some idea of what it is; daydreaming? Letting your imagination wander? Turning your reality into a fantastical adventure? What you actually have, Eddie, is possibly the greatest version of consight we've ever seen. And consignt, Eddie, is what this place operates under and strives so hard to keep secret.'

Eddie struggled with Mr. Jacobs' long strides and confusing words. They headed up two flights of steel railed-stairs, Jacobs quickening his steps and the conversation.

'Your ability allows people like me, your *headmaster*,' using the term humorously, 'to effectively put you in two places at one time.'

Ok, Eddie thought, sure he was Westlake's renowned leader but was it just a clever cover?

'So, you controlled my sight when you were coming towards the room back there?' asked Eddie.

'Try a little deeper than that, Eddie. How do you think you jumped to score that goal? Made that turn on Jonny? Found that room with the scratched door? Even back at Mildham… the intruder? You'd have had a surprise if you would have looked up in Puff's branches more closely. You'll understand connective sight more in the days ahead but for now just remember, there are more ways than one for your abilities to be used.'

Eddie had been in a whirlwind. The speed of the "tour" and this conversation was more than he was expecting and he had no real clue how he figured in all of it. In the back of his mind, the memories of the past few months and the connective sight he'd shared suddenly surfaced.

'So, Mrs. Andrews has this power too?' asked Eddie with intrigue. Mr. Jacobs was cold and quick to respond.

'Please don't ask me about her, Eddie. She has sacrificed more than anyone should ever have to. You will say nothing more about her from this point onwards…understand?'

Eddie was shocked at how quickly Mr. Jacobs switched tone. It frustrated Eddie. Why had she left Mildham? Was she part of this secret institution? Eddie needed to know what this band of brain charmers were up to. For now, Eddie stayed quiet and they picked up speed again, striding on through a blacked out, emblem-crested door that had automatically opened. A bright light caught Eddie off-guard, as did the breeze flying forcefully into his face.

'Here comes your first lesson, or should I say, answer Eddie Freeman…' said Mr. Jacobs, with relish.

In front of them was a communication room, resourced with countless technical components. It was a feast for his eyes but they were suddenly drawn away by something up above. A section of the roof was closing and through the small gap, a drone whined away into the dark behind. The ceiling sealed shut to join both halves of *the symbol*.

'This…' announced Mr. Jacobs '…is D.E.E.P. Control.'

For the first time in his life, Eddie Freeman felt harnessed, from the inside out. He wasn't afraid, he wasn't anxious, he wasn't anything. Eddie's senses were still; his imagination had met its match.

'Deep?'

'The Drone Engagement and Elimination Patrol; London's protection from rogue and criminal drones.' And so, Eddie's new world began to explain itself. 'Runners, piloting from their action bays,' Mr. Jacobs pointed out, 'they're the best there is and there's a beloved city above that relies on them,' he added.

The pilots, each handling a complex set of instruments, sat in elevated bays that banked around the room, much like those in the testing hangar. Eddie counted 9 runners in action, although a large section of balcony appeared unused and part of that, only half-built.

'Operations vary but this patrol works for agencies that need, let's just say, an immediate and direct response. We're no glorified taxi service,' continued Mr. Jacobs. Eddie nodded, understanding now, the greater purpose.

'So, do these runners have the same *vision* as us?' Eddie asked.

'Good question, Eddie old chap, that gift is………' Mr. Jacobs was interrupted by the announcement of a returning mission.

The roof broke open again and a rushing sound of air filled the room. The military dressed runner operating the drone swivelled his chair from his screen and efficiently guided the drone down.

This was the first time Eddie had seen inside of the bay; it was incredible. Holographic displays wrapped and encompassed the chair. Like a world within a world, a near true life view from wherever the drone travelled. A powerful hiss of air dragged Eddie's eyes back to the lower level of the control room. A vast section of the grey and oddly pimpled floor promptly elevated to provide a landing stage. A small platform within it became a brightly lit target.

With speed, precision and the sound of a violent rush of air the drone was docked. The platform reconnected with the landing stage and the whole assembly was lowered back. With Eddie wondering where the drone would be parked, the floor continued to drop. The machine powering-down disappeared out of view.

'Our engineers maintain them below,' said Mr. Jacobs, feeding Eddie's obvious curiosity. 'We'll get to that later, Eddie. Come on!'

Mr. Jacobs was already returning hastily towards the sliding doors they had entered the control room from. Eddie stepped quickly behind. In the narrow hallway beyond was a large harmless looking air vent. Mr. Jacobs crouched in front of the panel cover and used the now familiar double-handed technique. A secret access door separated from the wall.

'It's easy enough to open them, Eddie…knowing where they are, is the real trick,' Mr. Jacobs spoke with a gentle respect knowing what Eddie had already seen.

'It takes a bit of practice but we've found it to be safer than a lock,' he added, walking through the wall, 'I'm not very good with keys,' he looked on, joking with himself.

Eddie remained the follower, down a passageway, curving around the outside of the control room. Lights, illuminated by their presence, lit the doors in the passage. Along with a number, they all carried *the symbol* he knew now to be the logo of the D.E.E.P.

Mr. Jacobs stopped outside one of the doors and said, 'time we spoke properly eh, Eddie?' as it gently released.

'That symbol sir, what does it mean?' asked Eddie.

'Simul autem solus,' replied Mr. Jacobs, 'it's a reminder of how the D.E.E.P. operates, gives the patrol members a sense of collective responsibility…or at least it should.'

Mr. Jacobs tailed off with a sense of lost trust in something or someone.

'Anyway, let's get on!'

The moment passed and firmly tilting his thick, tough-skinned neck, he ushered Eddie inside. Mr. Jacobs sat down comfortably behind a desk that he was clearly well acquainted with.

'Take a seat, Eddie, please.' Mr. Jacobs gestured towards a brown leather armchair set with a low table next to it. Eddie obeyed while Mr. Jacobs rummaged around for something in his drawer.

The table that separated them was huge and solid. It had a back panel that spanned across and all the way down to the floor, blocking the view under and behind where Mr. Jacobs was sitting.

'Sweet?' He pushed a half-filled paper bag containing his *special* toffees across the table.

'Thanks,' responded Eddie politely.

He dropped the sweet into his mouth and gripped both armrests tightly. To one side of Mr. Jacobs, a wall displayed a number of images, like active drones being mapped and tracked. Behind it, pictures of people, prototypes and drones from D.E.E.P.'s yesteryear hung on the wall. It seemed bemusing to Eddie that this advanced and secret agency could have such a rich and unknown history.

'Relax Eddie, I am well aware of how daunting this all may seem. You will come to understand it more fully but I warn you now, no matter what I tell you, I can't promise you'll find all the answers you're looking for. Trust, for now, is where you'll find peace.'

The greying headmaster spoke with compassion in his voice, like someone almost apologising. He sensed Eddie's torment.

'You have been part of a test, Eddie...and still are. Through our sources, we learned of your gift quite some time ago. So, we started to watch you. A simple enough job when you were younger but as you've aged, so you have bloomed more quickly and powerfully than even *we* predicted. We had to move you. You'd become too disruptive and endangered our operations. You may not see it yet but Westlake is safest; for all of us as much as you.'

Eddie was guessing that Mr. Jacobs was talking about the Mildham intruder but didn't know how things could be better at Westlake.

'Safest? Who's after me? Why? What do my parents know? What am I being tested for?'

'As I've told you, I can't answer everything, Eddie.'

Mr. Jacobs looked frustrated but then the deep craggy lines around his eyes smoothed; pleased that a bright thought of something more positive had come to him.

'Let's talk about your training,' he sparkled.

The next hour disappeared in a matter of seconds. Eddie learned how drones were now the only source of secure transport of the kinds of documents, resources and equipment that needed to remain top secret. Couriers, Mail and even the Internet were slow, prone to interception and fraught with danger. Drones could be operated safely and either pre-programmed to follow a flight path or manually piloted by runners, over any distance, even across continents.

'Where do you fit in to all of this? I'm sure you've been wondering for some time, Eddie' concluded Mr. Jacobs.

'You need my mind to guide and control something? Or maybe you want to control me?' replied Eddie with a tone of inescapable inevitability.

'Our drones, as advanced and secure as they are, find themselves in danger of becoming unreliable. The information they carry is too sensitive to be risked. Our remote piloting is constantly under attack, our pre-programmed flights virtually redundant. So far, by using decoys and untraceable units we have stayed ahead but our enemies are closing in.'

Mr. Jacobs maintained a brisk and upbeat voice, as if he knew the answer to D.E.E.P.'s problems was staring right at him.

Eddie was inspired by his sense of enormous responsibility and the obvious faith Mr. Jacobs had in him.

In response, he stood up and declared, 'I'm ready, sir! Show me what you want me to do!'

He was committed, regardless of what would be asked of him or what danger he would face. He simply knew that if this Patrol needed him, then he was prepared to do whatever it took, especially if his dad *was* involved in this whole set-up.

'You are a courageous young man, Eddie Freeman,' Mr. Jacobs enthused as he strode around the table.

'We'll need every bit of that bravery from you. You are the DEEP's newest and possibly most significant recruit of its history.'

Chuckling with delight, feeling a deep attachment, Jacobs patted Eddie firmly on the back and ushered him to the door. They left the room, spurred by each other's character and headed back down the lifting then fading light of the curved corridor.

'My friends, can I talk to them? …What about my parents?' said Eddie, suddenly recognising the magnitude of absolute secrecy.

'First things first, let's show you the ropes of the Patrol's machines. Remember, mastery is reaching the destination. Your journey, however, may have more than one path.'

Mr. Jacobs' face widened with a gentle, wry grin. Instantly, Eddie's did the same.

As they turned back through the sliding doors into the control room, Eddie noticed even more than before, those around him seemed to be taking an interest in him.

'Don't worry Eddie, they're all with us. They've just heard a lot about you,' reassured Mr. Jacobs.

Eddie tried to give of an air of seriousness, raising a hand to acknowledge those looking on before nervously lowering his head.

'Each drone has its own purpose, Eddie,' began Jacobs, 'aside from relaying data and other important articles around London, we have to occasionally deal with unwanted attention. If an active mission is under threat, this I.M.P. unit provides us with the means to intercept and counteract any hostile interference.'

'Imp, sir?' quizzed Eddie.

'Immobilizing Patroller. It's the quickest we have, it carries nothing but its eyes and an incredibly efficient jamming signal that cripples other drones. Here, look at this.'

As Mr. Jacobs spoke, he displayed holographic videos of what he was talking about. They both stared at an aggressive, sleek-looking drone manoeuvring at speeds that seemed unreal. It reached target-locking range and a disabling pulse was delivered. The offending drone seized up, engine failed and fell terminally to the ground.

'Effective... but can leave a mess,' quipped Mr. Jacobs.

Eddie sat watching all the types and tasks of the Patrol's drones for some time, learning more about their significance.

'All these drones are incredible, Sir. They are much bigger than the stunt drones I grew up with but what about the machine that was just in the hangar? It was different from anything I've seen,' quizzed Eddie.

'Well that's a good question!' barked a clear and refined voice.

Both Eddie and Mr. Jacobs spun around to see Simon, eyes alive with excitement, striding towards them with an imposing looking figure, approaching close behind.

CHAPTER 9

AN EARLY INHERITANCE

Eddie rushed forward and the two friends shook each other furiously with excitement.

'Bet you were wondering when I'd finally show up, eh?' said Simon, trying to contain himself.

'Yeah, what kept you?'

'Well I had to wait in case you freaked out and lost it! They didn't want me to see the mess, you know, if this all got too much for you,' he ribbed jokingly. 'I told them, with your imagination, this place would seem like a home from home!'

The boys both laughed, thinking the same thing about how they wished it *was* their home. Simon continued to talk; exhilarated and breathless.

'No idea where we are. They covered me up outside.'

'Me too. Who brought you?' Eddie asked, thinking it impossible for Mr. Bird to have made it there and back so quickly.

'Ah, I think that's where I come in,' announced a tall, smart and official looking man. His thin stature and loftiness towered up high over Simon.

'Yes indeed,' Mr. Jacobs interjected, 'Eddie, this is the D.E.E.P.'s Mission Leader; Commander Michael Gibson.'

Eddie had noticed the men had both exchanged the same hand signal as Jacobs had done with Simon's dad. After he extended his arm straight down, tight-fisted to his side, Jacobs drew his hand across his chest holding three spaced fingers out horizontally. The Commander made the same three-fingered salute and bent his arm, making a fist in front of his shoulder on the same right side.

Gibson eased and looked down to make his first formal greeting.

'Pleased to meet you, Eddie. I trust you've been made to feel welcome. We're looking forward to having you with us. I'm hoping that you and your friend here will be of great use to us. Simon showed steady nerves whilst we *acquired* him today and I'm confident you'll thrive here too if you take his example.'

Simon was pleased of the compliment and smiled even though he had less of a grip on things than he was letting on. He'd dealt with so many *moments* with Eddie, he'd learned to accept life as a whirring mash of fun, fact and fantasy. He could never really piece all the twists and turns together but was nonetheless, content to suffer the journey.

'How far have you got along with bringing Eddie up to speed, Tom?' Both Eddie and Simon smirked at each other at hearing his first name.

'Eddie has got some of the background ok, we've just started on the hardware.'

'Good, good… Have you got any questions Eddie?' enquired the Commander.

'Just one,' Eddie replied without hesitation. 'Can you tell me what happened at Mildham that day? I think I understand about how I saw the chase now but I don't get what that man in the suit was up to.'

Both men looked at each other sharing an unspoken moment just as the boys had moments earlier but instead of surprise or joy, the sad and forsaken expressions they mirrored ruined the atmosphere and appeared to offer little hope of an easy answer.

'Our job here is often undertaken at great personal sacrifice,' began Gibson, 'There are no medals, no public notoriety or parades for our successes. We simply share a common purpose to serve, protect and where necessary, intervene using tactical covert technology. This and the secrecy we keep, burdens us all in different ways.'

The Commander's speech had started to take the boys' minds into a darker place. As he continued, Eddie tried to think of how his life might change with his family and Simon felt the cold lonely chill that came with the series of secrets and silence he'd been forced to endure. The Commander continued with a voice filled with anguish.

'The man you saw used to be one of us. He was a colleague, a comrade, a close friend, lured away and led down a path that is hard to return from. The rewards he betrayed us for were irresistible to him. So, instead of a man of solidarity we have an adversary. Instead of trust, we have stolen information and instead of a man of good, who needed no gain, we have a foe who would profit from our destruction. His actions compromised not just our base at Mildham but our whole Patrol. Nevertheless, it is not in us to lose our memory. Our hope remains that he'll return, that he hasn't wandered too far himself, as to forget.'

'But if he's let you down so badly, how could you want him back?' Eddie couldn't grasp it.

'Young man,' replied the Commander, 'betrayal is a deep wound but separation without hope is a failure of man's faith in what is right.'

He drew breath to hold back his obvious suffering:

'The forgiveness of others has the power to restore,
From despair and all loss; the scars of this war.
Like torn flesh that heals to smooth, mended skin,
Its power makes repentant, those souls locked in sin.'

As the Commander broke off, his enchantingly deep-set eyes welled. They spoke of the battle between broken trust and absolute faith. The moment offered a window into the confidence the men had previously shared. The double-crossing and deception that now threatened to expose the entire Patrol still somehow failed to shake the Commander from his belief.

'We live in hope, boys,' Mr. Jacobs said, 'and hope can be a dangerous thing. If anyone finds out about who we are and what we do, it's over… for us all. Eliminating a criminal threat is a delight and ruining their mode of villainy, utter joy. But trying to eliminate a threat made of flesh and blood, someone we know and will always care for, despite their flaws? No…there's always another way…though our options are limited. Therefore, for now, hope is the rock on which we stand. We are a small but powerful extension of what is right in the world. We'll succeed, or we'll fail but the truth remains; *simul autem solus*, we are together… but alone.'

Eddie and Simon had little time to ponder. Their thoughts became interrupted by the creaking of the steel platform and a mechanical high-pitched whirring from below. Another UAV was being hastily elevated into place ready for its mission. Its runner jumped into a vacant action bay, strapped in and grabbed the controls. Behind her, the rounded walls of the bay displayed flight data and mission information. Eddie and Simon watched on in fascination.

The runners all seemed well drilled during operations, looking highly organized in dark blue uniforms that all bore the logo of the DEEP.

Eddie could hear radio communication, though he couldn't see any communication link or headgear on the runner. As he and Simon watched the mission unfold, the Commander and Mr. Jacobs talked quietly together, a little way from the boys. Eddie felt the men's eyes park on the back of his head and

92

impulsively spun around. Though his instincts had served him well, they were of little use. The men turned briskly back towards each other leaving Eddie nervously wondering.

He himself had spent most of the day entranced but struggling to see how his gift would be of use to them. The time seemed right to try and find out more. If it was too much for the Commander to open up about the intruder, then at least he could explain what type of work they had in mind for him. Besides, Eddie was starting to think more about his dad and the tiepin; he still had so much to figure out. When the haunting echo of an I.M.P.'s blades faded deep behind the darkness of the exit tunnel, Eddie took the restored calm as his cue.

'What was your friend after, Sir? What was he looking for at Mildham?'

'Information, Eddie,' the Commander started to reply openly. 'Clues, anything that would lead him to this place. Each person you have seen here today shares a loyal commitment and dedication to the Patrol. Only a handful of people know the true purpose of this room. We have ways to cover our tracks to a point but if we can't protect what's in here, what chance do we have of protecting lives out there?

'Is he working for someone?' Eddie pressed.

'We're working on that, Eddie,' replied the Commander. 'We have our hunches but it's safe to say we have upset a lot of people in our line of work.'

Eddie hesitated before continuing his questions. Both Mr. Jacobs and the Commander's faces had become more serious, perhaps having started to share more than they had thought or wanted to. Perhaps having second thoughts on having *kids* brought in.

'I'm sure he'll come to his senses, Sir. I've learned that good friends can surprise you in ways you can only imagine.' Eddie

spoke with a bright and positive tone. It had the intended
effect and both men looked kindly at each other.

'Indeed, Eddie. Time for a lesson or two, eh?' said the
bristle-haired Commander, patting Eddie on the shoulder and
guiding him out.

As they left, the Commander paused (he was staring back at
the area under construction by the side of the action bays).
Then he spoke with a crackle of curious intent.

'When that's finished, Eddie, your training will really start.'

They made their way back to the hangar, or F.I.Z. (Flight
Induction Zone), as it was known. After having a quick 'Bird'
lunch of sandwiches, rolls and other homemade treats, Eddie
started his piloting practice. The design of the action bays
enabled a runner's eyes and ears to be in contact with the
D.E.E.P. wherever their mission took them.

Simon was able to take part in some of the tasks and even
persuaded the Commander to let them race after showing
some decent mastery of the both the I.M.P. and the heavy
duty M.E.R.M.A. (**M**ulti-Purpose **E**xtreme **R**ange **M**ail
Assistant). Using display screens in the action bay rather than
direct line of sight was new to them both and challenging. A
few spins and embarrassing bumps later though, the boys
found their feet.

The action bays made them feel like an active onboard pilot
with a huge curved screen surrounding the chair. Steering and
throttling these machines with such speed and force left
Eddie with no room for his imagination. This *flight of fantasy*
was real. Hard heavy turns, tight twisting corkscrews, gravity-
defying inverted loops; the drone mirrored perfectly Eddie's
movements around the expanse of the F.I.Z. and all of its
testing obstacles.

'You seem to be in your element here already, Eddie!' The
trip sharply ended with the face of the Commander
unexpectedly appearing on the screen. Thrown by his view,

eyes peeling, Eddie threw his hands up in shock and self-preservation. Gibson had caught Eddie unaware, opening his action bay without warning. He chortled, enjoying and reliving the same old trick he'd played on every runner who had ever trained in an action bay. Eddie shook himself.

'Yes Sir, that was...well, like another world!' Eddie had taken to his new *work* like a duck to water.

The boys' faces stayed lit with joy long after they had parted with the Commander and D.E.E.P. They were still glowing on their journey back home with Mr. Jacobs and it was not until Simon and his dad were dropped off that Eddie was finally forced to become a simple human being again.

'It goes without saying that I don't expect you to mention a word of this to me or Simon at school,' said Mr. Jacobs, returning to his familiar controlling and composed ways.

'Yes Sir,' Eddie replied firmly, knowing he would never risk losing this great new world.

The headmaster smiled. 'Good lad.'

He seemed reassured and directed his conversation to both Freemans as they got out of the car.

'Well, I'll see you both again during the week. Peter, I'll be in touch.'

Peter nodded, shut the door and followed Eddie down the homely brick-paved drive of his house. Mr. Jacobs' tyres gave a squeak and he was away.

'Fish and chips, Elf? Then a decent chat about today,' his dad suggested. 'Let mum know I'll be back in a bit, ok,' he called back as he started a lively jog.

Once inside, Eddie thought it best to not speak about his day in detail with his mum.

'Good time, Eddie?' she asked casually.

'Yeah, but I'm pretty tired.' He replied. Ally was surprised but happily welcomed Eddie's long hug. 'Dad said he'll be back in a bit. He's gone to the chippy.'

'Yes, he said he would bring dinner in tonight,' she said, stroking her son's untamed locks and trying to hold him for just a bit longer.

'Shout when he gets back will you? I'll be in my room.'

Eddie eased away and made quickly for his room, wanting to avoid any awkward questions.

'Of course, my lord. I'll have the maid call for you!' Ally quipped, as he thumped up the stairs.

After every scrap of batter and chip flake had been vacuumed from Eddie's plate, he and his dad started to tidy the dinner things away.

'Well, seeing as you men have this all under control, I'm going to relax in the lounge. One of your coffees sounds good right now, Pete?' she hinted and smiled expectantly as she left the room.

The moment seemed perfect for Eddie and his dad to finally talk. They had shared their lives together, yet how much of his dad did he actually know?

'Yep, give me a minute, Ally, I'll bring it through.'

Standing in the kitchen and after silently catching each other's eye, Mr. Freeman nodded in the direction of the hallway.

They both slipped upstairs. Eddie was led past his own bedroom and into the spare room. It was small and Eddie rarely went in it. Peter and Ally had used it as a makeshift workspace but it seemed more of a dumping ground now. Eddie believed that his dad must have thought it more private and out of earshot. He nervously prepared his thoughts, not really knowing what to expect.

'So, was that the type of flying you expected?' his dad asked. Peter's steely eyes pierced through his slim-framed glasses.

'I didn't expect anything like that dad, it was incredible!' replied Eddie, barely able to keep his voice down.

'Yeah, it's pretty impressive, right? There was a lot for you to enjoy I've been told…'

'You've been told? Don't you know about…?' Eddie hesitated with confusion.

'I saw those great new drones! So, were you allowed to have a go with one?' came the quick reply.

'Dad, you mean to say you don't know anything about that place?'

His dad gave a puzzled expression.

'Simon's dad said you'd have a day of flying and learning, I know that much. I guessed it was a state-of-the-art sort of aerodrome.'

'Why did you have to cover my head?' responded Eddie.

'That was all part of the surprise, Elf, I thought you'd enjoy the suspense,' his dad said.

'OK, you don't know anything.' Eddie despaired and sunk his hand deep into his jeans pocket. 'Well, what's this…?'

The silver tiepin seemed to gleam with the guilt of a life untold. Recognising it straight away, Peter's eyes gripped the object as hard as Eddie's tightly clamped fingers.

'Um, where..?' The colour and life in Eddie's dad's face vanished. His eyes grew panicked.

'…In the underground room at Mildham.' Eddie answered his dad's half-finished question.

For a moment, Eddie's dad looked as if he was trying to come up with a cover story. His words so far had seemed to oppose Eddie's reality. The two of them just stared at each other, almost too scared to go on, each thinking they had some knowledge the other dare not know.

Finally, Eddie's dad slumped dejectedly onto the one seat in the room and held his head in his hands. The person sitting there was a stranger to Eddie. His usually powerful frame, now wilted and weak, perched uneasily on an old, brittle wooden chair. Drawing his breath over his teeth and looking up with eyes tearing, Peter began. His tone was earnest and guilt-ridden.

'I'm sorry, Eddie. I was hoping this day would never have had to come. You've got to understand, I only wanted to protect you. We thought we could operate without your help for years.'

'What do you mean, without my help... Who's we?'

'I'm part of the Patrol, Eddie. I've been with them since the beginning, even before drones. It's torn me apart every morning that I've left for work, all these years, knowing that I can't tell you where I am going. I would leave early, before you were awake and if you ever asked, I just brushed you off. Though I hated it, time went by and I grew to accept it. It wasn't long before it became second nature to me to live my working day alone, in secrecy. But then there was the day... that day at school, when you first found consight and we struggled with... I'll call him what he is...a traitor.'

Eddie instantly knew that his dad must have tried to protect the room from the intruder and lost his tiepin during the chaotic encounter he'd only partly witnessed.

Peter confessed.

'I realised then, you were too valuable to us to be left in the dark. I just couldn't bring myself to tell you.'

Leaning closer to his dad, Eddie's disappointment turned into tight-lipped frustration.

'Why not?' he demanded.

A reply came that Eddie didn't like, though any dad would understand the reason for it.

'You're growing up so quick, Elf. I just wanted to cling onto the hope that you wouldn't have to worry about where I am or what I'm doing. I didn't want you to miss out on growing up, a carefree kid, like me. I knew you had a good chance of inheriting consight but if you didn't, I thought it best that you know nothing at all. My job has been messy at times, Elf, finding that tiepin has told you that already. We have a responsibility to protect the D.E.E.P, its people and those who rely on it. You have made me proud, Eddie and I'm glad there'll be no more secrets. It's our Patrol now.'

As Eddie saw his life through his father's eyes, he felt his own resentment dissolve. Throwing his arms out, Eddie gripped tighter round his dad than ever before. Mr. Freeman engulfed Eddie; finally sharing his true self and his undying affection. It was at this moment, Eddie felt the unmistakable sensation of a new and thrilling chapter start to unfold in their lives.

'Peter! Where's my coffee?' came the rather riled request from below.

Dad's duties couldn't be ignored! They let go and their choked-up expressions broke into sad comedy.

'Ooh Peter, it sounds serious,' joked Eddie, through his tear-stained face.

'Be even more serious if she finds us in *her* room,' chuckled Peter and bundled downstairs. 'I'll need that tiepin back, Elf,' he said, twisting round the bannister.

Eddie looked down at the shining clip sitting in the palm of his hand. Curving his fingers firmly over it, he thought he might have a better idea.

CHAPTER 10

AN UNESCAPABLE REALITY

Eddie and Simon spent the rest of the weekend messing around with some of Mr. Bird's castaway old machines in the Bird's back garden and in the field beyond. The trees, standing frigid and bare like ancient and forgotten statues in the open meadow, made for good obstacles to race around. The damp and misty air shaped the sound of the motors into ghostly whispers.

Strangely, the boys found themselves speaking mostly about the upcoming field trip as well as the football match scheduled for when they went back at school after the week-long break. Neither felt the need to talk about the D.E.E.P, thinking that if they did, their guessing would just lead to frustration or a fear of the unknown. Anyway, they were pretty sure they would be back in their buried bubble soon. For now, the Bird's house was enough for Eddie. It gave him a sense of safety and hiding; a place that knew him, giving so much and taking nothing in return.

As the muttering of machines and competitive taunts dwindled, a stillness descended. Looking out and away from the house, sitting on an old rotting log, they both let their eyes linger and reflect. The aura of this particular mid-autumn day was more magical than any Eddie could remember. His imagination took him on a tour, extending his view. Nature was slowly settling like an old man wilting before his rest. The features on each leafless branch, the deep and thick mire of the freshly turned soil, the woods that stretched out looming with darkness on the horizon all seemed to be magnified then crystallized in time.

With an eerie likeness, Eddie sensed the symmetry of his own life with what was in front of him. He knew that the things he had discovered, in time, would fully change his world, just as the season was sinking nature into a raw and desolate time. Eddie thought about whether his world would leave him just as cold and alone. Would he too, be isolated by this inherited surreal art of the mind? His imagination had always given him so much fun and excitement; he had found it easy to disguise its darker side. The constant fear of being abandoned by reality had recently started to nag at Eddie and now, like the mud-clogged boots hanging below him, he felt the weight of it.

Eddie's long-departed eyes had not gone unnoticed. Simon had grown to recognize the body language and expressions of his friend when he was somewhere else. He broke the silence, more out of curiosity than concern.

'Do you always go where you want?'

'Huh?.....oh, not always,' said Eddie. 'It feels like it's changing...or maybe I am.'

'Give it time, Eddie, we've found out way more than they wanted us to. It's a lot to take in,' Simon consoled.

Eddie was feeling both insecure and impatient. His tone became agitated.

'Dad told me that this connective sight is powerful and can be used in different ways. Apparently, the older I get, the more control I'll have. Right now, mate, it feels like I'm stuck trying to hold a cracked egg. Couldn't there just be a book I could learn it all from?' he finished rhetorically.

Simon stood up and threw the hood of Eddie's sweater over his head and wrapped it around his face trying to lighten his mood.

'Hey, talking of books, if Mr. J really can see everything, you won't have any excuses with your homework now then will ya?!' Simon laughed and face-washed Eddie through the fleecy hood.

'Oi! Get off!' Eddie muffled, wildly waving his arms around.

Letting go, Simon fled back to the house to warm up and more importantly, escape retaliation.

The next few days of their school break disappeared in a haze of adrenalin-filled adventure. Though Eddie and Simon were given great guidance and training towards their duties, it still had not become clear what their ultimate role would be.

Simon was mostly in the control room being taken through what the **R**emote **A**ssistance **B**ackup **I**ntelligence **T**eam (RABIT) did. They were a small team of communication and surveillance experts that acted as a failsafe for missions that became comprised. He learned how to operate UAVs to act as malfunctioning decoys and was drilled on other emergency procedures, both mechanical and human.

Eddie spent most of his time in the F.I.Z, working in the action bays and was taught about the astonishing covert abilities of each unit.

That is, until the day when the Commander summoned him and Simon to the control room. He met them in the waiting chamber with a look of great anticipation.

'Today chaps, your training really takes off, just as I promised you.'

'The action bays!' chimed Eddie and Simon.

The section of the room that had been under repair was now modified and the new recruits charged for their custom-built bays. From the personalized seats to the perfectly sized controls, every detail of their bays was tailored to improve Eddie and Simon's performance. The wall wrapped totally around them with only a small door to enter by that all but vanished when it closed. Eddie's bay was different from the others in that he lay forward on his seat on a small padded and curved bench. Harnesses came from above and around the snug fitting body support to secure him. Eddie, surprised at its comfort but sensing his purpose, readied for action.

'What's next, Sir?'

'There's an I.M.P. waiting for you in the Flight Induction Zone. Why don't you have some fun?'

On Gibson's command, Eddie's bay lit up. The curved sides gave him the view from inside his drone and to his joy and astonishment, the ceiling and floor illuminated to produce a complete 360-degree image. Eddie grinned and ripped his drone away from its platform. The sudden movement of his bench took him by surprise and his first few moves were slower and more precise.

Every turn and thrust was cleverly simulated by a variety of mechanisms attached to the body-gripping frame he was held to. Huge dives and wall-skimming high-speed turns gave Eddie the sense of actually being in the unit itself. Simon looked on, almost as excited as his pilot friend.

They both shared the remaining days preparing for missions and training in their bays. It was as if they both were in a constant, make-believe world, like two boys replaying a favourite dream over and over at will.

During this time, the exact location of D.E.E.P. headquarters remained unknown to the boys. Each time they were close, unexpected strategies were used to prevent them from having to carry the burden of another secret.

Towards the end of the week, both boys found themselves in Commander Gibson's office. Jacobs had led them into the same dark corridor and knocked on the first door; room number one.

'Yes, come on in,' came the Commander's invitation.

'Here they are, Sir,' said Jacobs, ushering the boys through the door.

'Thank you, Tom…Take a seat, chaps,' said Gibson, killing the seventies-style supermarket store music he regularly had jingling in the background.

He reached down into a drawer under his desk.

'I have been looking forward to this moment and I think you will both quite enjoy it too.'

He sat back up and leant forward, placing not more sweets, as the boys expected but two dark cylinders on the table.

'Before you open these, I want you to know that they are not presents or some sort of graduation gift for your hard work. They are a necessary tool, designed specifically for your work here…With that said, go ahead, they're yours now.'

The boys took the smart round containers in their hands and intuitively twisted each end. The cylinder separated and the contents elevated smoothly up. To their surprise, they were both looking at what seemed to be just a piece of thin, springy transparent plastic film.

'You don't seem impressed, lads. Let me show you how they work,' Gibson said, noticing the boys' bewilderment. 'Here, slip them around your wrists.'

Both Eddie and Simon looped the material around and allowed the flexy film to find a comfortable area along their forearms. A slim black band at each end of the material gently curled over and clasped together; it felt almost living. The Commander produced a large black tube from within his table.

'Now, here, step forward, Simon. Slide your hand through and grip the bar at the end,' he instructed.

Having slid his arm down the tube, Simon clutched the cold steel at its base.

'I've got it, Sir,' responded Simon.

'Ok, hold it firmly but don't strain. Just a few seconds…' said Gibson.

The black tube covered Simon's arm, up to his elbow and then lit up from the inside with a spinning blue circle of light.

'Good, Simon, nice and still,' coaxed the Commander.

Simon felt the material on his arm grip and warm slightly. He wanted to see what was happening but kept his arm motionless in the tube, out of sight. The light dimmed and Gibson looked proudly towards him.

'Now, slowly let go on the bar and ease your hand out, Simon.'

The material that had given a warming hug, inside the tube, had vanished as Simon looked down at his bare arm. Just the two fine black lines remained.

'What now?' he asked.

'Tap your first and middle finger alternately against your thumb twice, please.' Seeing puzzlement in Simon's eyes, Gibson directed him with his own hand. 'Like this, nice and smooth.'

'WOAH!' exclaimed Simon.

The motion triggered a light that seemed to brighten from within his own flesh. An image formed within what was now a glowing emerald green forearm. Simon's spellbound face illuminated, revealing a mouth gaping down in astonishment at *the symbol* of the D.E.E.P.

'You'll see that it operates only with your own fingers. It should have everything you need to do your work here.'

Sure enough, the display appeared very similar to what they had grown used to with the Patrol though as Eddie went through the same procedure, they both had trouble believing what they were seeing.

'Each of you now has the power of the D.E.E.P. literally at your fingertips. You will always be able to find us with this and more importantly, we will always be able to find you.'

'What's it called?' asked Simon, still looking down at the device.

'It's a **C**ontact, **L**ocation **a**nd **W**arning device. More simply, C.L.A.W.'

Gibson and Jacobs explained the ways in which Patrol members communicated with each other. Every imaginable function was available but with a simple tap of their fingers, any sign of its existence disappeared from view. Most remarkable to both Simon and Eddie was how they could speak and listen to each other as if wearing some sort of microphone and earpiece.

'Donkeys in dressing gowns,' whispered Simon to himself, in amazement.

'Yes, its task capacity is a bit more than you're used to,' Jacobs smoothly bragged.

'Eddie…Simon…you are part of the Patrol now and as such, I expect utter loyalty. Our family relies on it.'

The Commander's final comments struck home but the boys left the room not knowing how to show their gratitude.

'Simul autem solus,' they both uttered; prompted by the words inscribed above every door of the D.E.E.P.

It did the job of pleasing the two men. The boys headed out along the corridor, feeling dazed with excitement. As Eddie stared down at his arm, bent in front of him, he paused, as if reminded of something.

'Hey Simon,' he started to ask, 'you know that salute they all give each other down here…? Do you know what it means?'

'Yeah, I think I've worked it out…look,' replied Simon, 'The first fist is the D,' he continued adding the hand gesture, 'the three fingers closed and opened twice, like this…that's the double E and then the last part is P.'

'Huh,' Eddie grunted. It seemed obvious *now*.

Their time at the D.E.E.P. headquarters quickened to an end and school life returned, roaring rudely up at Eddie and Simon with its deadlines and cruel captivity of their time. Since the Monday back, Eddie had been on the receiving end of the unnerving death stares of Mrs. Crandall. Try as he might, he couldn't understand or evade her bitter scowl. Perhaps she still had not forgotten his early year misdemeanours or maybe it was something new. Either way, her cold grimace suggested that she had it in for him.

Rain had been falling throughout the week and during a soggy break, the football team had got together to chat about their next match. Eddie had hoped the old saying of "safety in numbers" would put a temporary end to the menacing presence of the school's black, bobbed-haired, deputy. Keeping low and tight inside the huddle surrounding Bobby, the conversation started.

Eddie was half-listening but at the same time fidgeting and swaying his head, trying to get into a well-hidden position.

'Alright, settle down lads...' started the skipper, '...big game this week. I hope you've all been keeping fit over the break, haven't seen much of some of you.'

Eddie and Simon's eyes met, both fighting smiles from their faces. Macca piped up between bites of his mid-morning *snack*.

'Don't worry, Bobby, I've been on the treadmill every day!'

They all laughed and the usual wisecracks bounced around the group. The upcoming game against Hanfield was dismissed as a walkover so the conversation focused on the importance of a big scoreline to improve their goal difference.

'We've got to be at our best at both ends of the field, lads,' reminded the skipper to his whole team.

Bobby had noticed Eddie's jumpiness during the team get-together so he picked the right moment and took him to one side.

'Hey, Eddie, are you wondering about old Cranky Crandall over there?' Eddie nodded, eager for an explanation. 'Let's just say Jacobs is like a cuddly koala compared to her when it comes to punctuality,' he chortled.

'What do you mean?' asked Eddie.

'You arrived late for "*an important school event*". That didn't go down well with the old grump. Don't worry, she turns school traditions into torture at the best of times. Just wait and see what she does to the house football tournament. You know she sometimes referees the games; it's torture.'

As Bobby bemoaned her, Macca started to imitate her. Using a gruff voice, over-the-top prancing and gesturing he held an imaginary whistle to his lips.

'Play forward...Off line...Corner pitch kick!' mocked Joe, making fun of Mrs. Crandall's general incompetence and ridiculous body moving.

The group broke up and made their way laughing, back inside.

'She's as useful as a solar-powered foghorn!' Bobby said smiling with a wink towards Eddie.

Eddie tried to hold back his delight at Bobby's lampooning. Whilst it seemed harsh that she should find his lateness such a big deal, at least he knew she had a reason for her crazed stares.

He enjoyed an easy walk back to class despite getting steadily soaked as the rain began again in torrents. Eddie thought about Simon and how he had avoided Cranky's mistreatment. Although it seemed strange, he was happy to take the heat for him.

Drifting away, Eddie paddled in an imaginary kayak across the wild water that was cascading down the stairs from the school building and onto the playground. The distraction of the ripping current and wind-lashed surf meant his journey took a little longer than his friends who had all scampered for shelter.

Eddie ended up being the last in line outside the music room. With no real cover outside, the group had taken the decision to head in, even though Mrs. Longstaff, the school's enigmatic music teacher, had yet to arrive. As the crowd of students spilled through the door, Eddie turned his head and noticed the distant figure of his teacher scurrying across the courtyard towards, what she called, her "auditorium" (it stood alone and was more modern-looking, unlike the main building).

She was struggling to tame her umbrella in the stiff breeze that was angling the rain into her face. Instinctively, he waited by the door and seeing her distress, tried to offer some polite assistance.

'After you, Miss,' Eddie said, as he stood to one side.

Mrs. Longstaff, shocked by the scene of disorder and looking like she had just climbed out of a swimming pool, blurted her frustrations.

'What?........ Why is everyone?.......Who told you to?.........Oh, never mind, in you all go…Thank you, Eddie.'

'That's ok, I love storms,' Eddie said, as he looked up to the sky only to be belted by another gusty deluge.

Mrs. Longstaff was overcome by the same whipping wind and her brolly was thrown out of her hand, completely showering the children in front of her. Eddie's image was of a fierce wave breaking over poor Mrs. Longstaff and carrying her crashing over the class, leaving the whole room awash with bedraggled bodies. Eddie was brought back by a single distressed cry.

'AGHH!'

Jonny Wilson, wildly overreacting to the discomfort of a little spray down the back of his neck lurched dramatically and fell into a stand loaded with tambourines, cymbals and other lively instruments. The crescendo was hilarious and no one laughed louder than Eddie.

'Play it again, Jonny, I missed the chorus,' he joked.

'EDDIE FREEMAN!!' an indignant voice screeched from behind him and some fatefully familiar footsteps closed in.

Mrs. Crandall had arrived unnoticed and captured the last moments of the debacle. It was obvious that she had come to the conclusion that Eddie had caused the chaos and was now standing back, amusing himself at his handiwork. The noisy clicking heels stopped and Crandall's hostile scowl descended darkly over Eddie. It creased with contempt as it prepared to dish out its feverish fury. Her mouth looked more like a gaping cave and her stony skin seemed to have the appearance of a weather-beaten cliff-face. She wailed with a voice like a raging hurricane.

'How dare you, boy! Follow me!'

The whole room hushed and even the storm outside seemed to fall silent. Eddie went with her across the small courtyard to the school offices. Walking in dismay behind the broad and bowed stride of the school's Deputy, voices spun in Eddie's head;

'What did I do..?' then, 'She didn't even see what happened…' next, 'What's she got against me…? and finally, 'I was just trying to help!'

Cranky led him into her office.

'Shut the door behind you!' she ordered. Fearing that he would need a quick escape if Cranky lost it completely, he pushed, leaving it slightly cracked. There was no one else around apart from Perry the parrot, perched at the back of his cage and he was hardly likely to offer any kind of shelter from her wrath. Eddie attempted to diffuse the moment.

'Miss, I was just….'

'Oh, this should be good,' countered Crandall, 'you were lost?' she mocked, 'couldn't help it?'

'No miss, I wanted to…' Eddie pleaded but the seething old bag interrupted him again before he could be heard.

'ENOUGH!' she screeched, seemingly frothing at the mouth with speckles of spit caught up in the remnant rainwater that had yet to steam off her face.

As she ranted at Eddie, the words and purpose of her nasty outburst were lost on him. Perry had deftly flicked his beak, unlocked the cage door and exited. He flew down, close behind Cranky and started his transformation to human size.

Perry then rocked some funky moves in time with Cranky's bizarre squawking melody. Eddie was caught between the beat-boxing bird and Mrs. Crandall's eye-popping, head-shaking, shoulder-rolling rabid animal histrionics in front of him. His imagination was out of control! Strings of saliva whipped round her bulldog cheeks and slopped across the room. Caught in the line of fire, Eddie had to jolt his head left and right as the furious phlegm fired his way. Perry's ridiculous dancing now mimicked Eddie's body shifting as well as Cranky's crazy headshakes.

Like a record being scratched, the door creaked and the action died. The voice of a concerned girl called in.

'Miss, can you come upstairs, please?' It was Howie.

Eddie had never been so glad to see her. She stood waiting for a response, trying hard to ignore the weird atmosphere.

'Why, what's happened?' snapped Crandall.

'There's a toilet door that's locked and the loo won't stop flushing. It looks like it's going to flood the whole of the girls' toilets.'

'Honestly,' Cranky grumbled, marching towards the door. 'Where's Mr. Scrivener? Isn't it enough that I have to…?' she caught herself mid-sentence as if she had lost the purpose of her rant at Eddie.

'Go!' she commanded, 'I'll be watching you, Edward Freeman… and your little football friends.'

Saying this, she looked briefly and curiously at Howie before charging off down the corridor. Eddie gave a look of relief but before Howie could do as much as smile back, Mrs. Crandall was barking down the hall.

'Come on, young lady! Show me where the trouble is.'

As Howie followed, Cranky missed a step halfway up the staircase in her fluster. A Perry-like yelp rung out as she crashed and slid down the carpeted stairs; fumbling for the bannisters to catch her fall. Pulling herself up, she did her best to correct her clothing and made a point of not looking back down as she called again for Howie to follow.

Howie returned Eddie's wave of thanks from the hallway below. Trying to hide her smile, she covered her mouth. Her muffled laughter faded away up the stairs as she chased Crandall with her customary athletic ease.

Eddie made his way back, pondering the timing of Howie's appearance and the equally baffling telling-off he'd just had. Only when he looked back, much later, would he understand the reasons for Crandall's scorn.

After the match against Hanfield, Eddie was more satisfied at having avoided Cranky for the entire week than he was for scoring his two goals in the 5-0 drubbing. For the record, Simon may as well have taken a hammock with him to put up between the posts. The opposition lacked any real skill or strategy, despite their pluckiness.

It was a good day for Callum who scored with a cracking volley into the roof of the net after a great team move and he played some extended minutes as Mr. Jacobs took advantage of the weak opposition. With the whole squad in action, every player grew in confidence. Simon was a spectator in goal; Bobby, Max and Charlie Croft were equally underused at the back. George and David ran the show from midfield whilst Eddie and Howie made the Hanfield defence feel like they were in a washing machine that was stuck on fast spin! Their faces were greener than their shirts by the end of the game.

Everyone was great. That is apart from Jonny. He was still grumbling about having to come off towards the end of the game and sat moodily on his own. He moped, watching the game out of the corner of one eye, trying to act uninterested.

Everyone came together afterwards and the bonding was brilliant fun. For Eddie, however, his emotions went beyond the strong team spirit. The more he was around Howie, the harder he found it to stop looking at her. He began to experience a heavy and consuming weight deep inside him. At its worst, it was like being thumped in the stomach by an angry kangaroo; robbing the breath inside him. No one else in the room even noticed but Eddie felt emotions he had no experience of and clearly no idea how to handle.

'Games like these can set a team on the road to great things,' Jacobs started his theatrical debrief, 'the more we work for one another, celebrate in each other's success and expect more from ourselves, the more invincible we will become. This game was your solid foundation…now let's build the tower!'

Cheers of encouragement broke out as Jacobs left the room, his words ringing in their ears.

After Howie had left for the girls' changing room, Eddie's focus gradually returned to how he had played. Teammates and parents had been continually praising him and the attention, though flattering, had made him feel awkward. It crossed his mind whether Mr. Jacobs might use consight during competitive games though he greatly doubted it. Mr. J's integrity was the virtue that stood out most. He was gracious to opponent players, coaches and even the interfering parents. He would always insist in his team not just shaking hands but finding positive words to offer, regardless of the result. No, Mr. Jacobs liked to win the right way and anything else would be an empty and worthless victory. It was both his and the school's tradition and most noticeable trait. Not that he was ever thanked for it; especially when players would have numb fingers from taking the nets down during winter or enduring conditioning sessions where footballs did not even make it out of their bags. Nonetheless, *'Character above all'* was a motto longer lasting than the memory of victory or defeat. Jacobs had a different identity away from the D.E.E.P. but his character could never be disguised.

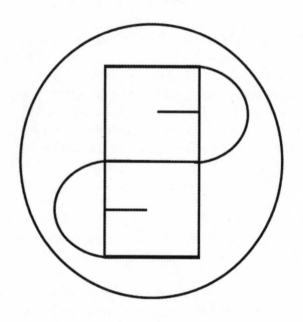

CHAPTER 11

AN EXCURSION FROM THE EVERYDAY

'Hey, slow down lads!' ordered a gruff and extremely tired-looking coach driver as a pack of overexcited boys climbed up into the coach. A school outing, to learn more about London's history, was translated as a day off by Eddie's history class. As long as you could avoid all teachers, undertake minimal work and arrive at meeting points on time, the joyful sense of freedom and escape was there for the taking.

The coach ride, however, was an anarchic adventure in itself. The noise onboard the coach destroyed anyone's ability to think straight and with the teachers still outside, everyone was clambering all over each other, squeezing through the smallest gap, trying to get the best seats.

'Get off me!' shouted David, half-wincing, half-chuckling at Jonny's efforts to prise him out of his seat on the back row. Jonny was encouraged to give up the attempt by a couple of well-aimed carrots to the head.

Meanwhile, Joe was sitting down nearby, seatbelt fastened and pale-faced, preparing for the onset of the green grogginess he was famed for. This, before the coach had even started its journey.

'Oh, poor Joe,' commented Simon to Eddie, 'he hates coaches.'

117

The two boys had been kneeling up on their seats, just past halfway down the coach, chewing sweets and chuckling at the backseat bash-up.

'Sit down, boys!' called Mrs. Boone, the late-arriving, scatterbrained history teacher and unconventional trip organizer.

It may have been because of, rather than despite her giddy vagueness that she was one of the most loved members of the Westlake faculty. The long flowing velvet dresses, flat dank hair, even her thin and pale frame were all part of her charm.

'And get strapped in before we lose you,' she added.

Eddie and Simon twisted and slid back down into their seats. As they settled, a familiar voice then came from the seat behind.

'You seem to be trying to upset everyone this week, Eddie.'

Before realising who it was, Eddie span round and peered through the small space between the dusty cloth seats. Howie was staring back with a grin, wagging her finger sarcastically towards him. Eddie smiled sheepishly, he hadn't noticed her arrive and was quick to jam himself back hard into his own seat.

Just before setting off, as the engine started and shook the coach into life, one more passenger boarded. Simon looked forlornly down the aisle and jabbed at Eddie.

'Oh no, I don't believe it,' cried Eddie as he saw the unmistakable figure of Mrs. Crandall boarding and striding down the coach with the grace of a charging elephant.

'Why did she have to come?' he moaned under his breath.

She stopped a couple of rows in front of them and screamed the voices to a halt.

'That's quite enough noise, thank you! I don't care if you're in the classroom or on a coach, your disgusting manners will not be tolerated. You will listen and follow my instructions now and every time I speak!'

The excitement inside the coach was sucked away as the old windbag replaced it with her oppressive moaning.

'Now firstly, you will all sit properly and get your se….'

Cranky's angry demands were suddenly and abruptly halted as a great gasp went up on the coach. Right in the middle of her moaning, Mrs. Crandall had been yanked backwards down the bus, by the scrawny and angry looking driver. He had seemed to have taken offence to her bossy, time-wasting, rant.

'I'm not getting paid by the hour, love, I've got other runs to make,' he said as Cranky, with heels dragging, yelped and clambered to get her footing.

She was lifted off her feet and launched from the front of the coach down the stairs, tumbling in a flapping mess of arms and legs. The coach broke into rapturous cheers. The driver strode back down the aisle triumphantly, waving gloriously and receiving great cheers from his adoring audience.

'What are you looking at me like that for?' he asked as his head lowered just in front of Eddie's seat.

'Huh? What?' Eddie replied as the thin, wrinkly, grinning face of the driver instantly transformed back to Mrs. Crandall's harsh scowl.

She had once again snatched the joy from his wishful imagination.

'Are you listening, Freeman? Away with the fairies? You'd be better off back in the river with the rest of your fish-faced friends by the looks of you.' Her cruel berating could be heard even by those off the coach.

Eddie quickly closed his gaping mouth and once again, pushed his head back hard against his seat. He remained silently still along with everyone else on board as the coach pulled out of the school drive and on towards its destination; *The Museum of London*.

As the coach rattled into life and slowly drove away, Mr. Freeman, Mr. Bird and Commander Gibson passed by in the opposite direction unnoticed and pulled into the school car park. They came to an abrupt stop, parking discreetly away in a quiet corner. Briskly leaving the car, the men slid off down a sidepath that led towards the maintenance area and quickly hurried out of sight.

Inside, Mr. Jacobs silently greeted them and following his lead, the four men made their way along the disused corridor towards the room with the scratched door, Room 13.

In the narrow hallway, having spoken not a word to each other, the men took on various positions in front of the door. Although the heavily worn door had the appearance of being hinged, it instead slid to the side as the men worked it open. In place of the old squeaking sound that you might have expected, the door sounded mechanical and weighty and instead of a room, the opening offered just a small recess, just like the one at Mildham, with metal steps leading down.

'Did you really have to design every one like this Jonathan?' quipped the Commander, 'I'm getting too old for this.' he said as they all made their way down. Mr. Jacobs went last and having had one last look along the passage for straying eyes, sealed the door back in place.

After an uneventful journey, the ride was almost over. Simon turned to Eddie with a telling look. 'I'm pretty sure we're not too far from you know where, Eddie,' he said under his breath. 'I definitely recognize some of this.'

'Don't talk, just look. Maybe between us, we can work out where it might be.' Eddie said quietly.

As they looked out, with Simon furthest from the window, Eddie had the sensation of his head being covered by the feeling of two hands pressing down around his ears. His head lurched in shock and a small whimper of fear fell from his mouth.

'Woah! You're a bit twitchy aren't you,' joked Howie, 'you're not on a ghost train, I just thought you might want to listen to this. You said you like them.'

Knowing they shared a similar taste in tunes, she had tried to put her retro headphones on Eddie.

'Oh, right.....yeah, ok.' Eddie, now relieved, readily agreed and sat back in his seat as Howie put the headphones back over his ears.

The music that played took Eddie somewhere else and he enjoyed a sentimental moment he hoped Howie shared.

After a time, Eddie knew he should say something. With the headphones still on, he turned and spoke at an awkwardly loud volume.

'Thanks for bailing me out the other day!'

Howie and her friend Lily both looked at each other and laughed.

'I don't think the driver heard you,' Lily said, leaning forward and nodding towards the front of the coach.

Eddie spun round and noticing Mrs. Crandall turning in her seat, dived back into his own. He passed the headphones through the seats and quietly mouthed 'thank you,' to Howie.

'That's alright, you can pay me back by setting up a couple of goals next week against Brockton,' she boldly replied.

Howie was always so confident and sharp. Since the day they had met, Eddie had thought it was an unfair match. Her athleticism and looks made the situation all the more desperate for him and though he tried to disguise it, a type of suffocation nagged away from his insides.

'We'll be arriving in just a few minutes,' came the announcement from Crandall, at the front of the coach.

She had rudely snatched the driver's microphone and whacked it up to an ear-piercing volume.

'Clean up any rubbish before you collect your belongings. Don't leave any of your things on the coach, anything left behind will be thrown away. And make sure you all disembark in an orderly fashion.'

The journey came to an abrupt end with an amateurish attempt at parking by a befuddled driver, who was clearly put off by Cranky's commands. He hit the side of a kerb as he wrenched the coach to a halt. The heavy braking caused the standing adults to lurch down the aisle.

'Aghh!' screamed Cranky, bumping clumsily off chairs, armrests and stray bags. Rearranging her hair and trying to compose herself, the fuming Crandall made for the door, leaving the other teachers to usher the remaining passengers off the coach. This was far easier to accomplish with the Deputy and her painfully screeching wail out of the way.

The students got off the coach and were bundled into groups by Mrs. Boone who remained cheerful and detached. Crandall was frustrated and crushed by how simple her subordinate made things look.

Back at the school, the men had gathered underground.

'You still think it's a good idea to shut all this down for good?' asked Mr. Jacobs, turning on the dimly glowing lights, back in the underground patrol room, 'it's the last one we have and these action bays could still be useful in a jam.'

'I'm afraid, that's a luxury we can't afford,' said the Commander. 'If he *is* hell-bent on uncovering us, it's only a matter of time before this gem will quickly become something we simply cannot defend.'

'Seems such a pity,' remarked Mr. Bird. 'How about we fire her up one last time...? Just for old times' sake?' he suggested temptingly.

The men looked at each other, smiled and without a word set to work. Their faces illuminated like the displays across the room, their fingers feverishly lit up action bays and remotely activated some unassigned units back at Control.

'A little race, gentleman,' announced Gibson.

Mr. Bird manned the main control chair, from where he could see the view and activity of each of the drones about to be launched. With them all standing by, the Commander gave out the course rules.

'First to the creek barrier, over the alps and under the Air Line!' he challenged, 'Then, upriver to the finish line behind the dome. Our units will use the coordinates for the Blackwall tunnel to notify course completion…On my mark.'

All of them knew the area, east of the City, like the backs of their hands and the overhead route to each landmark was familiar territory. Gibson gave his final words.

'Stay over water where you can, men, we don't want to cause unnecessary attention. Ready…the operation deck is live…3,2,1 UP!'

The drones took off in military like formation out of the Patrol's well-covered tunnel exit before diving in a mad dash towards the nearby water. Two units split, turning downriver but Mr. Jacobs' machine headed in the opposite way.

'Not the Thames barrier, Tom!' chortled Gibson.

Jacobs had misunderstood the Commander's mark but turned sharply and made for the correct barrier, up Barking Creek.

'You've always been taken by the shiny things in life!' laughed Commander Gibson, referring to the nine, silver, gleaming piers that stood like steel stepping-stones stretching in stunning symmetry across the capital's waterway.

'Ahhhhh!' exclaimed Tom, quickly finding himself well behind already much to the other's amusement.

'You've got your work cut out now,' jibed Mr. Freeman, 'especially in that old fighting machine you're trying to fly.'

Mr. Jacobs always preferred the tough armour-plated and brutal looking M.A.D. (**M**ilitary **A**rmoured **D**efender) drone. It had served him well, despite its age and limitations.

The two in front now powered on, the downthrust of their machines painting a sharp line of whitewash on the surface of the water, just a few feet below.

Two, forty metre concrete posts came up fast on the northern bank where Barking Creek runs into the Thames. The Commander split the posts first and flying low between them and well under the icy blue metal barrier that was lofted like a mighty boat guillotine. Mr. Freeman followed, swinging smoothly through the gap a few feet higher. "The Alps," that the Commander had referred to, was the huge grassy hill in Beckton. The local kids skulking around on it were caught by surprise as the drones thundered over. They felt the full force of the unit's downthrusting blades. The overgrowth and nearby bushes shuddered with them, as the machines hurtled overhead.

'I think they enjoyed the show, Peter,' remarked the Commander.

Meanwhile, Mr. Jacobs had made up time by craftily cutting the corner of the hill. He turned at a steep tilt, back south, in chase of the others. The east London Air Line came up on the three raging drones. The shimmering wire and cable-cars hung like a laundry line of space capsules, pegged out in the sunshine.

Zipping under them, Commander Michael Gibson was only just ahead of Freeman. Jacobs, with a bit of cunning, had also closed the gap. The once-maligned, now iconic and proud white dome, situated where the river bends at almost 180 degrees to form a peninsula, offered itself up as the final obstacle. At that moment, Freeman's unit suddenly disappeared from the others' view. Unfazed, Jacobs hugged the exhilarating final curve, no more than a few metres behind Gibson.

'Come on, old girl,' begged the desperate headmaster, bleeding the last ounce of effort from his machine.

'Not this time, Tom,' said an already celebrating commander, 'just a few more seconds and.......'

'Yeaaahhh!' wailed Mr. Freeman, interrupting the leaders with a euphoric scream.

His drone had crossed over the top of the capital's big top, buzzing those on the walkway above it. The result of the stunt was enough to finish at a faster speed and overtake the other two, almost taking out Jacobs in the process.

'Course completed…unit 4 wins!' came a soft-spoken voice heard by all three men.

'No, no, no, no, no! That was an illegal manoeuvre Peter,' responded Gibson, in a tone that suggested surprise as much as anger at losing.

'Illegal manoeuvre? Not sure anything about this would fly with the law,' laughed Peter.

'You flouted the rules, man! Stay on the water I said.'

'You have to admit, Michael, it was a clever move,' cooed Jacobs.

'It didn't impress me, I'll teach you a thing or two on the return leg,' fumed Gibson, refusing to acknowledge the crafty expertise.

'Actually, can I suggest you all separate now, gentlemen…' Mr. Bird interrupted, subtly reminding them of their actions. 'And make your journey back a little more discreet!'

'Agreed,' said Peter, 'Our lot aren't far from here. I'll take a quiet fly-by and look over them at the museum.'

'Ok, I'll head back south of the river. Tom, you take the north.' said Michael. 'You can see if that crowd on the hill have recovered.'

'If it's all the same to you, I'll take an autopilot river cruise for my return,' said a drained Mr. Jacobs. 'I could do with a cup of tea.'

Back at the museum, the group had been allowed some free time and Eddie, Simon, Howie and Lily were strolling through *Sailortown*; a Victorian exhibit of life on the Thames back in foul and treacherous times. It was a maze of narrow and dingy doorways with passages supposedly frequented by the era's most notorious sailors.

The four of them enjoyed the shadowy feel to one of the rooms and acting like sloshed seafarers, sat around a table in a saloon bar of the time. The place was dark and deserted. The seclusion allowed for some boisterous behaviour.

'Arrrrr, fetch me a tankard of your finest ale, wench!' demanded a theatrical Simon.

The girls looked disbelievingly at each other and hummed, as if in thought. Lily then walked around the back of the table, behind where Simon was sat.

'I'd love to get you your drink, master,' she started in character, 'but if you're thinking I'm going near your pale, toothless, scurvy-ridden face, you must be more drunk than you look, you festering old scab!'

The girls were in stitches and Howie high-fived the gloating Lily. Much to Simon's dismay, even Eddie was chuckling.

'I don't have to sit 'ere and put up wiv these insults,' Simon snapped back and slid his chair back to leave.

Unfortunately, he did not allow for Lily's foot; resting, as it was, against one of the back legs of his chair. As he jammed it, the chair tilted. Lily yelped as Simon flew back right at her. His long legs, for once, worked against him and he lost all balance, the chair caught still as it was round his feet. It followed him sprawling across the old stone-cobbled floor. Lily roared with laughter. Simon tumbled painfully.

'Cats in cardigans, there was no need for that!' he complained, leaving his chauvinist sailorman character behind.

'Beggin ya' pardon, *Admiral*, I didn't realise you only had one leg!' scoffed Lily.

She and Howie started to walk out of the room back into the dimly lit alley while Eddie went to help his stricken chum to his feet. Simon shook him off and stomped after the girls, trying to recover his pride.

Eddie tidied the area as best he could and left. He was still a little way behind them walking through the gloomy exhibit, when he suddenly felt a sick draining sensation of someone watching him from the dark alley he'd left. He turned around impulsively, his face creased and eyes squinting into the gloom. A silhouette appeared slowly, out of the shadows. Eddie started to make out the figure of a man, looming with purpose and pacing directly towards him.

Howie was a step or two behind the bickering Simon and Lily. She noticed Eddie not beside her and turned around whilst the other two walked on. Lily and Simon were too preoccupied with teasing and putting each other down to notice their friends.

After taking a few steps back towards Eddie, Howie froze. Just a few feet away from her and within arm's reach of Eddie, the frame of a smartly suited man emerged hauntingly into vision.

'Hello Edward,' greeted the man, with an echo in his breath and a posture of grim assurance.

CHAPTER 12

AN INSISTENT OUTSIDER

A frozen chill wrapped itself around Howie and Eddie's necks and dread crawled up their throats at the sight of the sly looking man. The same man who had intruded at Mildham. The same man who was the subject of Eddie's first consight vision with Mrs. Andrews. The same man who had betrayed the D.E.E.P. And the same man who now posed the greatest threat to the operation of the entire Patrol stood coldly in front of them. Time and space abandoned Eddie. In that short moment, he was aware of only one thing; the unsettling presence of 'the *Suit*.'

Ripping his body from its paralyzed state, Eddie dropped his head and pivoted away. In perfect time with Howie, he tore off down the alley; in terror, they ran. Their renowned speed seemed to double as their feet echoed off the cold concrete tiles. The tight and unknown confines made it hard for the two to know which way to go.

'Eddie, here! QUICK!' yelled Howie, noticing what looked like an exit at the back of a room off the main passage.

The two smashed through the door with their shoulders and fell, sprawling into the passage that lay beyond. Boxes of unused artifacts, sitting on nearby shelves were still toppling as they both frantically got to their feet. Taking a sharp breath as she looked one way then the other, Howie grabbed Eddie and dragged him up and frantically searched for safety. Eddie threw the door shut in the vain hope that they wouldn't be followed and picked up pace, charging along after Howie. At the end of the hallway, they turned tightly and bounded down a flight of stairs to the ground floor; all the time breathing too heavily and smashing off walls too loudly to tell if the *Suit* was even chasing behind.

The small stairwell at the bottom of the steps led to a double door that had a large metal bar across it. They both gave it a decent push but the door didn't give. Eddie suddenly remembered his C.L.A.W. While Howie whacked away at the bar that was blocking their escape, Eddie put out a signal to the Patrol. A few seconds passed then Howie turned back, wondering why her friend had stopped. Seeing him, head down and distracted, she screamed.

'What are you doing, Eddie…? HELP ME!'

'Yeah, sorry,' Eddie blurted, covering his arm quickly and returning to the doors.

Then, before they could get back to their useless door thumping, back along the corridor came the sound of something falling and smashing. Adrenalin took over and they belted harder than ever on the metal bar, shoving it violently. With a scream of jamming metal, a small slither of daylight broke through.

Eddie, wishing not for the first time that he was bigger, did his best to push open the door with Howie. Over and over, they hammered hard onto the bar, each time causing the door to scrape slowly open further.

'Come on Eddie, together!' cried Howie and they both stepped back a few paces.

They stared hard at each other.

'Ready? – GO!' they chorused and ran at the door with everything they had.

Forcing their will on the bar and with a screeching whine of rusted hinges, a welcome gust of fresh air filled their lungs. The door gave way to the sun's harsh glare, signalling their freedom. The sense of escape, however, was instantly replaced by disorientated thoughts.

'What now…? Where are we?' Howie begged.

Her squinting eyes searched for a landmark that could lead them to safety.

'Which way now?' Eddie pleaded.

They circled each other, trying to regain their bearings in the shadow of the steel and glass that made up the high rises of Canary Wharf. Eddie and Howie had found themselves on a busy quayside.

'Ok, let's work this out,' reasoned Eddie.

They started walking along the water's edge but instead of Howie's affirming voice, the next sound was the scream of the door that they had crashed through. It swung wide and there, standing menacingly, fixing his penetrating stare on them, was the *Suit*.

His appearance was as sharp as the chill of the autumn air that had greeted them. Carrying an easy style in his gait, he smiled, approached and started to speak in his stony, persuasive way. The creep of terror returned to Eddie. His eyes met with a sinister glare while his ears were forced to endure false words of friendship. There was no way of knowing the *Suit's* intentions or next move.

'Eddie, you don't need to run. Look around you, what am I going to do?'

His voice was controlled and firm, his arm stretched out as he extended a hand, open and upturned towards the busy scene of lunchtime workers around them.

'I have so much to share with you if you'd only stop and listen.'

His deep purr almost convinced Eddie that there could be something to what he was saying but his instincts left him with no time to dwell on the idea. He turned and fled once again with Howie picking up by his side. It was lunchtime and

131

the walkway was awash with coffee-guzzling pen-pushers, heading in all directions. Eddie thought they at least may now hold the advantage of being out in full view. Perhaps that would put off their traitorous tail. That hope was quickly cast away by those nearby, scuttling along obliviously around him. Their perpetual state of self-importance was more than a match for the threat facing Eddie. They remained detached from their surroundings and seemingly unaware to the ongoing chase.

As Eddie and Howie ran, trying to duck and dodge around the city's high-flying worker-bees, they both sensed that they were in need of an escape route but outrunning this man required a strategy beyond their fear-crippled minds. With nothing inside but sheer panic, Eddie spun away towards a side road.

'Howie! This way,' he called, leaving both the problem and the protection of the pedestrians behind.

Breathless, bewildered and with things looking desperate, there came a powerful rush of air along with the *Suit's* tired and gasping plea.

'Ok, you win!' His voice echoed around the high-walled alley that Eddie and Howie had fled down.

Howie seemed confident enough to slow a little and look back over her shoulder. To her shock, a drone now occupied the alley, hovering at head height right in front of the *Suit* and blocking his path. It tilted left then right, humming menacingly, mirroring the *Suit's* movements and at the same time edging forward towards him.

'Alright… ALRIGHT!' The *Suit* raised his hands in submission, as if knowing that the machine had the upper hand.

He paced backwards, imprinting his intense stare on Eddie and Howie before running back into the crowds on the walkway. Eddie recognized the machine as a M.E.R.M.A. The heavy, wide body looked like two wheelbarrow buckets welded together. The sharp nose along with its cameras and red, glowing sensors gave it an angry-looking face. Its thunderous fan blades were pounding the air down around them, whipping up anything not stuck down. The two of them both stood and stared, waiting for its next move.

Back in the action bay at Westlake, Peter Freeman's face had paled to a pasty grey. Having closed in on the distress signal, he had witnessed the chase from above. The line that Eddie and Howie had made through the crowds caught his eye as he'd flown overhead. It hadn't taken him long to work out what was happening and he responded without a thought for D.E.E.P. regulations or procedures. Every sinew in him strained, trying to stay composed and poised as he carefully rotated his drone towards Eddie in the narrow lane. Eddie and Howie were still stationary and gaping up at his machine. Mr. Freeman lowered the nose of the drone and tilted the machine down, sweeping forwards in a robotic gesture to the children.

'Run, Eddie, RUN!' he begged, feeling helplessly detached from them.

'I think it's telling us something, Eddie,' said Howie.

'Me too,' replied Eddie.

They both twisted round and scrambled towards an overpass that seemed to offer an escape route. As they heard the resonating sound of an overhead train, an exchange of glances decided their next move. Hastily, they made for the nearby station, thinking that a train could create some distance, that is, if time and chance were on their side.

Ahead now, the glass-covered footbridge spanning the rat-running lanes of Aspen Way on the A1261, was all that separated them from Poplar DLR Station. Dashing up the steps, Howie followed Eddie as he cut sharply into the see-through walkway. Their hearts and feet were in rapid rhythm as they peeled over the metal bridge. In the middle of the crossing, a flight of stairs offered a route down to the station.

'Look, Eddie!' shouted Howie.

The view of an incoming train underneath provoked a look of excited relief between them.

Within a few paces, their excitement evaporated. Eddie gasped,

'AGHHH NO!!'

His legs strained to a stop and battled to absorb Howie as she fell awkwardly against his back. The tragedy and pain in Eddie's voice drained every good thought from Howie's mind. They froze together and in that moment were dismayed, once more, at what was ahead of them.

A shadowy shape had filled the entrance to the platform, halfway along the crossing, casting a looming intent. An unwelcomed voice followed, seeping through their whole bodies.

'Please children, you need to be told what they'll do to you. I just want to help.'

The words were as confusing as they were intriguing. Though Eddie and Howie were full of fear, there was still something mesmerizing about his tone and presence that was hard to resist.

Pacing backwards, instincts returning, they turned to flee. However, a powerful and steady humming signalled that their only means of escape had also been blocked; the M.E.R.M.A. had returned. Trapped and fearing nothing good could come of their predicament, it was all they could do to stand their ground. The drone tilted and calculated its path. Suddenly, its fan blades quickened into a throbbing beat and it thundered at Eddie and Howie.

'Get down!' yelled Eddie and they both dived desperately to the ground, expecting the worst. Eddie covered his arm round Howie and simply clung to her while fate took its course.

Instead of any impact however, the drone swept past, leaving a downdraft and fading pulse that told them they were safe. Easing his hold, Eddie looked up to see the machine closing in fast on its intended target.

With a groan of annoyance, the *Suit's* expression changed to one of frustration.

'This is getting tiresome,' he lamented before fleeing the opposite way.

The M.E.R.M.A. took up the chase.

Eddie had glimpsed quickly at his C.L.A.W. as Howie lay under his arm and interpreting its simple message of "TRAIN - EASTBOUND", shot up and took off, down into the station. Although much had happened, only a few seconds had passed. The train was still at its platform and they both jumped on with doors sliding shut.

'Who..? What was..? Why did the drone do that?' quizzed Howie.

She was bent down but looking up, catching her breath as the train pulled out of the station.

'I think I know who, but I don't know why,' Eddie puffed, being careful what to say whilst his lungs refilled.

'Well that's a start, who was he then?' badgered Howie. 'I'm not sure of his name and what I do know, I can't really tell you.'

'I think we're past the secrets stage, Eddie,' Howie announced. 'I know about the D.E.E.P. In fact, I know a lot more than you realise.'

Drawing back her sleeve, *the symbol* appeared emblazoned on her forearm. Eddie's earlier actions had been all too obvious for someone of Howie's talents and he now stood dumbfounded by what he thought was his own secret, gleaming back from the arm of this ever more beguiling girl.

'What?' he uttered, barely able to breathe the word.

'I'll explain later,' said Howie abruptly, re-covering her arm and glaring in horror at something over Eddie's shoulder.

Eddie spun round and stared through the train's rear door glass window. There, holding on to a rail on the outside of the accelerating train, was *the Suit*.

He stood motionless, though the train's draught whipped furiously around his long coat and thick, dark, flowing hair. He remained there as the train barrelled along, statue-like, never once taking his piercing eyes off Eddie. The sound of squeaking brakes that slowed the train into the next station brought back the same feeling, to Eddie and Howie, as the grating door at the back of the museum.

'What shall we do?' cried Howie, urging Eddie to think of something.

As they both scanned along the train, they saw that their carriage was nearly empty. The few people onboard seemed unaware. An elderly lady, near the front, sat reading a heavy novel that was resting on the small shopping trolley clenched between her knees. A scruffy paint-covered workman was in the middle of telling his friend a joke. He spoke in what seemed like an Eastern European language so the punchline was lost on all but his pal, who was roaring with laughter. No one else had noticed the *Suit*.

A short chirp signalled the doors opening. Both Eddie and Howie bolted out onto the platform. At the same time, the *Suit* leapt from his precarious position, confronting them before they could reach the exit. He spoke on the emptying and quiet platform with growing confidence and familiarity.

'You are different, Eddie, but not in the way you've been told. They'll mistreat your gift, like they mistreated mine. I'm not a monster, please...'

The *Suit* walked slowly toward Eddie, arms open again, face warming and eyes that still seemed to hold some sort of spell on whoever they were cast on.

'What have you got to lose, Eddie…? Just a little chat.'

His voice was pleading and endearing and as the train pulled away, Eddie and Howie were left to consider the suggestion, seemingly now with no alternative.

'What do you say… hmm?' proposed the *Suit*.

Both Eddie and Howie shared an accepting glance, part with reluctance and part curiosity and this time, they did not run. The *Suit's* magnetic persuasion concealed their fearful instincts as he advanced calmly towards them. As he did so and without warning, a huge rush of air pummelled down on them and angling aggressively under the platform canopy, there appeared the M.E.R.M.A. again.

'Please don't run children, don't be scared' implored the *Suit*, trying to regain eye contact and be heard over the rushing air now separating them.

The more Eddie and Howie watched the struggle, the more concern they started to feel for this man's fraught attempts. Another deep throbbing hum descended, marking the appearance of a second unit. Then, a sudden and horrific sounding strike! The second drone had blindsided the *Suit*; hammering into him with its armoured underside. The *Suit* lay on the floor, writhing.

'Tom! What are you doing? We don't want to kill him!' shouted the Commander.

'Yes sir,' came the repentant voice of Jacobs. 'I was trying to fly across to distract him. I didn't mean to…'

'Hold back, cover Peter…' ordered Gibson, furiously '…and wait for *my* next instruction!'

Slowly, the *Suit* twisted onto his back and recognising what faced him, retreated on all fours, crab-like, up against the back of the platform. Stunned and taking evasive action, *the Suit's* attention was now forced away from Eddie and Howie. He closed one hand over the side of his forehead and held his other arm out, upward at the unyielding drones. Under the cover of his hand, a line of blood spilt into his hollow cheek and seeped down, casting a scarlet brilliance against his snow-white skin. The second unit took its position behind the first as the sound of another train came down the line.

'We need to get away Eddie....now!' screamed Howie, walking backwards towards the platform exit.

'Hang on!' shouted Eddie, over the sound of the drones and the approaching train. His head owled round, firstly at the stand-off between the man and the machines, then the stopping train, before fixing back on Howie.

'Not that way, we'll get more distance between him and us on here,' pleaded Eddie.

His C.L.A.W. had told him that the train was the better option and they both reached the closing doors with an unnatural speed, even for them. Both on board and with the train winding up, they watched the continuing stand-off at the far end of the platform behind.

'I think he's done chasing us for now,' said Eddie.

'What do you think they'll do to him?' asked Howie, 'he's hurt.'

'He knows drones and he knows how to protect himself. How do you think he managed to catch up before?'

Back at Westlake, in the underground bunker, what had been a final flight of fun had soured into a desperate and very public skirmish.

'What now, Commander?' asked Eddie's dad.

They both had the *Suit* still pinned against the platform wall but as he scanned the platform, Mr. Freeman saw an approaching station guard.

'Looks like we've done all we can for now, Peter. Follow the train and see if you can get them to the *Captain's Cabin*.

Jacobs, get a welcoming party on deck for them. I'll do my best to watch him from further away. We don't need the attention of a downed UAV. Peter, be safe and get your unit back into the D.E.E.P. as soon as you can.'

Safe for the moment, the two runaways with faces aglow, sat down on the train and gathered their thoughts. The escape had brought down the wall of secrecy that had been between them. Eddie's outbursts during the getaway had stirred Howie's conscience about what she knew. She had only so far hinted, now she was burning to talk. Before Eddie had the chance to ask the obvious, Howie spoke. She did not want to appear as if she was playing games or forcing the pain of hidden truths on him. She, of all people, knew the suffering *that* brought.

'Listen, I don't ever speak about this, no one at school knows and neither do any of my friends. I've been staying at my uncle's, ever since the rest of my family went away last year.'

Eddie replied understandingly. 'Yeah, we all know that, Howie. Jacobs gives you a ride there from our away games and you always have to wait, late after school, for him to turn up.'

'That's all true, it doesn't seem that big of a deal, Eddie, but what you don't know is that Tom *is* my uncle and my family are away 'cos they're part of the *Patrol* too…'

Howie slumped back in her chair, gathering herself. 'Like yours, like Simon's and who knows who else's.'

She had always been frustrated by not knowing where the family of the Patrol began and ended.

Eddie looked away from Howie and just stared down, trying to think how he couldn't have known and what clues he must have missed.

'But they went with your brother to America to help him settle in to university,' he said, half-stating, half-questioning.

'Well, there's some truth in that but they had more to do than find Dan a place to stay and buy him some books to read,'

Howie was hinting at knowing their real reasons for being in America but her bluff was a mask, an act disguising her feeling of rejection for being left behind. Though it had been months, she knew no more than Eddie, apart from the empty chats she would share with her family from time to time about her brother's university life. Her parents wouldn't or couldn't speak of their involvement in their D.E.E.P. *mission*. Like Eddie, Howie had enjoyed a fun and carefree life with her family before. Things had changed now.

Perhaps from this sense of a robbed childhood, an unspoken bond had developed on this day, perhaps even on the train ride. It went beyond the crush and the romantic pictures of Eddie's dizzy mind. Behind their deepest thoughts, a place now appeared, secret and safe. Though invisible, it was a place where they both belonged and understood in some ways more than ordinary things. They began to feel like puzzle pieces; pressed down where they truly fit. As they talked, both slowly seeing their own burdens reflected in each other's face, a unity, deeper than their struggles, awoke.

'So, what has he told you? How much has he shown you?'

Eddie asked, with a mixture of apprehension and warm cheekiness.

'You know how he is; so proper, so kind. It can be a downfall for him. He tells me and shows more than he wants… out of sympathy, I think. He's always apologizing for mum and dad having to be away for so long.'

As they passed through quiet stations, knowing D.E.E.P.'s orders on communication, Eddie and Howie both sent vague, almost misleading messages to Simon and Lily but enough that they would know they were ok. The line wasn't busy and their end of the carriage remained largely empty as they began to share fragments of their concealed lives; the pieces that they thought the other could not have known about. Eddie spoke about his training and the drones, Howie volunteered information about a team of secret engineers helping Mr. Bird. They also had a good laugh at all the different ways they had been stopped from seeing the way into the underground headquarters. Some things they both knew but neither of them had any idea of who the *Suit* was and why he had betrayed the D.E.E.P.

Despite the obvious and complete trust he had in Howie, Eddie had not spoken a word about consight.

'Dare I mention it? Will she know?' he thought.

Eddie had a mind to confess but as he pondered the thought, Howie jumped to her feet and shot to the other side of the train.

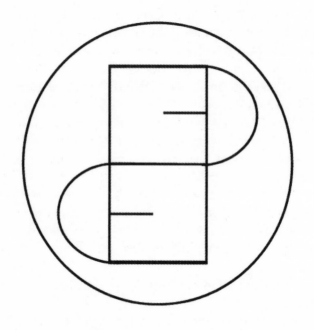

CHAPTER 13

AN
EAR
TO
THE
GROUND

Lifting above the train and flashing in the corner of Howie's eye, the same M.E.R.M.A, sent as their saviour, was soaring by.

'Eddie, quick, it's back!' called Howie, her face pressed right up on the window to see.

Eddie joined her and their eyes clung to the drone's movement, each minute detail within its glossy metallic skin was crystallised by the purest spans of blue surrounding it. The other passengers looked on, unconcerned with the view beyond the window. It was of little significance to them even as it drifted closer, changed its path and raced up and over the train. Tracking its path, Eddie and Howie sped back across the carriage, ruffling a couple of grumpy commuters in their haste. It powered ahead of the train, curving round, following the line of the track and hovering above the platform of the next station.

During their time on the train, they had all but forgotten the fact that they needed to find a way out of their spiralling situation. The M.E.R.M.A. had brought them this far and as it lowered over the station's ground level exit, Eddie and Howie obeyed its mechanical instruction. They jumped off and speedily made it through the small station concourse.

Once outside, however, the drone had vanished.

'What now?' Eddie asked with concern. The display on their arms showed a map of the area and highlighted the large roundabout just ahead of them. They looked out across a scene of double lane traffic, circling it. Dense bushes and hedge-like growth had overrun the few ailing trees in the scrubland that it was made up of.

A large concrete building rose from behind the overgrowth though it appeared to be secured by a high iron fence. There was, further away behind a long line of tightly growing trees, a row of cold and empty looking properties but nothing obvious. The clear path or trail they thought would have been left for them was nowhere. Helplessness slowly imprinted itself on both of their faces.

The flow of vehicles eased and a silence fell (the drone they had followed had skilfully slowed down the traffic approaching the roundabout, out of their view).

Precisely then, Eddie and Howie heard a strange, soft, warble-like sound from the other side of the road. Turning together, they noticed a chirpy looking, middle-aged man hovering by the pathway that bordered the roundabout. He looked calmly towards them before turning his bald head to scan the roundabout. Seeing the road was still clear, he punched out the sign of the D.E.E.P. Eddie instinctively responded. The man nodded and with a wry grin wheeled his lumbering body away, his portly build clumsily smashing through the growth as he bumbled out of sight.

He left Eddie with the fleeting sight of a gold etching on the back of his regal navy overalls. The emblem sent excitement and relief pouring through his veins.

'Come on!' he resounded.

Howie, equally energized, tore across the road after him and through the thicket the jolly rescuer seemed to have disappeared behind.

A faint trail of disturbed long grass wove its way through the growth and they darted along it beating between large bushes and bramble, outside of the view of the traffic. Swatting and tumbling into a tiny clearing, they came upon the man, crouching over a rough patch of scrub. After working on some sort of lock laying deep in the undergrowth, Eddie and Howie's disbelieving eyes widened to see him lifting a concealed, grass covered, metal hatch in the ground.

'Welcome to the Captain's Cabin.' The man said, offering a friendly grin as he stood back up to face them. 'After you, Miss.'

Howie had spent so much of the last hour of her life in a state of astonishment, she could do nothing other than stare blankly back. Noticing her hesitation, he nodded his wide-jowled face in the direction of the steps leading down from the opening.

'It doesn't look great, I grant ya,' but it's a whole lot better than waiting 'round 'ere,' croaked the stocky, pug-nosed protector.

With that, Howie stepped over the surrounding weeds and down through the opening.

'Now you, Sir.' The man spoke in a familiar tone and winked reassuringly at Eddie.

As he passed by, Eddie's shabby mane was given a playful flick.

'There's enuf' for both of us up 'ere! Seen less 'air on a grizzly!'

Eddie smiled and swiftly slipped down the rungs after Howie, into the blissful unknown.

'That's it, they're safe!' exclaimed Mr. Bird, spinning away from his desk in Control.

Gibson remained focused and briefed the men.

'I'm going to trail him… At least while he is visible, which knowing him, won't be long. There's nothing more you can do. Get yourselves back to Control.'

Both Freeman and Jacobs switched to auto-pilot and flew out of their action bays. Their drones took simple flight paths along standard navigational lines from their position, back towards the D.E.E.P. The Commander remained high above the scurrying *Suit*.

'He's heading back towards the underground. He knows it's busy and also safe from our units there,' reported Mr. Bird.

'Gentlemen!' hailed Gibson as he called without taking his sights off his target. 'This is a testing time, please remain vigilant, for all our sakes.'

Peter and Tom stopped and looked at each other, pondering Gibson's words.

'Of course, Commander,' they both replied firmly then swiftly vacated.

'Just wait at the bottom, Miss, and I'll start your delightful and enchanting tour from there,'

Eddie and Howie's new friend jested, as he descended behind them. Howie reached the last rung noticing the loss of daylight. The hatch above had been firmly shut leaving the glow from her C.L.A.W. as the only light. The steps ended some way short of the ground. First Howie, then Eddie dropped awkwardly from the final rung onto a hard and dank floor.

They stood each other up and scoured round, noticing old shelves holding a few dusty tools, some old worn-out gloves and some kind of small, metal supply box. The only break in the brick wall circling the bunker was a steel door. It lacked a handle but the two of them, by now, had grown to expect anything but simple ways to enter to the D.E.E.P.

'Right, here's our first delight,' chortled the engineer, 'the great door to the D.E.E.P! 'Ere do me a favour and get ready with your fingers when it pops open, will ya?'

'Sure!' they eagerly replied.

Together they approached the door as the engineer started to work on part of a bracket attached to the wall, his hands either side of the shelf it was supporting. Looking over to see if they were in position, he noticed their curious faces.

'Oh, this? It stops people gettin' in on their own. Crafty villins rarely creep aroun' wi' company,' explained the engineer.

'Will this take us to Control?'

The engineer smiled and answered with a vague yet wry response.

'We got a few of these lil' routes on standby. You know, in case of the odd awkward moment.'

He grimaced at the wall, made a groan like the croak of a bullfrog and the door twanged open with a resounding vibration. The small gap immediately started to close.

'Pull it back, 'ang on to it!' ordered the engineer.

Eddie slipped as much of his hand that he could back into the crack. He dropped his weight, leaning and heaving away as the door tried to close itself. Howie joined in, reaching above with a small metal pole and quickly wedging it into the gap.

'That's it!' called the engineer, 'They said you're a sharp pair. Good work. Now just 'ang on a mo.'

He shuffled over and flipped the clasp of the supply box and creaked it open. Being ham-fisted, he shuffled noisily through the container for some time. Finally locating the desired tools, he wandered wearily across, puffing his cheeks. The heavy entrance was counter-balanced and hard to shift.

'Stay there, young man. Don't mind me,' buoyed the engineer, lowering himself under Eddie before reaching his

147

arm through and looking up as he released the weight. Eddie's face was just above his with Howie's right behind.

'By the way, in case you're wond'ring, they told me to tell ya' that Cranky knows you're safe and that she won't be after you for this one.'

With a clunk of heavy metal, the door lurched free, sending those who had been gripping to it, sprawling across the *cabin*.

'Come on, stop messin' about, you two,' teased the engineer, looking back as if he had nothing to do with their clumsy tumble.

Howie had fallen, smack-bang on top of Eddie and her face hovered inches above his. Both unhurt, her frown curved into a smile that seemed to light up the space around them. She pushed her hands down on Eddie's chest and springing to her feet offered her hand back to Eddie. He grabbed past it onto her forearm and scrambled sheepishly to his feet.

'Very funny,' said Howie sarcastically as she passed the engineer, now politely holding the door.

The man responded with shoulders hunched and that innocent pose, reserved only for the mischievous at heart.

'Don't know what ya' mean, luv,' he replied.

They walked on for some time; through a myriad of low, arched tunnels. Some were lined with old Victorian brickwork that seeped dank water through its worn-away and cracked openings. Others, covered by corrugated iron and diagonal timber braces, were like passageways to a bomb shelter. The only commonality these shafts, paths and channels shared was their direction; they all led down. Flights of rough rutted stairs broke up the journey.

'I barely get out these days. I hope I can remember the way. That's the problem round 'ere, our protection is that no one knows we're here so if we get lost, who's gonna' 'elp us?'

He continued laughing at his own wisecracks as they carried on. All the time, the endearing engineer made the *tour* entertaining with his kindly way and easy humour. He made up for his pranks by handing them snacks, although Eddie and Howie weren't so thankful having worked out they must have come from the crusty old tin box back in the bunker. Regardless, they were both too hungry to care and munched madly on them as they funnelled along behind "Mr. Funny".

'And 'ere we are,' announced the engineer, coming to a turn in the tunnel.

A light could finally be seen that wasn't tinged with emerald.

'Welcome home, kids!'

He held the door as Eddie led Howie into one of the storage areas that lay at the back of the F.I.Z.

'Thanks, er…… sorry, I feel like I should know your name but….'

'They call me Hackman down 'ere. Why don't we start with that, eh? Oh, and while we're on the subject of introductions, come wiv me for a sec. I've got a couple of friends you should meet.'

They turned away from the direction of the F.I.Z. and walked along a wide, picture-lined corridor, behind the drone storage rooms. Eddie and Howie passed images of engineers holding parts of machinery and odd-looking mechanisms. There were also copies of what looked like programming code, framed and commemorated with an inscription below each of them.

'Them?' Hackman proudly clarified, 'well, they are to remind us of what we've done to stay ahead.'

A holding room, identical to the one Eddie had passed through on his first ever visit, linked the passageway from the F.I.Z. to the lower level of the control room. As the second door became see-through, a quiet man in Patrol uniform appeared on the other side along with more delights of the D.E.E.P. The platforms and metalwork in the middle were surrounded by drones that had either recently completed, or were preparing to go out on, their duties.

'We're below the Control room,' said Howie.

'Have you been down here before?' Eddie asked.

'That would be telling.' Howie commented glibly, while her eyes took in with glee all the works going on.

Hackman called towards two technicians, hard at work, sitting opposite each other at a small workstation nearby.

'I gotta treat for you two young'ns!'

To Eddie's surprise, they saw that the two workers were only a little older than them. They both shot up from behind a tall, cylindrical, part holographic screen and looked at each other, exchanging faces brimming with anticipation.

'Eddie…you're lookin' at the D.E.E.P.'s finest weapons… Soda and Chips.'

They exchanged polite greetings and Hackman explained that their nicknames showed what they meant to him; he had been addicted to greasy hot chips and ice-cold club soda for longer than they'd been alive.

Howie stood back, arms folded, waiting for Eddie to take things in.

'Aren't you going to say hi, Howie?' asked Eddie, thinking she was being quite rude.

The others all laughed as the penny dropped and Eddie realized that they already knew each other, very well. Howie half-started the sign of the D.E.E.P. then leapt forward, laughing with her arms out wide.

'There's always something to learn around these two, Eddie. Don't worry, you can't be expected to know everything!' she joked, turning back from her hugging friends.

Eddie then watched in amazement as they went back to their jobs. They worked in partnership, using all manner of technological skills to show how they could remotely take over and disrupt the workings of factory machinery, office networks and most importantly, other drones.

Chips was a boy barely a few inches taller than Eddie, with unparted short black hair and a kind, smiling face. He relied on Soda to act as interpreter as they spoke. She joked with the group, saying that even hearing people need help working out what Hackman was saying most of the time. Chips signed that it was easier decoding *Sky Bugs* than his boss!

Hackman's team made the Patrol's drones not just impregnable but incredibly powerful.

'It's child's play, so to speak, with these two. You put their brains and our drones togevva and it's 'avoc for the scum of this ci-y,' bragged Hackman. 'Betcha glad they work for us good guys, eh?'

Eddie and Howie nodded in awe and appreciation.

'Just remember them when you're in the air. You're in good 'ands. Now, cam'on; time you were gettin' where you're goin'.'

Eddie left the room astonished yet again, by the Patrol and its secrets.

'Thanks, Mr. Hackman.' Eddie shook his hand and Howie smiled gratefully.

'Back through those doors and you'll be in the F.I.Z. You should remember the way from there, eh?'

As they parted, Mr. Hackman couldn't resist one last cryptic crack and stopped Howie before she headed away. 'I said he wouldn't fit but looking at him now, he'd still have room to rattle if he was dropped in a toaster!... *Simul autem solus.*'

Howie was clueless as she watched him shaking his head and chuckling to himself as he made his own way out of the storage area.

'What was that all about?' asked Eddie.

'I wish I knew. They seem to have their own ways down here. Perhaps it's the lack of daylight.'

They found the funny side and restored with energy, made their way into the F.I.Z.

Back in the museum meanwhile, the group had gathered outside and were eating lunch. Simon was staring down at his wrist and, once again, having to play dumb. Eddie had sent multiple messages, all of them short and only clear to Simon. The simple updates had described the last hour's events and Simon's nerves were in tatters. He had kept himself and Lily close to others, just as Eddie had told him, though he was left guessing why he needed the safety of numbers.

'What do you think this message even means?' Lily asked, then read the projected words. 'It says, *found someone to help with coursework, catch up later.*'

Simon looked up.

'Huh?' he said, giving him time to replay Lily's question in his head. 'Who's it from?'

'Howie, you melon-head. It's the first time she's messaged since she disappeared with Eddie.'

'Oh, I'm pretty sure they've just lost track of time. Anyway, Crandall doesn't seem to be bothered that they're not around. I reckon we should just carry on with the others. Fancy a D.D.T.?'

'D.D.T. What's that?' Lily asked curiously looking into the paper bag Simon was holding out towards her.

'Dog Dirt Tart. It's one of mum's specialties.'

'Er, no thanks,' Lily came back in disgust.

'It's actually much nicer than it sounds. Mum calls it something far more tempting,' said Simon. 'You sure?'

'Yeah, you're alright' replied Lily, watching him bite down on the brown lumpy mixture that sat on top of some kind of dark and crusty pastry.

Simon munched merrily on the treat while Lily conducted a search into her own bag for something to eat.

'Wish someone baked for me,' she quietly and sarcastically lamented to herself as she took each processed packet out.

'Ooh great, cheese flavoured play-doh, rolled up rubber fruit, or a delicious pack of crumbs.'

Lily was finally won over by a bland looking snack bar.

'Mmmmm….tasteless,' she announced and ironically smacked her tongue off of the top of her mouth, mocking its sorry lack of flavour.

Simon smiled and shook his head.

'Can't say I didn't offer,' he said, holding up what he hadn't already shoveled in. Then, nodding towards the remainder of the group nearby, he chuckled, 'Monkeys in mittens, look at that lot.'

Half the team were amusing themselves by tossing Joe's lunch around and mocking his lame efforts to recover it as it sailed through the air between them. The game was brought to earth by Cranky who threatened them with her usual charm but the fun had not quite finished. As Joe started to stuff away his pulverised sandwiches, he had not noticed that his bag was sitting on the very edge of the table.

The force of his heavy-handed packing sent it toppling over, slamming down on to Jonny's foot. A classic Wilson overreaction included screaming, hopping backwards and finally sprawling over his own bag. Throwing his arms out to catch himself, he smashed Max's fizzy drinks bottle out of his hand and sent it spinning skywards.

Like a field of crows fleeing from the crack of a shotgun, everyone around took flight; all of them flapping and floundering their way clear of the sticky spray that was spewing out.

'You wouldn't believe how well they play on the pitch together,' said Simon, ironically.

Jonny had fallen at the feet of where he and Lily were sitting and overhearing the remark, decided to retaliate.

'What are you tweeting about Birdy? Oh, and where's your friend? You left him in the museum with the other little dummies?'

Simon could have played the situation in many ways but considered silence and a smile his strongest suit. Lily also obliged by clipping her ear buds out of her trendy "*bud grip*" ring on her finger and losing herself to the music video projected from the grip onto the back of her hand.

Filled with angst at being so dismissively blanked, Jonny had little else to do other than shake his head, pick up his crushed belongings and stomp away, muttering furiously.

After the encounter and having left Room 13 being dismantled, Freeman and Jacobs drove to D.E.E.P. Control in a car fuelled with intensity.

'Perhaps they've figured it out. He may have even told them,' said Peter.

'We cannot assume anything *he* said or didn't say, Peter. We can only find out what he said to them by what they say to us.'

'So how much should they know?'

'If we speak about things that we aren't even sure of ourselves, then how are we going to be of use to either of them? It was pure luck that you were so close when they signalled. Would they feel any safer knowing that? Let alone the whole tragic story. The Patrol is compromised with them in it.'

'But unthinkable without,' countered Jacobs.

Eddie's dad sat staring in thought. He had brought his son into a world of danger. His only solace was its fateful inevitability. Eddie would soon have to face greater challenges than he had earlier, along the train line. That being so, Mr. Freeman's better judgment gave in to the greater cause.

In the hangar, Eddie and Howie noticed eyes were turning their way. They carried on, following a metal rail that took them under the action bays hugging the curved walls above. The glances of those they passed became fixed stares and an expectant hope flickered in the shadow of each one. All work had ceased and Eddie sensed in the silence, the expectation the Patrol had bestowed on him. He had felt it throughout his training but this moment was different. Never, during all of his visits, had he felt so surrounded by so many and all with such a weight of expectancy.

From his frail and hollow feeling body he bleated, 'Hi-i-i.'

The nervous smile and goat-like greeting was the best he could do.

'Sorry, sorry, sorry!' called the voice of a well-spoken lady, trotting towards them in an enthusiastic fluster. 'Welcome, welcome, welcome!'

She smiled and shook both Eddie and Howie's hands vigorously.

'I've only just got things ready, we weren't really expecting you,' she announced.

'That's ok. Got what things ready?' asked Eddie.

'Oh, of course. You wouldn't know, would you, given today's, shall we say, circumstances? Well, I trust you both have worked out that the other… well, of course you have, you're both here together! So silly of me, I'm so sorry. Right, let's start again,' said the delightful and unnecessarily apologetic lady.

Her fractured words came in a frenzy, making them hard to follow. Eddie looked up at her, waiting for something he could understand between the flurry of mumbled phrases and spoken thought.

'Yes… right… so, you've both seen what happens here and, Eddie, you've spent a long time learning about and working with our beautiful machines. That means it's time; *come on!*'

She led off before Eddie could speak but her sharply focused eyes, set intently behind her oval-framed glasses, had put Eddie in no mind to question her anyway.

As she hurried along and led them both towards a group of uniformed men, standing in the open arena, her lavender scent, two-piece bottle-green suit and black and kitten heel shoes, took Eddie to another place. Her strong, thick-set appearance was more suited to a bygone era.

A mist lowered, reducing Eddie's view, as he came across a scene reminiscent of war times. Eddie studied the lady's face, as she turned reassuringly back at him. Her cheek-bones were strikingly pronounced and rounded high and wide, curving beautifully under the frames of her quaint lenses. Her smile was subtle but enough to reveal the warmth of her heart.

Eddie, now clothed in a flight jacket over a chocolate brown shirt and white silk scarf, marched with purpose through the hangar towards his fighter aircraft. On his head, a strap lay over a dark leather helmet holding at each end, rubber ear-cups. Sewn on the forehead of the helmet, just below his flight goggles were Eddie's initials E.L.F. in bold black embroidery.

He marched with other pilots along the flight deck, proudly striding with heroic valour and taking in the sounds of the rasping motors that were cranking into action. Although the lady had meanwhile slowed her stride, the blindly daydreaming Eddie had not.

Unwittingly, he caught her step and fell against her soft-suited elegant frame. She toppled sideways and gave a sort of yelp before instantly gathering herself and making an excuse for Eddie's untimely contact.

'I am so awfully sorry, I've forgotten my manners completely. I am Dr. Eleanor Walsh and I am the operations officer here inside the F.I.Z. and this, my two young friends, is... the *Tear*.'

A group of men stood, facing away, in front of them. For a moment, Eddie was confused. But as they peeled away, what remained engulfed Eddie in electrifying memories. The same drone that had blistered unbelievably around the course on his first visit, now sat poised gloriously on its launch platform. Its strange shimmering surface overloaded his and Howie's senses.

The click of a catch releasing bulged their eyes to near popping. A small door opened from the side of the *Tear* and slid forward. His premonition had been realized as he saw the glow of flight instruments inside.

Looking back at Dr. White, Eddie's heart had already answered the question he uttered;

'Am I going to fly this?'

'For now, I'd like you to see how it feels. Perhaps a small flight here, in the hangar. But yes, Eddie, you *are* going to fly this.'

She spoke with a relaxed expectancy, as if she knew that Eddie sensed things had been leading up to this. 'I should think you'll get acquainted quickly. The controls have been set up just as they are in your action bay.'

'Mrs. Walsh?' interrupted Howie, just looking to be noticed.

'Oh, my dear, I'm so sorry. Please, if you'll come with me. We both have so much to share.'

As they left, Eddie heard Dr. Walsh muttering to Howie the relief of having a bright young lady to assist her but the rest of the conversation drifted out of range. He turned back towards his craft and found a gathering of eager eyes all peering back at him. Though the excited engineers conveyed their anticipation with few words, it was obvious that much had been made of this moment.

'Well, come on my lad, let's get you ready,' ushered one of them.

Looking inside again, the darkness awaiting from within was strangely inviting. The windowless craft's black interior was broken only by the illumination of the control lights that shone from the curved sides towards the front of the machine. It somehow beckoned Eddie and a warm, magnetic sensation started to overwhelm him.

CHAPTER 14

AN
UNDAUNTED
COMRADE

Nearing D.E.E.P. Control, Eddie's dad and Mr. Jacobs left the main road onto a partially hidden and deserted access lane. The cracked concrete track was lined with featureless hedges on one side and wire fencing on the other.

'Drop D.E.E.P. gate 2,' instructed Jacobs. His voice, transmitted through his own C.L.A.W., activated part of the fence just ahead of the car. It lowered and disappeared into the ground. Violently changing direction, the car skimmed over the curb and headed down a ramp that appeared from a dark open cavity in the ground, out of sight. The fence restored itself back into its place and the road returned to its desolate silence.

'Perhaps your way is better, Tom, but he'll discover it soon, either way,' Said Mr. Freeman as the car left the early afternoon daylight behind.

'I'm sure you're right, Peter, his consight is like nothing I've ever seen. You've always needed a line of sight to exchange and even then, power transfer is directly proportional to distance. He watches through walls, inside buildings, we have no idea how far his range extends. And this is all with him taking part in our *tests* unwittingly!'

Then, in a low and thoughtful tone, Peter asked, 'Do you think Gibson really can develop him for Patrol work?'

'I don't know. How do you harness a force you can't measure? That task maybe for Eddie and Eddie alone to solve.'

In the F.I.Z., Eddie had been fitted with a navy blue flight suit. It was constricting and clearly built, from his feet up, to protect him from extreme forces. He walked with an engineer over the dusty and wide expanse of the F.I.Z. and squatted alongside the *Tear*.

'That's it, headfirst, Eddie. Pull yourself up into place with the side rail.'

The *Tear's* interior now explained the set-up of his action bay. Eddie lay forward and rested his chest on a padded surface, the top of which curved up to allow him to drive his shoulders firmly in. This meant his arms fell beside his body and bent at the elbows, under the chest plate so that his hands could reach the controls beneath him. As for his legs, they slid in and formed a v shape with his knees fitting into padded cups fixed on the narrow floor. To ease pressure, a final support elevated from the floor and softly sunk across Eddie's waist. His body became incased as a final section lowered and surrounded his torso. It all made sense now.

The Patrol had developed this drone with maximum capability and minimal space. The craft's shape had more reasoning to it than just its awe-filling look. The engineer crouched at the door.

'It's a snug fit, Eddie. You ok?'

'Yeah, it seems fine,' Eddie replied, finding himself compressed but with the familiar comfort of his action bay.

Each part of the *Tear* had been meticulously constructed, just like his bay in the control room. The simple yet perfect controls and display panel provided solid and intuitive feedback as he went through a pre-flight system check and briefing.

'See you up there, Eddie, and good luck.'

The engineer slid the hatch and it sealed shut with a whisper. Once enclosed and taking hold of the controls that had tilted up to find his hands, Eddie's attention turned to the crystal-clear images and information on the screen directly in front of him.

'Once you're up, don't force the controls,' Dr. Walsh's voice resounded with authority in Eddie's ears, 'the turning forces can take you by surprise. Trust yourself and keep an eye on your readings.'

Eddie's mind went back to when he had watched the *Tear* in flight before. The sharp, vicious way it moved sucked at his confidence. The routines of flight training were a long way from the inside of this tiny and terrifying machine. As Eddie gripped down with clammy hands and anxious thoughts, he drew breath, fought off his fears and prepared for the ride of his life.

A deep pulse signalled the fan blades' initiation. Then, the silence in which the *Tear* hid its irresistible energy. The only thing cutting into the quiet was the fast rushing air that gently swayed the unit on its rigid platform.

'All systems are go, Eddie, you're clear to start your ascent,' announced Dr. Walsh.

The darkness inside broke as a rectangular window appeared in front of Eddie. Two more followed on each side, giving him both a natural and simulated sight of the arena.

'Enjoy your flight, you lucky duck,' Howie added with both pride and envy mixed into her reassuring voice.

Eddie smiled. The unerring horn bellowed and with tightened lips, he tensed himself and pulled back on his controls.

The *Tear* thrusted upwards, sending the air underneath curling across the hangar floor. In the air, Eddie instantly became an extension of the machine. His hands, eyes and whole being, all tuned in to a machine that already knew him. Dr. White was right about the controls but Eddie was soon in synch; each move becoming more aggressive and less strained.

When Peter Freeman entered the F.I.Z. he found Eddie completing a series of training manoeuvres. Jacobs had rushed into the control room and charged up to his niece; seizing Howie with an uncharacteristically emotional squeeze of affection. Dr. Walsh was distracted by the events around her. By the time she returned to her screen, Eddie was buzzing low to the ground and clearly delighting himself with the attention of the onlooking engineers.

'Eddie, stay high while we prepare the course for more advanced work.'

The sharp instruction hit Eddie like a gust of gravity. With the familiar obstacles in place, Eddie lowered and hovered in place with a feel of an astronaut before launch. Dr. Walsh spoke again;

'You've flown well so far, Eddie. You're going to use the *open sight* mode for this task. Arm your drone on my command.'

'Arm the drone?'

'Oh yes, of course, how silly,' remarked the doctor, chuckling to herself, 'the pad below the screen, slide the cover to the right and leave your finger on the symbol.'

Eddie flicked the cover quickly across. The D.E.E.P. emblem shone brightly back at him from the centre of a small panel. He paused. That symbol had served as a constant reminder of his importance and that this was not a game. He lowered his finger and as it rested, the pad gave off a golden glow before shining a bright emerald green.

The main display read: *Open sight mode activated* and dropped into a recess below, leaving his finger momentarily suspended in the air. All around him, the dark metallic surface of the *Tear*, the entire shell, became like glass. Eddie was able to see completely around him as far as his body position would allow and the F.I.Z. appeared before him in direct sight.

'Woah, I can see everything!' marvelled Eddie, 'can you see me?'

'It's one way, Eddie.' replied Dr. Walsh. 'It's called open sight and hopefully should feel something like you do piloting from your bay. The course is open, are you ready?'

Eddie's eyes took in his surroundings, 'I'm ready,' he replied.

As soon as he had heard the low booming siren, Eddie took on the course. The speed and skill with which he cleared complicated obstructions was astonishing. He ignored the warnings on his display and the panicked screams of Dr. Walsh that told him he was pulling too steeply into turns. It was as if he was immune to the natural forces on his body.

Forces that should have caused a loss of coordination or even consciousness. Instead, Eddie experienced no more than a gentle exhilaration. In fact, his simulation seat seemed a poor imitation of flight now. His body swayed effortlessly with each turn, pivoting and oscillating within the confines of the *Tear* whilst outside, the forces and action of the drone ripped the air in a terrific and brutal way.

Thinking his job was done, he eased back as he cleared the last part of the course. To his surprise though, there was more. A dark cave-like hole appeared towards the top of the F.I.Z. wall, above the action bays.

'Eddie, listen carefully,' came Dr. Walsh, 'pilot your craft into the opening you see. Follow the shaft all the way…follow the lights… You're going out.'

Eddie's choked throat swallowed dry. Regaining composure, he replied 'Ok, I'm on it, Doctor.'

'After you leave, speak only if absolutely necessary and don't use my name. You've got every imaginable defence in here to protect you. From magnetic shielding, scanners and jammers to good old-fashioned concrete walls. Out there is different. From now on, you will be referred to as Patch 3. Remember, we see what you do.'

Eddie wasn't sure if somehow the Doctor meant consight but realized that his on-board cameras would nonetheless relay every angle of his run back to Control.

The tunnel was thinly lit along its roof, just enough to pilot at a good speed. Ahead, a bright circular light shone up from the shaft floor. Looking down as he flew over it, Eddie caught a quick glimpse of the control room. He thought he saw Howie standing by Dr. Walsh but before he could be sure, the opening had flashed behind him. Building speed, Eddie now knew exactly where he was and exited the shaft at speed. The lingering moan usually heard from the shaft was replaced by a forceful gust that became instantly distant, then evaporated.

'Will he be safe out there?' Howie asked.

Thoughtfully and in her own quirky way Dr. Walsh replied,

'I haven't found myself saying this before but I'm quite glad of the early nights that winter has brought. It allows for some protection without having to burn the midnight oil.'

She turned her attention back to the trainee.

'Patch 3, we have your visual read from outside and on board. Your zone of reference should be appearing in your sights.'

Sure enough, Eddie was guided in flight, throughout his drill, by two lines of navigation that somehow fused his craft to the outside world. He continued in this flying lane as he headed low, down river and performed some larger sweeps around the uprights of the Dartford Crossing. His body remained relaxed, despite the flashing warnings. Eddie sensed that this wasn't just down to his uniform and the encased angle he was flying at. Regardless, he piloted aggressively on, finding time to take in the silhouettes and structures around him. It was like wrenching a chewy toy from a stubborn dog when Eddie was finally ordered back to Control.

His dad had followed every turn of the assignment and as soon as the fan blades wound down, with the *Tear* resting back on the platform, he was the first helping him out.

'Not bad, eh?' he said coolly.

'Yeah, not bad. But I get the feeling I wasn't alone up there,' Eddie replied.

His dad looked long and hard into his eyes and without words, gently acknowledged the comment. A small ripple of applause from those standing by soon erupted into an ovation and Eddie stood up from the craft. He stared blankly and slowly, lifting one hand up in appreciation. The shock and thrill of his experience was etched all over his face.

'You've got a lot to be grateful for, Elf,' said Peter, 'they've been working long hours for this. You've just shown them it was worth it.'

Eddie was ecstatic. His dad's words of approval meant more to him than any amount of cheering and handclapping. Looking back up at his dad, Eddie's thoughts started to pour out. 'but how...?' he started to ask.

'...Let's talk somewhere else. There's a few of Mrs. Bird's flapjacks with your name on them in my room. You hungry?'

After helping the engineers wheel the *Tear* back out of the F.I.Z., Eddie and his dad gave their thanks and slipped away. Back at Westlake, the Commander and Mr. Bird had finished their hasty dismantling of Room 13 and then made for the car park.

'The quicker we get back the better, Jonathan,' stated the Commander.

'I'll be as quick as I can,' replied Mr. Bird, walking away from Gibson's car, towards the returning coach.

The mid-afternoon grey had left for the onset of dusk and a strong smell of winter as the school day ended. Simon jumped off the coach, eager to hear news.

'Dad, what are you doing here?' he questioned.

He wasn't really surprised to see his dad but put on a decent show for the sake of those piling off the coach with him. Mr. Bird put his hand on his son's shoulder and turned him to face Mrs. Crandall. She was checking children off the coach with a cold shrill that added to the already harsh chill of twilight.

'Ah, Mrs. Crandall, I wonder if it might be permitted for me to whisk this one away early today. We have a family function this evening and a head start on the evening traffic would be very much appreciated.' Mr. Bird pulled his collar up and hunched himself over Simon for added effect.

'Well, school isn't over yet, Mr. Bird.' Cranky replied bluntly.

'I understand that completely. Any work Simon misses today, I will personally make sure he catches up with later this week.'

Mr. Bird was full of charm, giving his son a telling squeeze on his shoulder and a gentle smile to the cold-hearted killjoy.

'I suppose that's acceptable, just on this occasion but please give the school proper notice in future, Mr. Bird.'

'Of course, Mrs. Crandall, of course. Thank you so much,' said Mr. Bird and hustled away for the car park with Simon.

'I don't know what you mean, Simon, she's so soft, demure and considerate,' he said sarcastically in a low voice, 'Cranky indeed.' The two laughed and escaped in Mr. Gibson's waiting car.

In a darkened and desolate tower block, some stories up, well away from the heaving exertions of the city below, the *Suit* sat alone on a leather-backed chair, in the corner of a large regal room. His surroundings opposed the other levels of the broken-down building. Plush patterned rugs, expensive looking art and antiques occupied the floor and walls of the room. It was like a drawing room in a country manor, though its contents were more likely pillaged than passed down. The grand luxury made the *Suit's* wounded and dishevelled appearance look harsh and out of place. A large, ornate wooden door was opening and a dark presence arrived.

The man entering the room appeared slowly, wearing a dark, turtleneck sweater under a half-fastened black leather coat. The chain of a gaudy gold necklace snaked down from his stunted and stocky neck. A huge calloused hand, loaded with gold rings, reached towards the *Suit*.

'Not really your style of headwear, Felix,' quipped the man, pointing at the seeping dressing barely holding around the *Suit's* head.

'Never mind that, I didn't sign up for this, Birrell. The boy is too well protected; you've seen that now.' He spoke in a begrudging and impatient way, as if he would rather be anywhere than there.

'You didn't sign up at all. We both know this is a free and mutual agreement, right?' asserted the colossal aggressor.

Adam Birrell had a reputation in the London criminal underworld of being as starved of compassion as he was hungry for money.

'Right...' The *Suit* spoke with the sound and look of resignation.

'We'll just have to come up with another way,' continued the surly and heavy-set leader of lowlifes, 'Once we have him alone with us, we can have a little chat. I'm sure he'll change his view of the D.E.E.P. then. After all, you're Felix Banks; the man who's convinced the world he doesn't exist... well almost.'

The brutish man smirked at the bleeding and suffering *Suit*, showing interest in only his need of a drink, which he started to pour himself.

Although filled with rage at the insult to having his real name used, particularly in the covert and criminally organized world he was surrounded by, the *Suit* simply tightened his lips and responded, giving nothing away.

'Unless he falls into our hands, I can't see what we can do.'

'You better *see* something soon, Felix, for your good, as well as our guest's,' the criminal mastermind snapped back.

He lowered his dark eyes and thick brow towards a lilac-coloured sweater resting on the arm of an empty chair. The uncontrolled expression of pain on the *Suit's* face seemed to please Birrell. Gulping loudly out of his crystal-cut tumbler and swaggering across the room, he spoke mockingly.

'Perhaps one of his friends could do a better job *investigating*. At least they might do as they're told.'

'I need time,' the *Suit* begged in desperation as the conversation ended abruptly. He was left to repeat the plea to himself. Birrell was already onto other schemes and dismissed the *Suit* with a flick of his fat fingers.

Back in Mr. Freeman's office, Eddie was still coming to terms with the events of the day. Snacks helped Peter speak without fear of interruption.

'It worked, Eddie, even out there! The turns, the speed of thought, you were incredible. In every test we've run, you've gone off the charts.'

Eddie looked back, face stuffed, with a look of bemusement.

'Very few people have consight' his dad continued, 'Out of all those that possess it here in the Patrol, no one has anything like your skill. To engage consight over such huge ranges is unheard of. The energy shared in the link is usually lost or weakened by distance. I was with you for the entire run but your consight made it like I was in the *Tear* with you! What's more, Elf, I don't think we've even found your limit yet.'

Eddie had hoped his dad would add more but could see the conflict in his father's eyes. Consight could do many things but sadly for Eddie, discovering how to read the thoughts of others was not one of them.

'These are difficult times, Elf. As much as you've enjoyed it, sending you out in a drone has always been the one thing we wanted to avoid. Before now, we had certainty, we had solidarity. But now?... now things have changed and you need to know the reasons for the burden we're about to place on you.' Eddie's chewing stopped.

'The *Suit*.'

Those two words were said in a whispered breath and Eddie then waited, motionless, for a response.

'He's dangerous, Elf. I can't tell you what he'll do, I can't even tell you what he did. He left us and now spends every waking hour trying to find us. He was once the man that the D.E.E.P. trusted more than anyone outside of this Patrol. We know him as Patch 1. He was the first to cover our trails and provide protection for us, from the outside. The thing is, Eddie, he was part of us but at the same time you wouldn't be able to find any link between us. We know he doesn't know where we are, that was his choice. He wanted to work with minimum communication and maximum trust. It looks like that trust has been lost now and his decision of not wanting to know where D.E.E.P. Control was is our only saving grace. So where does that leave us? Work to do but no ears and eyes on the outside. The D.E.E.P. only ever trusted a few and that hope in those few is now depar… all but gone.'

Eddie thought his father seemed more angry than tormented by the events. His words showed a loss of faith in these outsiders and feeling his father's anguish wanted to offer his own hope.

'So, can *I* go out to do his work?' he asked.

Mr. Freeman leant forward, put his hand on his son's shoulder and spoke knowing that the answer betrayed his own wishes.

'I'm so proud of you, Elf. You've learnt so much in these past few weeks. You're the only one we have now that can keep the D.E.E.P. operating. The truth is, consight has always picked someone, in its path through history, for times of trouble like this.'

Eddie listened on. What the *Suit* had done on the ground, Eddie was now going to attempt from the air. The recovery of sensitive items, intercepting rogue drones as well as defusing potential conflicts with other agencies would now be Eddie's role but only first, if his consight could be proven.

The two ended their time together knowing that without putting it to the test, Eddie's potential could not be fully measured. However, putting it to the test meant immeasurable danger. The quandary lay heavy with Peter Freeman and struck chords of despair in his heart. How could he risk more suffering to his own family, especially Ally?

By the evening, Simon and Howie had had time to eat and catch up. They met with Eddie in the holding room.

'Eagles in evening gowns, Eddie; flying now? You're ridiculous.' Simon spoke in admiration as he punched Eddie's shoulder, reflecting on the momentous day.

After clearing the holding room, they all headed back through the Flight Induction Zone together towards the exit. Simon thought that Eddie and Howie needed a dose of reality after their incredible journey.

'You two going to be alright to play tomorrow? In case you've forgotten, it's just the big game against Mildham, that's all. I understand if you're not up to it.'

'Nice try but we'll need more than a quiet day trip to the museum to take us out of the action,' Howie proclaimed, making light of the day in her typically confident way.

CHAPTER 15

AN ELEMENTAL OPPOSITION

The next morning, as Eddie hauled his exhausted body out of bed. The soreness in his muscles was almost unbearable. Heading downstairs, groaning on each step, he noticed that his dad had already left the house; he assumed that he was already back at the D.E.E.P. The fatigue of his consight-aided flight had left Eddie goalpost-stiff. Zombie-like, he started to piece yesterday back together.

'Morning Eddie, sleep well?' his mum asked.

'Hmm? … yeah,' he slurred, as he sat slumped over his breakfast.

Eddie was still tuning in to the world when the back door suddenly burst open. Clattering in, out of breath and looking like he had just been swimming, his dad caught Eddie and his mum completely off guard.

'That's the way to start the day! A refreshing run in the stinging rain. How you feeling, Elf? Your mother didn't want me to drag you around town after your school trip but you're looking pretty good on it to me.'

His dad winked down at him out of Ally's view, grabbed a piece of toast and sped upstairs.

Despite his aches, Eddie was in a hurry to use the *Tear* again and with it, test the limits of his consight. Still dreaming about it, he forced himself out of the house to meet Simon in the usual place. Putting his hood up and his face down, he ambled away into the dreary downpour.

'Your kit, Eddie!' screamed his mum from the front door. Eddie rolled his eyes and blew a raindrop off the end of his nose before heaving his aching legs back towards his house.

'Of all days, how could you? You've not forgotten about playing your old team, have you? I thought you couldn't wait for it.'

'Yeah, yeah. I couldn't... I mean can't.'

Eddie covered for his distracted mind but worried how he was going to get around the pitch with his concrete legs.

Down the road, Eddie met up with Simon who was hastily pacing and clearly anxious about something.

'Apes in anoraks, Eddie, this rain could ruin it.'

'Ruin what?' replied Eddie.

'The pitch! It won't take much more before it'll be waterlogged and they'll call it off.'

'That doesn't sound a bad idea right now, Simon,' Eddie said, struggling to keep up with his friend's speedy pacing.

'My whole body feels wrecked!' Simon chuckled unsympathetically but his laughter was short-lived as he glared despairingly upwards at a fresh and worsening torrent of rain.

'Oh, pack it in will ya'!' he wailed.

By the time they both reached the school gates, Simon's cloud-begging had been rewarded; the rain had all but cleared. The playground was empty but for the puddles that were collecting the shower's last drops.

Passing Crandall's office window, Eddie exchanged an upbeat glance with the human-sized Perry. He span in his office chair, then made for Cranky's desk and a pile of papers resting there. Perry made short work of them; imitating his owner's elaborate writing style before whipping each page high into the air with a comic flick of a wing. From floor to ceiling, the room was teeming with flapping paper. Like oversized confetti, the pages danced and waved in the air. The scene escalated further, as Crandall returned.

Her bulbous frame standing wide-legged in shock at her door, her face grimacing with misshapen teeth, flashing and gritted with fury. Clutching her head in horror, she pulled at her hair (which made for two horns sticking up and out) and erupted, spewing spitty howls of disgust off walls and windows.

Eddie left Perry running for his life, feeling less achy and greatly cheered by the plucky parrot's mischief. Even the charcoal-etched sky seemed to brighten.

Most of the team had gathered in their usual spot, beneath the balcony and they were in full swing. The rain stopping had seemed to spark a frenzy of excitement and players were chanting together the words of a playground favourite, "*football pinball*". With arms folded and feet together, they each jumped on the word football which was repeated twice before launching at a friend on the word pinball. The aim was to knock over someone, or at least force them to uncross their arms. In a tight circle they all leapt around, attempting to keep the rhythm of football, football, football, PINBALL! going.

Joe Mackenzie bounded with a spectacular lack of control, out of the pack and clumsily towards Eddie and Simon. It was obvious Joe couldn't stop himself now from an almighty impact.

'Easy Macca!' Simon shouted, who took the full force while fending him away from a joyful but vacant-looking Eddie.

Both Simon and Joe fell then scrambled against each other to get up off the wet, muddied playground tarmac.

'What's up with you Eddie?' Joe said, noticing Eddie's detachment from the mucky messing around.

'Nothing,' he blankly replied.

'Nothing to do with yesterday then?' Joe probed.

'Yeah, we heard you had extra work or something. Why weren't you on the coach back?' Bobby added.

The conversation started to draw the attention of the rest of the team and as they all came closer, Jonny Wilson took up a curious position, craftily concealed but within earshot.

'We tried asking her,' Joe said, staring over at Howie. She and Lily were staring back, unimpressed, leant up against a pole under an overhanging balcony. 'But you know what girls are like,' he concluded.

Eddie couldn't believe that he hadn't prepared some sort of story or clever line for this moment. Instead, he smiled meekly and stuttered into an awkward excuse.

'It was nothing really, my dad just dropped by and had some extra research he wanted me to do,' he casually said.

'So, you weren't smuggled down the river by pirates then, or abducted by aliens?' joked Bobby.

Max pitched in as well.

'You didn't get lost with her… on purpose then?' he teased.

The suggestive comment ushered a chorus of whistles and laughter. Never one to let her friends suffer at the hands of juvenile boys, Lily sauntered over and weighed in.

'I think about that a lot, you know… aliens. I hope they don't exist… they're so slimy, aren't they? Gives me the jeebies just thinking about them.'

Bobby, Joe, Max and the others nearby turned to each other, faces crooked and bemused. Her outburst, though odd, had at least put an end to the interrogation.

'Yeah, well, it'd be hard to tell most of you lot from 'em if they did appear anyway!'

The team started to split away, fearing one of Lily's character-destroying put-down parties. Eddie and Howie's gaze met quickly but then also parted. Paranoid and for obvious reason, they resolved not to look at each other again.

Lily finished staring down the last of the hastily retreating boys and proudly linked arms with Howie back to their bags. Eddie got away in a different direction with Simon. He tried

174

to make himself scarce for the rest of the day to avoid any more awkward encounters.

To the Westlake players, there was something beautiful about playing on their rain-soaked field. Perhaps it was the teasing nature of the day; with reports of the game being on, then off, then on again. Or the way the ball would slip and skim across the glistening turf before jamming to a stop in the mire. Or the fun of sliding and tackling on a surface like an ice rink. All these elements added to the expectation of what was sure to be a heated encounter.

'Alright, Eddie?' greeted Sam Stratton, one of the ogreish twins who had helped to make Mildham a so far unbeaten force.

'Alright, Sam,' replied Eddie. They both stood a little distance from each other, either side of the halfway line, stretching and trying to get warmed up.

'Can't believe your lot still haven't lost a game,' Sam muttered dismissively, clasping his hands above him and powerfully arching his body back, 'with a shrimp like you and a girl up front. You're hardly a deadly strike force are ya'?'

Eddie had heard worse and frankly, quite enjoyed him and Howie being so ignorantly underestimated. Plus, the Mildham badge on the chest of Sam's claret and blue shirt was bringing back fond memories.

'We've got by so far, Sam,' said Eddie, 'we'll give you a good game.'

Stratton pulled a face as if his nose had been dipped in manure while continuing his laughably fancy stretching routine. He swung his head to and fro like a boxer dodging punches and performed a weird backward roll type move before firing another conceited comment Eddie's way.

'Can't see it, mate. Anyway, your unbeaten run ends today and as I don't expect to see you at the regionals, we'll leave it at *"better luck next year"*, shall we?'

Not waiting for a response, Sam turned back and rejoined his squad, his arrogant strut, brimming with self-importance. It was just the motivation Eddie and his worn-out body needed!

Though the rain had long since departed, its effects had left the pitch barely playable. From the kick-off, it was obvious the game was going to be anything but straightforward for Westlake. For one, the quick passing and skillful running game, with which they had torn apart other teams, was impossible on this bog of a pitch. The smash-and-grab type of football Mildham played left Westlake lucky to be level at half-time.

Although games in the rain were often swashbuckling battles, full of slides, skids and splashes, today was different. Simon had to be sharp; saving countless shots from the dominant bulldozer twins whilst Bobby seemed to be the only Westlake player who could put up a fight. By half-time, Mr. J was ticked. He dropped the drinks holder dejectedly down on what was left of the grass.

'We haven't even come close to scoring, lads. Come to think of it, we haven't come close to keeping the ball for more than five seconds,' he lamented.

Mr. Wernham stood over his team on the other side of the pitch clearly enjoying the scene. His rosy, fat face bubbling with satisfaction and his thick black moustache curling with glee.

'Sir, they're more interested in kicking us, than the ball.'

Whitey was right. He'd tried but Mildham's brutal thuggery was punishing. The gashed knee he was tending to was just one of the war wounds the team suffered. Only Bobby's imperious and resolute defending, had kept their team alive.

'Ok, let's try and get the ball moving in the air more. Eddie, Avery, try and find space wide and round the back of their defenders. George, Jonny, get that ball forward, high and quick, look for their runs. The ball will hold up in the muddy turf and we can use our pace to attack them without getting caught up in the ugly stuff.'

Mr. Jacobs was clearly biting his lip. Westlake was a test of his poise as much as his tactics. Players that Eddie and Simon had once called friends were now footballing foes. When Mrs. Andrews had left Mildham, many changes had taken place. Eddie felt to blame in some way for her disappearance. It didn't help that no one would speak to him about it.

Worse still was his old school; now a pale shadow of its former proud style. Mr. Wernham had lost his way completely and hadn't time for the niceties of the game. He was always competitive but his *"win at all costs"* mentality seemed a poor example and wrong for schoolboy football. Nevertheless, he continued to force it on his team despite their misery and lack of enjoyment (except for the Strattons). They followed his orders, glumly.

Vicious tackles flew. Shirt pulls, holds and niggling studs to the ankles ruined the game. Westlake's cause seemed hopeless. Eddie's weariness was becoming obvious and when those bursts of speed faded to stumbling splutters, he suffered the agony of being substituted. In front of the players and large crowd of spectators present from his old school, he trudged sadly to the sideline. It was as much as he could to lift his hand up towards Callum as the switch was made.

Oh, how he wished that Jacobs or his dad had shared consight with him rather than their head-taps of sympathy. Fight as they did, led by their mud-covered and battered skipper, Westlake were losing their grasp. Despairingly, each of them suffered more cheap shots and clattering thumps from the opposition. The rain returned and seemed to mask the referee's view of the events. The swamp-like pitch became a combat area. George and Jonny had nothing left and were also substituted as Mildham overpowered them. With around ten minutes remaining, the inevitable happened. As a corner swung in to the Westlake box, Sam's brother Ben took out Bobby, plunging his knee vilely into his hip as he tried to leap to meet the cross. Stratton was left with a free header from six yards out. He twisted his neck and thrusted his head down through the ball with authority, towards the bottom corner. Bouncing away from Simon's straining dive, the ball skidded off the turf and inside the post, rippling down the side of the net. Beaten but not defeated, Simon was quickly up, trying to pick up the rest of his team. He'd been an inspiration all year and his team owed it to him to persevere.

'Come on blues! Let's get back in this!' he rallied.

His words united the team and for the remainder of the game, Westlake threw everything at Midham, trying to get back in the game.

Mildham were penned back in their half but despite the territorial advantage, Jacobs' team just couldn't find a way to equalise. It had come down to a desperate last push with seconds remaining. Bobby, Whitey and Joe had charged up the field to support the attack and as Howie tricked a Mildham defender one way then the other, she produced the perfect cross towards the onrushing boys. Bobby rose first and highest, towering over a Mildham defender. The unerring sound of his head meeting the ball gave the sense that the shot was on its way in. With their keeper rooted on his line, the soaring ball powered goalwards. CLANG! It smashed off the crossbar and came back out towards the edge of the area where Whitey gave it another mighty crack; surely goal-bound. This time the ball missiled against the post and shot across the box, hitting one Mildham player and flukily falling to another. He quickly cleared it away with the groans of the Westlake parents still reverberating.

To worsen the despair, Sam Stratton collected the clearance and bounded freely upfield. Westlake's defence was hopelessly out of position. The sickening glee in his voice and plastered over his face was unbearable as he turned back to his teammates having struck the killer blow of a second goal.

'Looks like they forgot there's two ends to the pitch, eh lads?!'

That was it. A hollow shrill ended the game and the onsetting anguish began. Jacobs held back his feelings enough to shake hands with the Mildham coach and remind the team to offer their congratulations to the already gloating visitors. It added insult to injury but Mr. J wasn't about to lower his standards despite the revolting gamesmanship of the opposition.

'Told you, Eddie,' smirked Sam Stratton, as Eddie shook his hand, 'looks like you chose the wrong school … unless you *wanted* to play with losers, that is.'

The smug smile on Stratton's wide and square-shaped face would have drawn a reaction from Eddie in times gone by. Now, however, standing there, suffering and sore, Eddie was better for it and simply stared through him. The lack of response riled both Sam and his brother, nearby. Their rising taunts and rude remarks met with Eddie's calmly waving hand as he walked away towards his teammates.

Burning with fury, the twins looked angrily at each other. Like two trolls enduring someone crossing their bridge unchallenged, they grimaced and growled. The small victory widened and cheered Eddie's perspective of the day as equally as it had narrowed and tainted the twins.

Westlake's unbeaten run was over. Their ultimate success as league champions would now require Mildham to slip up. Each player and especially the coach knew how unlikely that would be.

Over the following weeks, heading to the Christmas break, Eddie had no time to dwell. The simulated missions he ran from the Patrol were just after twilight or before dawn, when the darkness would offer the *Tear* greatest protection. His dad would always stay with him, in consight range, staring at the screen while sitting secluded and alert, in his room.

Dr. Walsh's portion of the Patrol secured all drone communications. Hackman and his team enabled all flights to be tracked and protected from interference. At the same time, the Patrol's machines, with their jamming capabilities and disabling pulses, disrupted and displaced unlawful operators across the London skies. Such was their skill, they could now take complete control of even the most physically and digitally shielded dark drones. They would also regularly capture the location of the originating signal; passing the information and confiscated hardware on to London's premier law enforcement agencies.

The best weapon still, of course, was the virtual non-existence of the Patrol to the outside world. They were untouchable and superbly protected, patrolling every corner of the capital. Eddie's skills increased with every mission. He chased down and captured dark drones with Soda and Chips always one step ahead of the villainy. From burglaries and bank raids, to trespassing and terrorising; Eddie was quicker and more equipped than anything else in the sky. He enjoyed most, the rare but ever more challenging outdoor tests. His C.L.A.W. became invaluable for the times he would have to leave his machine; warning him of danger and guiding him to targets.

The task of transporting and delivering secure and classified items remained with those runners in the action bays of the control room. The Patrol was functioning efficiently and successfully. Every member was as valuable as the next and everyone had their own role. Its motto became evermore befitting. The upper hand the Patrol enjoyed over the *Overland Legion* was not going unnoticed, however. Birrell's desire to disrupt the D.E.E.P. and particularly its most vital member, grew with every *Sky Bug* he lost to them.

Between the missions, there were more matches. Westlake recovered their form quickly and easily won their last few league games. The annual grudge match against the black and white stripes of Brockton had been a walkover, with Bobby winning it almost single-handedly from both ends of the pitch. During the encounters, Eddie had started to build more endurance and thanks to his duties inside the *Tear*, he felt stronger than ever as his body adjusted to its new routine. He and Howie were now the team's joint top scorers and though the league was out of their reach, they were looking forward to the regional finals that were taking place the week back after the Christmas holidays.

The last week of school before the break was a vain attempt to harness the efforts of pupils who had grown daily more excited and impatient for the holidays. The final day came. Cards were shared and kits packed up as friends said their goodbyes. Eddie left for home, eager to increase his shifts at the Patrol.

Meanwhile, Jonny Wilson had been one of the first out of the gates. He strutted merrily home, thinking only of what was in store for him this Christmas. As he turned a corner and without warning, he was confronted by a man who seemed to have appeared from nowhere. They both exchanged unheard words before turning and walking together. All the time they acted in a secretive way, obviously not wanting to be seen together.

'As agreed, here's your early Christmas present,' said the man, tapping the screen on a device pulled from the inside pocket his jacket.

Jonny checked his watch and nodded to signal he had what he wanted.

'Are you going to tell me what this is all about? I could still be of use to you…for the right price.'

Amused by the comment and with a wry smile, the *Suit* responded.

'I'll be in touch if the need arises but for now, you can lower your periscope, ok?'

'But Mr. Pearson!' Jonny cried as he watched the man glide across the road and away in the opposite direction.

The call fell on deaf ears. *Mr. Pearson* blanked Jonny and despite his fury at the boy's inability to maintain stealth or cover, did not break stride. Jonny shrugged ignorantly and continued on home. He looked down again smugly at his reward. The receipt displayed electronic credits, deposited in a virtual account in his name. Good for use on custom-built, online stores and gaming sites.

During the days that followed, Eddie travelled with his dad to the Patrol. When his mum sent them off each morning, no more was said than if he was just off to school. Eddie had learnt just to go with it. He hadn't the courage to ask his dad how much she knew. The only hint he had picked up on, was in the knowing look that his mum and dad would share before they left. Either way for Eddie, his trust in his parents more than made up for what he lacked in knowledge about them.

Simon and Howie developed their friendship with the fascinating Chips and Soda. Their short quirky interactions were a lot like Dr. Walsh and Harry "Hackman" Ackerman's. They were a superbly skilled and smart quartet. Though fun kids, Soda and Chips' speed and complex skills made it hard for Simon and Howie to stay with their interactions. Their topics varied and overlapped whilst their hands danced between holographic screens, keyboards and signing to each other. Their skills somehow complemented each other. Soda could operate multiple components at the same time and specialized in redirection. Units would sometimes need to change routes to preserve the safety of *items of value* or even to engage dark drones. She adjusted frequencies and methods of coordinate recoding, to avoid potential interference (The D.E.E.P.'s procedures were not always popular with those who regulated the skies). Her ability was matched only by Chips'. Using cameras, navigational and scanning equipment, he had become a master of target-locking and placed all kinds of digital weaponry at the fingertips of his grateful runners.

Hackman helped, mainly during spells of heavy traffic but seemed to find mysterious other ways of keeping the Patrol one step ahead and out of harm's way.

Eddie's flights, whether quick drills or important operations, helped him get a better understanding of the Patrol. As he soared over the city, he would keep in the back of his mind how his size had turned out to be a great asset and his consight ability invaluable. His short body and daydreaming mind had turned into an unexpectedly powerful combination. The purpose he served, though daunting, was greater than even *he* had ever dreamt.

CHAPTER 16

AN AIR OF DANGER

It was the day before Christmas Eve. Eddie was on his way to the D.E.E.P. with his dad and as usual the last part of the journey, east of the City, was a dark and invisible one.

'I think it's alright not knowing where it is you know, dad,' Eddie remarked from inside his latest head covering.

'Sort of makes me feel like the Patrol is always with me. I can see it wherever I am.'

He had grown glad that the control's location was a mystery. It was a burden he was happy no to bear.

'So, what's happening today, Sir?' he asked, curiously scanning the screens of the control room.

'Ah, morning Eddie,' replied Commander Gibson, 'it's been a quiet night and now everyone seems to be shopping or working from home this morning.'

Simon arrived soon after, with his dad.

Hey, Eddie, fancy one of mum's mince pies?'

By the size of the box Simon was carrying, it seemed the Birds had bought enough for the whole Patrol! After taking a couple and enjoying an exciting chat about the presents they were expecting, Simon headed down with his dad to the maintenance area. They were shortly followed by Howie and Jacobs who also did not hang around for long. The Patrol was full of industry and everyone seemed to have much to keep them occupied. All but Eddie.

The day seemed to drift slowly for him. Training in the F.I.Z. had become routine and hardly compared now with the thrill of his outbound missions.

Late that afternoon, Eddie sat impatiently in the control room. He was waiting for his tireless dad to call it a day, when the Control's alarm sounded. Overhearing the details of an aerial robbery in progress, Eddie quickly tried to influence the Commander's thoughts.

'Send me out, Sir. I know how to keep out of trouble and I'll have the jewels back in no time,' Eddie pleaded.

Half-listening to Eddie but more tuned in to the call, the Commander offered unwelcomed words,

'Remember Eddie, you going out is our last option. As much as I admire your enthusiasm, you must understand, you only go if the runners are out of options.'

Eddie frowned and paced around. The comms operator turned to Gibson and relayed the call,

'Single unit involved in a theft at the Muscovy Jewelry Store, Commander. Police are in pursuit of two men on the ground but the drone carrying the stolen items hasn't been acquired.'

'Send out a couple of I.M.P.s to intercept,' Gibson calmly instructed.

Almost before their action bays had lit up, two runners gusted in and hastily prepared themselves. All eyes turned to the screens. The two units were positioned on the platform and within seconds, in the air; sleek, efficient, unerring.

The echoing tune left by the drones faded along the tunnel then died; swallowed by the darkness and her frozen sky. The mechanical twins tightened their path then vanished, along with the last trace of dusk.

'Knightsbridge…it's a big one!' relayed the Commander, 'a jewelry store…two men… gems and stones transferred onto a dark drone. The police are in pursuit on the ground but their units can't clean the sky.'

Eddie, with his dad standing alongside him, was absorbed by the images relayed from London's network of motion activated cameras. This surveillance equipment had turned the city's rooftops into its eyes. Any rogue UAV craft could be viewed in detail as it shot over them, each camera following its path like dominoes pivoting, one after another. Along with motion sensitive cameras were the pulse cannons. They were located in strategic positions, high on buildings, designed to hit suspect or off-course drones with a disabling signal. In this case, they had so far failed. Police H.U.M.M.E.R.s were also seen struggling to match the agility of the fleeing machine.

'It will stay low, between buildings, where there's cover. It probably has a rendezvous point somewhere close,' said Mr. Freeman.

The Commander's thoughts raced ahead. He spoke over the hum in the room, conveying developments from those on scene. 'No sign of the robbers on the ground. Patrol engagement, ninety seconds and counting...' His words carried urgency yet remained composed. The I.M.P.s still had terrain to cover when Gibson made his decision. Though he said nothing, his intentions were obvious to Mr. Freeman. Recognising the signal and situation, Eddie's dad obediently ushered his son away to Room 3. Once there, he turned to face him and spoke simply... 'It's time.'

'What's happening, dad?' Eddie questioned, trying to resist the excitement inside. 'The Commander wants you prepared, just in case.'

Mr. Freeman's voice seemed detached and business-like. He dared not allow Eddie to see his true emotions. The family gift seemed more and more like a curse to him each time he readied his son for flight.

'In case of what? asked Eddie.

'In case our two I.M.P.s struggle out there... This isn't just about a robbery, it's about our effectiveness. These moments are what people rely on us for…Not that they know who it is they are relying on.'

Eddie was all set in a matter of moments.

'So, I'm going after this dark drone?' Eddie's voice sharpened.

'You need to be prepared…' his dad blankly responded. He collected himself before looking up. '…just in case.'

'Ok, dad,' came as serious of a reply as Eddie could muster.

'*Simul autem solus,*' he said loyally. His dad's eyes glistened and creased as he proudly smiled.

'Let's go, Elf,' he gently breathed.

All of Eddie's previous missions had given him experience and great expertise. His instincts, size, skill and of course, consight were now a supreme force, as was his machine; illuminated on its platform.

'They've had a couple of shots at it but they're in a real dust-up Peter,' Mr. Jacobs informed them both as they stood watching the screen, just behind the Commander. 'This is no good … no good at all,' scowled Gibson, 'No suspects apprehended on the ground and the air is getting filthier by the second.'

The Commander hated long and drawn-out operations and always asserted the need for being *"clean, efficient and precise"*. The chase had been on for more than ten minutes and just as Mr. Freeman had predicted, the fugitive drone was banking steeply between buildings, finding cover for itself as well as a route to escape. The Patrol's drones hadn't been able to engage it or disrupt its progress.

'Enough!' resounded the Commander, ripping away from his display and swivelling sharply in Eddie's direction. He paused; his face softening as he addressed Eddie.

'Why send a drone to do a man's job, eh, Eddie?' he quipped. 'Ready?'

Eddie did not wait to be asked twice. Like a whip cracking, he flew and snapped himself in place. The rotor blades were already thrusting upwards before the exit hatch could be fully opened and after abandoning take-off procedures, Eddie made a charge for the small, widening gap into the tunnel behind. He thundered through with inches to spare on each side.

London brightened on the landscape with the colourful illumination of streets and skyscrapers that Christmas time had brought. Eddie, oblivious of the cheery glow, powered to full throttle along the river. He synched his coordinates and switched to open sight. Dr. Walsh's voice then filled the craft.

'Patch 3, we have the target in view heading east from Hyde Park Corner over Green Park. Leave the river, north from Hungerford Bridge and await instruction.'

Eddie navigated the river, cutting the sharper turns just as in his training runs, though never before at such a speed. As he left the water, the navigation lines continued to show his flight path. After flashing by Trafalgar Square and starting along The Mall, he received an update.

'Patch 3, we've had to disengage our I.M.P.s. Suspect is now in cover, low to your right between trees in St James' Square. You'll have clear line of sight over the building lit on your display. We'll try and paint the target.'

'Yes, Sir,' he replied.

Eddie turned sharply and swept over the marked building. Behind it appeared an open area ringed by the glow from lampposts and nearby buildings. Scanning feverishly, Eddie immediately located the dark drone.

'Target acquired,' he called assuredly, feeling confident that he would be able to take down the hiding drone before it even knew it had been found. Closing in and preparing a jamming signal, Eddie was shocked by what he saw.

The dark drone plummeted, as if powerless. It fell wavering towards the path below. Eddie tracked the drone to its doom but instead of the expected impact, the unit span away just inches from the ground, sparking off the pavement as it swerved very much alive again. Rapidly on it flew, under the cover of the tree line in the square.

Eddie had not engaged with anything as elusive as this machine. Down he followed, ripping through the fragile fingers of a low-hanging limb and levelling up before bursting forward after the dark drone.

The crafts lifted and skimmed over the metal railing that bordered the square then chased around traffic, up a narrow street and towards the conspicuous shape of St. James's Church that was dead in front. Hard and fast, the suspect banked left and charged along Jermyn Street. The most traditional and stylish of streets met with the two modern monsters. The machines rudely stole away the calm, leaving behind ornate lattice shop windows shaken and the hustling Christmas punters cowering for cover.

Eddie felt a strong force as he followed. His consight was fully engaged; helping him gain on the rogue machine. A locking tone let him know the drone was in range and he lifted his thumb over the flashing ELIMIMATE signal. As he did, the drone turned ferociously and seemed to disappear through a wall. The street was a narrow rocky canyon of high-sided buildings. Throwing himself in the same direction, Eddie found himself flying through the entrance to the Princess Arcade.

The crowds along the store-lined path inside, hearing the chilling wail of the rogue drone, dropped to the floor and ducked into shop fronts. Throwing themselves behind the immaculate Christmas trees and richly decorated pillars that stood between the doorways of each shop, the well-heeled folk crouched and shuddered as the drones shot along.

Eddie stayed close behind but alert to the peril of the enclosed shopping parade. Then, a muffled communication crackled through the *Tear*.

'PA……OUT…..N…..AIR….ST…'

He could make out the Commander's unusually ruffled voice but not the message. Regardless, this cold and calculated chase carried on down the warmly-lit and festively decked precinct.

'We're losing him on comms,' panicked Gibson, 'do we have visual? Peter, are you still with him?'

The control room was in a panic. The scrambling quest to bring down this dark drone was unnerving the Patrol. 'I'm with him,' confirmed Mr. Freeman, moving with consight precision in his action bay.

Relieved by the news but still concerned for the mission, the Commander gave an ultimatum.

'Patch 3, take down the suspect immediately or disengage… We can't risk innocent people!'

Eddie received the message as he surged out of the arcade and onto a busy street.

'I'm right with him…just about…WOAH!'

The two units narrowly avoided the side of a passing double-decker bus that was chugging, chocked full of commuters along Piccadilly.

'GET OUT PATCH 3, DISENGAGE AND ABORT!'

Gibson ordered as Eddie climbed steeply over the giant red bus. Without responding, Eddie clung to the escaping machine as it twisted down into the densely-populated Burlington Arcade. Shoppers were, once again, scattered and left strewn all over the walkway. One figure remained motionless, however.

A man wearing blacked out glasses and a long dark overcoat crouched, lowering a briefcase to the floor. He poised himself and calmly focused. Without expression, he snapped open the

191

case and spun it around to face the onrushing machines. The first drone squealed past. Precisely then, the man pressed down on some sort of remote device, hidden in his hand. Time, at least for Eddie, seemed to stand still. All around him was silent and somehow frozen in that moment.

From outside, an enormous and piercing light pulsated out of each end of the arcade, then vanished. Eddie's display flickered, faded and died. He was losing control of the *Tear's* movement as it juddered towards the end of the walkway.

Behind, the mysterious man calmly crouched down once more, fastened shut his suitcase and walked purposefully in the opposite direction and onto the Piccadilly street outside. Sliding his glasses into an inside pocket of his coat, the narrow-faced and grim looking man immersed himself into the teeming river of people who were flowing along the pavement.

Inside Eddie's capsule, mayhem had ensued. He had flown through a sheet of blinding, white brilliance and lost almost all vision. His open sight had failed. Through the three small slits, in the front of the *Tear*, Eddie's best efforts offered only the squinting sight of a fast escaping drone.

'No...NO!...ELF!!' gasped Eddie's dad from his action bay.

All visual contact was gone despite Mr. Freeman's desperate attempts to recover the link. The Commander's head shot around. His eyes lurched across the room. Clutching Mr. Freeman, they froze with fear. 'Peter!' he screamed.

Eddie, still determined pulled hard left out of the arcade, struggling to stay with the dark drone.

With his controls now operating without support, he felt the huge strain of G-force over his whole body. Grimacing and groaning, Eddie's turn was weak and he lagged towards the buildings on the opposite side of the street at a dreadful speed. With nowhere to go and sensing the impending impact he pulled up hard on what was left of his crumbling controls…

…The pressure on Eddie was too great and like shadowy curtains drawing across his eyes, the hero of the D.E.E.P. slid out of consciousness…

Eddie's stricken machine maintained its line but spiralled miserably up, into the gaping black. The doomed drone was now failing, sailing lifelessly above the cityscape. Without mercy, gravity tightened its grip. Levelling off then arching back towards the ground, the *Tear* gave its all to protect its pilot from the inevitable impact. Internal padding and cushioning surrounded Eddie whilst air packets burst from the outside of the capsule in an attempt to soften the landing.

A single explosive thrust threw the *Tear* into a shallower dive as the cold boggy ground of Berkeley Square came up fast. Clipping the branch of a large Plane tree, Eddie's once invincible craft cascaded into the turf and started rolling, throwing mud and long-dead leaves up over its lifeless body. The pointed rear of the craft finally caught the soil and ploughed along, heaving it to a stop.

The quiet returned, as did the tranquillity of these kindly situated gardens. The remnants of autumn drifted back down, falling gently around the wreckage.

'DEPLOY! DEPLOY!' cried the Commander as he hurried to help the frantic engineers prepare all units for action.

Peter Freeman was already heading out of the room.

'He's not moving, can't hear me G-LOC…' (gravitational loss of consciousness). 'I've got to get to him, his positioning will still broadcast from his C.L.A.W.'

He mumbled his thoughts and actions aloud, more in shock than duty.

'Peter, he's in Berkeley Square,' Jacobs said, 'it's the rush hour,' he added, trying to think, himself, of the best course of action. 'Hang on, I'll come with you!'

Grabbing his jacket from the back of a chair. Eddie's dad charged on, darting through the doors and to his room. Tom chased after him, quickly looking to reassure Howie who was standing helplessly with Simon and Dr. Walsh. In their rooms, both Peter and Tom sat in their chairs, flipped a control panel on the armrest and after selecting a route, fell with their chairs down through an opening and out of the D.E.E.P.

As drone after drone scrambled from the control room and made for the crash site, Eddie lay in a haze of confusion and alarm.

'Why did I fly down that passageway? What happened?' he thought to himself as slowly, his mind replayed broken moments from his disastrously failed mission.

Light from dusky lampposts filtered in through a crack in the unit's side hatch that had been partly prized apart from the force of the collision. The drone itself was still in surprisingly good shape considering it had not been designed to be smashed into the ground at high speed.

Eddie had started to unlock his restraints and push away the protective dampening material from around him when a forceful jerk on the door from outside startled him. After two or three more wrenches, the door gave up its resistance and then gradually, in a measured and deliberate way, it was eased fully open. In the same way, Eddie's mouth gaped open as he saw who the clasping hands that had freed the door, belonged to.

'You?' Eddie gasped in disbelief.

'Hello, Eddie…' The voice was familiar though the charming tone seemed unnecessary, given the circumstances.

'Do you think perhaps we can chat now?'

The *Suit* and his accomplices had trapped and captured their prize. Eddie, semi-coherent and barely able to stand was eased out of the wreck and helped to his feet. Even though

194

the intercept and takedown of Eddie's drone was anything but, everything the *Suit* did was troublingly considerate.

'That was quite a stunt, Eddie,' he remarked whilst lifting the casualty to his feet.

He dropped down and draped Eddie's limp arm over his shoulder; propping him up.

'I wish it hadn't come to this but you're better off outside of the D.E.E.P. than in it. Now, let's get you in the warm, my friend.'

His words were comforting as well as captivating. The *Suit* always had the ability, when working for the Patrol, to be on the scene of any incident with uncanny swiftness. The talent clearly remained. Why his motives and allegiance seemed so altered though, was still a mystery.

The separation of Eddie from his custom-built craft meant the D.E.E.P. were now tracking his signal on their displays. As the pulsing image headed slowly away from the crash site, the Commander's concern for Eddie's wellbeing, after such a long unresponsive period, was eased slightly.

'He's ok! At least he's moving.'

His relief was short-lived as an engineer commenced a countdown.

'Pilot is now outside the zone of devastation; *Tear* drone destruction initiated. Commencing in ten…nine…eight…'

Part of the Patrol's protection and defence of itself included leaving little or no trace after any failed missions. Countless hours of development and design were decimated and given up to the night in the historic London square. Tiny but fiery detonations split the shell and sparks crackled over the controls inside. The entire structure then seemed to liquefy as it surrendered itself to its fate. The snapping and whispering light, shimmering amongst the empty branches of the trees around Eddie, acted like ice water being poured over his head. Shocked into consciousness, Eddie turned his head feebly at the wreck and watched it vaporize right in front of him. Flames licked at the cold and empty air, then vanished.

The *Suit* paused and turned to the inside of his coat. Eddie recovered what he could of his thoughts.

'Before we slip away, Eddie, let's make sure our journey isn't interrupted, shall we?'

He rolled up Eddie's sleeve and slid his arm into the sapphire glow of a dark cylinder. It seemed identical to the tube that the Commander used when Eddie and Simon first received their C.L.A.W.s. Before Eddie could work out what had happened, the thin, see-through film lay lifeless in the *Suit's* hand. He studied it, tilted his head and gave an underwhelmed expression.

'This won't do either of us any good,' he said, tossing the flimsy material into a litter bin as they left the square.

After a few strides, it was obvious that Eddie's shaky walk was catching the eye of those passing by.

'Right, let's not cause any more of a scene, Eddie,' the *Suit* said, straining with Eddie's slumping strides.

He crouched down and Eddie gladly slumped onto his kidnapper's back, resting his face inwards over his shoulder. The *Suit* piggy-backed Eddie along the beaten paths of Mayfair offering a cryptic explanation to those walking by.

'The poor lad. He's been flying around all day.'
Within a few short seconds, the Patrol had lost its two most valuable possessions. The loss of the *Tear* and its most valuable member were the D.E.E.P.'s worst fears, realised.

CHAPTER 17

AN
ACCOUNT
OF
CONSIGHT

The Patrol used every conceivable method of surveillance intelligence. Still there was no trace of Eddie. Runners operated in shifts with Simon, Howie and Dr. Walsh added to their numbers. Mr. Freeman and Mr. Jacobs had scoured the crash area for a trace of Eddie's whereabouts. They discovered his deactivated C.L.A.W. but little else. Using consight, they had darted desperately all around the streets surrounding the square. Peter scaled some of the trees and nearby buildings to get a wider view of the area. The attention this caused compromised the secrecy of the D.E.E.P. It was of little interest to the men; time, fast fading, meant that usual rules were being abandoned.

'Any news?' Tom asked Control as he stood still, allowing Peter to combine their powers once more, stretching his search to the limit of their consight.

'We have everything in the air but we're just guessing... we have no trace on him.'

The Commander spoke sorrowfully, 'Keep looking, Tom, you know what's at stake.'

Jacobs didn't reply. He was already exploring his mind for every possible reason for Eddie's disappearance. Peter rejoined him, breathless from his ghostly chase. Tom looked up and stared hard into his comrade's dread-filled eyes. Voice falling, he uttered the inevitable...

'He's failed us before, Peter…We knew he wouldn't give up…Could he somehow have..?'

Tom stopped. He could tell by his friend's pained expression that the words were already torturing him. Since contact was lost, they had avoided this moment. Neither their consight nor the Patrol could release Eddie from the *Suit's* hold now.

Eddie, head throbbing, felt a billow of warmth from a door that swung open in front of him. His whole body was aching fiercely and the heat was gladly welcomed as he was cradled inside. The smell inside carried the scent of brushed suede, tinged with a faint mustiness and further in, through the foyer, the aroma of a busy kitchen.

The *Suit* lowered Eddie and exited through a swing door on the far side of the room. Eddie was left on a long, padded seat in what appeared to be a dining area for the lords and ladies of a more regal time. The lavish tables were set for dinner. Gold-rimmed bone china plates sat between parades of fine silverware. Thick crimson napkins nestled in crystal glasses and tasty condiments held in silver dishes completed a setting fit for royalty.

Lifting his woozy head, Eddie's eyes widened as he took in his new surroundings. Windows draped with lavish patterned curtains, large crystal chandeliers and a dense burgundy carpet gave the room a theatrical feel. A tinny-sounding bell rang twice from another room. A door opened and the *Suit* sauntered in, carrying a plate under a silver dome lid.

'You look like you could do with a good meal, Eddie,' he said, gently laying the plate onto one of the prepared tables. 'Come on, we can catch up while you get your strength back.'

Eddie rose from the bench and was cheered by the appearance of one of his favourite dishes.

'Liver and bacon ok?' teased the *Suit*, knowingly.

They sat down opposite each other. Eddie gazed with intrigue as the *Suit* slipped his jacket off, casually flicked his cufflinks onto the table and turned his shirtsleeves up a couple of rolls.

'Eddie, let's start at the beginning, shall we?'

Instead of creeping him out, The *Suit's* elegant tone simply sharpened Eddie's thoughts.

'What's this all about...What do I want...Who am I?' he purred.

'I know who you are,' barked Eddie 'you're a traitor!'

'A traitor? Is that what they call me?' The *Suit* looked away, over Eddie's head and gasped with frustration and hurt by the outburst.

'Well, you are, aren't you?'

'I can understand why they would say that. I just hope they don't believe it.' The reply confused Eddie.

'Why wouldn't they believe it?' snapped Eddie. 'You walked away from them and now you've kidnapped me. YOU'RE A TRAITOR!'

The *Suit* maintained a stunned look, filled with self-pity. Gathering himself, he asked,

'And do I get a say on who I am?' Eddie looked up and with his mouth preoccupied, just shrugged.

'Yes, you eat and let me talk now,' the *Suit* continued, 'you see, your view seems a little one sided. Perhaps my words, or at least my actions, can help balance out those scales of injustice I'm being weighed by.'

Eddie was unsure who to trust but reasoned that if the *Suit* wanted to harm him, he would have already taken the chance. In any case, his hunger was more than a match for his suspicion.

'Eddie, let me make it clear. The D.E.E.P. isn't my enemy but neither, at the moment, can it be my friend. You don't just have consight, Eddie, but a greater, unbridled, untapped,

199

unchartered power. People have watched you perform great feats, yet no one has been there to say how you achieved them. What if I told you that this power, this *gift,* isn't in fact, yours at all?'

Eddie was confused but the softening rich tones of the *Suit's* voice had him hanging on every word.

'Let me explain in a way you can conceive, without dispute. If your consight *is* natural, then the next few minutes of your life couldn't possibly happen… enjoy your supper.'

With that the *Suit* rose and collected his cufflinks and jacket. Staring down with a look of utter assurance, he unfastened his expensive, vintage wrist-piece and placed it by the side of Eddie's half-empty plate. Calling back, echoing his own voice, he left the room,

'Ten o'clock sharp Eddie…ten o'clock.'

Eddie frowned with confusion and stopped chewing long enough to read the time; a little less than five minutes to ten. The tastes stirring in his mouth soon enticed his jaws quickly back into action. The food was the most impeccable he could remember eating and Eddie savoured each bite as he watched the second hand creep ominously in the dial.

While the night sky offered its long wintery quiet above, the D.E.E.P. was humming manically below. A hive of agents, runners and engineers worked as one; hovering over black rooftops and hunting through the festive streets. The Commander and Mr. Bird were discussing the ensuing and compromising operation when Jacobs walked in with a vengeful-looking Freeman. Peter stormed across the floor and attacked Gibson the moment he saw him.

'He's your friend, Michael, what's he doing? WHERE IS HE?!'

The Commander, after hours of futile hunting, had nothing left, not a word. The muscles in his long and weary face struggled to express his total desperation and a deep longing for the moment to explain itself.

Mr. Bird tried to calm the situation.

'We don't know for sure what's happened, Peter. Let's not turn on each other...not now.'

At that moment, the channel that the Commander had been begging a voice from became active.

'Michael, I realise that I haven't covered myself in glory but I have motives beyond my loyalties. I will keep the boy 'til such a time comes that my motives change. Pray they do, for all our sakes.'

'He's transmitting from a moving source, Sir,' called an engineer, 'heading south over Horseferry Road.'

The Commander snatched the headset from the engineer, gestured to redirect drones to intercept and attempted to keep the deserter talking.

'What have you done with him? Think about what you're doing to us all...your family,' he implored.

'Don't worry, Michael, your salvation is resting.'

The *Suit* was relaying his communication using a drone as a mobile messenger. A camera hidden in the high back rest of a chair facing Eddie, transmitted a video signal directly through the drone and into the control room. With sublime precision and for just a split second, Eddie's well-fed image blazed across every display and screen within the D.E.E.P.

'Eddie!' yelled his dad, instinctively.

Eddie himself, charged unknowingly by his father's consight, pulsated with renewed energy. At the same time, he looked down and read the hands of the watch lying on the table...ten o'clock...to the second.

The drone had served its purpose. It gave out and plummeted into the Thames, sinking beneath its grey rippling gloom. The river buried its inheritance; leaving behind the gently quivering reflections from the cheerily coloured lights along its banks.

'We've lost the signal, Sir. It broke off as it crossed the river.'

'What about the relayed signal?' asked Gibson

'It was…we needed more time, Sir,' called Mr. Hackman apologetically.

'He knew how long he had,' muttered Gibson, feeling empty and strung along like a puppet.

Lifting himself with the Patrol's expectations on his shoulders, he summoned up what little hope he had left.

'Conduct a search along the banks and under the bridges, upriver from Westminster.'

The Commander knew that it was a long shot but the Patrol needed something to give them hope and a purpose. Drones scoured along verges and skirted under piers but despite their stealth and systematic efforts, time and tide made the cause hopeless.

'Ah, Eddie, you look like a different person,' remarked the *Suit* as he re-entered the room and saw Eddie transformed by his supper and comfortable surroundings. 'How was your food?'

'Good…thank you,' Eddie replied, 'how did you know?' he asked with intrigue as the *Suit* tidied Eddie's finished plate to one side and sat down.

'Know what?' came the innocent reply.

'I felt something, how did you know it would happen at ten?'

'Eddie, there is so much to understand, so many things to tell you, the first of which is learning to trust against your instincts. It would be beautiful if consight was all so natural and flowing between your 'family' in the Patrol. But that's just a little too improbable, don't you think?'

'So, what do you say it is? It doesn't seem like you have it, so what would you know anyway?' challenged Eddie.

'The digital world we live in is the power, Eddie. I can't show you what happened when that watch reached ten o'clock but it was only me who could have known. How else can we explain it?'

Eddie grew even more mystified. The *Suit* did have a point but how could it be? Had he been deceived all this time? Doubt was now swarming around the words of those he had trusted, even his dad's.

'From your youngest day, I've been there, Eddie. Remember the school field? I was trying to prove it to you then and I'm trying to get you to understand still now.' He softened his voice sorrowfully. 'They will do anything to stop you knowing.'

As he spoke, he lifted his thick wispy fringe to reveal a long scar crawling out from his hairline and down the side of his forehead. It was fresh and reminded Eddie of the incident on the station platform.

Compassion and perhaps even a little sympathy were added to the cocktail of emotions stirring inside Eddie.

'So, what now then? If what you're saying is true.'

Eddie had heard enough to make him question everything now.

'We'll get there soon, Eddie,' the *Suit* replied assuredly, 'but for now, you need rest. Come on, my boy.'

After climbing a wide and elegantly carpeted staircase, Eddie plodded along an equally broad landing and through a set of heavy oak double-doors. On the other side, a luxurious bed and a change of clothes draped over a large studded leather couch met his eyes.

'Here, sit down,' said the *Suit*, pointing towards the sofa whilst switching on a device shaped like a rounders bat. 'Now this thing is just to make sure your insides didn't get scrambled after you fell from the sky.'

Speaking reassuringly, he ran the baton over the length of his body. It produced a thin blue line that traced the outline of Eddie's torso as it passed over him. A few short beeps later and the *Suit* was satisfied. The pain all over Eddie's body ceased. Whether it was the *Suit's* medical gear, or the comfort of his new and sumptuous surroundings Eddie wasn't sure but as he turned and fell on his bed, he found himself strangely at ease.

'I'll leave you to your rest now; tomorrow will be easier after sleep,' the *Suit* said.

With no energy to resist, Eddie surrendered to a soft pillow and the gentle hug of his bedcovers.

The evening provided the opposite experience for the Patrol and especially Eddie's parents. Peter had gone home to try and explain things but reassuring words had failed to calm Ally. It was hardly surprising. He only partly believed what he was saying himself.

'It's no use saying that he's ok, Pete, he's not here…he's not with me!' Eddie's mum was frantic.

A pain was returning to her that she hadn't experienced in years and along with it the empty feeling a missing family member leaves behind.

'We know he's safe. I know you don't want to hear it but we just have to wait.' Mr. Freeman's words only made things worse.

'You're right, I don't want to hear it. I just want him home. I can't stand this, Pete, can't we call someone?'

'You've known about the danger all along, it's the curse of the gift. The police, special law enforcement, even the army won't be able to help, we're involved in something that doesn't even exist, you know that. Please Ally…trust me, we'll get our boy back. He's smart…resourceful…he'll be ok.'

They had nothing but each other to cling to as the night wore on.

By the morning, it was obvious that the Patrol couldn't carry on searching so fiercely without causing alarm to London's waking eyes. The drones returned to SNL flight paths, remaining vigilant but now restricted.

It was mid-morning when Eddie finally woke, revived once again, by another tempting smell. After dressing, he made his way down the stairs.

'Ah, good morning, Eddie. What perfect timing,' remarked the *Suit* as he crossed from the bottom of the staircase into the room where Eddie had eaten the night before.

Eddie paused, pawing his hand over a gracefully curved bannister. He looked over it, between the flights and noticed he was many floors up. Carrying on down the staircase, he imagined the building with butlers, maids and servants all industriously going about their morning duties. Two men with their daily newspapers harrumphed along together, bustling with self-importance in this merry made-up scene from history.

'Come on my lad, chop, chop!' snapped the *Suit*, parting Eddie from his daze.

The two shared a hearty, late-morning breakfast and as the fog of a long night lifted, Eddie began to wonder about all that he had seen and heard.

'My parents will be worried; can I at least speak with them?' he asked.

'Already done, Eddie, they know that you're safe. Today, you have something more important to do,' the *Suit* briskly responded.

He neatly cleaned up the table and summoned Eddie out of the dining area.

'Questions, questions…you must have so many questions, Eddie,' he continued as he led Eddie down several grand flights of stairs. 'Not tempted to run again are you?' It was a rhetorical question that conjured images from their last eventful meeting and designed to guide Eddie's train of thought. 'Trying to talk at the museum with you was a gamble on my part. I apologize for being a little too bold that day but honestly, Eddie, I really had no choice.'

On what Eddie figured must have been the ground floor, the *Suit* pushed through a stiff wooden door. A colder, damp-smelling hallway followed by a narrow concrete set of stairs took the two further down. Their journey below ground ended in a small windowless room with little in it. A filled laundry bag sat on an old and scratched table. The *Suit* pulled out an uncomfortable looking wooden chair from under the table and offered it to Eddie.

'Why are you here?' he asked, not waiting for Eddie's guess. 'I've shattered your consight world, now it's time to show you a real one.'

He circled around the table as he spoke. 'Why did I leave the D.E.E.P.? Ah, good question! Sometimes, in life, Eddie, you need to feel appreciated. Money can often reward you in a more practical way than the kind thankful words of the virtuous. And that leads me to why now...Why have I got you involved now? It was a matter of timing. I had to wait 'til you were ready, Eddie.'

The *Suit* broke off his version of things to chuckle at his rhyming wisecrack and fish out a second chair. He spun it on one leg and straddled down with vigour.

'The tiepin told me you had found the Patrol. So nice of the Headmistress and your team to be so accommodating.'

Eddie quickly recalled the day at Bobby's when he had found his bag unzipped.

'You were there! You moved it!' spouted Eddie.

'Not really, let's just say I had a willing friend whose betrayal of you was cheaper to buy than mine. I say friend but he doesn't seem to really care about anyone. The picture he sent me was the beginning and here we are now, about to make our own ending.'

Eddie knew it could have only been one person.

'Speaking of ending, I must leave you now...just for a while. You can enjoy your afternoon thinking of ways to thank me for freeing your mind.'

He slung the laundry bag over his shoulder and made for the door. Leaning against its frame, he turned and spoke with a mixture of delight and cunning. 'Did I mention that I can teach you to trigger your *consight* to access others, even those that can't be seen. A very useful skill for where we're going tonight.'

As the door was closed and bolted shut, Eddie had new questions to ask. The four vacant walls surrounding him however, were all that remained to hear them. What were they doing tonight? Where were they going? What did he mean by *those that can't be seen*? Consight always needed some sort of line of sight or proximity, didn't it? Downhearted, he looked around the insignificant and featureless room. Eddie gave a long sigh of dull disappointment that even his daydreaming couldn't help him escape from.

The D.E.E.P. shared in his suffering. The anguish and despair amongst its people radiated as powerfully as any consight. Christmas Eve brings with it a promise of joy and celebration. For the Patrol, all that remained was a fading hope and the fragile faith in a fallen friend.

Across the glowing city, where lights and last-minute presents were brightening spirits, a darker event was also taking place. The *Suit* was waiting again, in the room where the heists and hold-ups of Adam Birrell's *Overland Legion* were hatched. A gruff, bragging voice punched through the door along with the strutting, oversized frame it belonged to.

'Felix, I've heard you have good news...You've got him!' he exclaimed, holding his fists up like a champion fighter.

His hands flashed with showy rings, while gold bracelets and a loosely fitting watch, rattled on his wrists.

'It's about time! You cut it close.' He nodded in the direction of one of his doubting henchman. 'Jenkins here told me you would never get him… He had me worried.'

'It was just a matter of time, like I told you,' replied the *Suit*, coldly.

'So now there's nothing in our way for tonight…GREAT! I feel like putting a daisy in my hair; I'm giddy.'

He spoke with arrogance and an unnerving superiority over his blackmailed adversary. He chomped and gnashed in anticipation of a chance to gloat face to face. 'We need him here before a blade so much as turns tonight. I want to know exactly where he is before we roll this party out. It's going to be a night to remember, Felix!'

'With any luck…it will,' came the stony, whispered reply.

'What was that?' barked the malicious mastermind, his crooked smile twisting into a scowl.

'It will…but I need assurances that you won't harm the boy,' bargained the *Suit*.

'Have I harmed the old lady?' he snarled back, sliding his hand across the screen on his desk before brashly putting it in the *Suit's* full view.

The display revealed an image of the frail figure of Hazel Andrews; former head at Mildham and now a pawn in the conflict between the D.E.E.P. and Birrell's airborne army of dark drones known as the *Overland Legion*. She was sitting alone and quietly reading in what seemed like, a well-furnished cell. Steel bars covered the high, block glass windows and a single, narrow wooden door in the opposite corner seemed to be the only way in or out.

'Everything alright for you, ma'am,' mocked the villain, as he called through to his tiny captive. The *Suit* fought his feelings. The fury he held for this shameless scoundrel was almost uncontrollable. His composure was only held together by the resolve in the lady's eyes.

'Don't worry, Felix…what do I look like, a monster? I just want a monster pay day. I'll have no need for your mum, you, or even the boy after that.'

The words failed to reassure the *Suit* but nonetheless, he agreed to return later as instructed.

'Be here by eleven tonight, with the boy. The operation is set, we've got everyone and his drone ready for the show and now you've done your bit, it'll be like stealing from a blind man.'

Shutting the screen off and leaving with his ogre of a sidekick, he scornfully crowed, 'Merry Christmas, Felix!'

--

As nightfall came, the entire Patrol gathered in the F.I.Z. Standing on the platform that Eddie's *Tear* had never returned to, in the centre of the arena, Commander Michael Gibson gave his brief for the evening ahead.

'As I stand here, the future of this Patrol is unknown. Questions are being asked by those that keep us alive and flying and they're questions I can't answer. We've suffered loss, we've suffered betrayal and now, we are without the one person we all have strived to protect. The survival of this family relies on us finding our son. If we fail, then the search for Edward Freeman will be our last mission. Now we could wait this out; he doesn't appear to be in mortal danger. But does this patrol wait for others to dictate our destiny? Does this Patrol give up in the face of irrefutable odds? Does this Patrol stand with me tonight, to serve and to search throughout our beloved city and prove that the D.E.E.P. will overcome any adversity for a lost and mortally endangered member of its family?!'

A roar of support had built and now boomed around the F.I.Z.

'Then let's save Eddie and recover the reputation of this Patrol…Simul autem solus!'

Cheering and with the passion of an attacking regiment, the people of the D.E.E.P. charged to their posts. Amid the roar and as the crowd separated, Howie stood still and alone. The only movement was in her welling eyes and the tear that had escaped, now creeping down her cheek. She drew a deep stuttering breath, wiped away the watery track and raced to her position.

AN ABANDONED TRUTH

Eddie had never sat for so long, so alone and with so little hope. He had resorted to adding to the scars and scrapes in the table with a small chip of stone that he had found on the floor. His heart and head squabbled about the words of the *Suit* and the teaching of the Patrol.

Convincing and conflicting thoughts pounded through him. He could not explain the events of last night so perhaps he had been fooled about his powers. One thing he *had* worked out, by the groans of his stomach, was the absence of at least one meal. It must now be nearly night-time, he concluded, as he stood and worked his way around the room again. He had probed and prodded each wall and even whacked at the ceiling, trying to find some chink or gap he could pry apart. The remains of a chair lay in pieces on the floor; the splintered leftovers of his effort to break down the door. His useless attempts only reminded him of how limited his strength and abilities were without his consight power, or whatever it *really* was.

As he sat back down and slouched his elbows on the table, he let his chin and sullen face fall despairingly into his hands. It was in that total silence and pitiful moment when an image then appeared holographically in front of him.

'Hello, Eddie. I admire your patience, it will serve you well.'

The well-tailored clothes, familiar hushed voice and intense but caring face were unmistakable.

'As you listen to this, feeling trapped and confused, please remember one thing. All I want is to open your mind wider than they will ever allow. The truth you're about to hear will give you that opportunity.'

Each word the *Suit* uttered drew Eddie more intently to him.

'Your whole life, as I have seen it, has been a test. I watched you as a young boy being used and manipulated; all in the name of Patrol *development*. Your body's natural rhythm has been altered by them. Digital and biological mutations have left you at their mercy like an experimental weapon. They control your power, Eddie, to use at their command. I showed you last night that I can break their hold on you. Let me set you free, Eddie. Not from your family or friends, not even from the D.E.E.P. but from the machines they have harnessed you to. If you trust me, I will be able to make things right…for you and perhaps…even for me.'

As the message continued, Eddie sat breathless, lost, desperate.

Across town, in their darkened den, three men stood plotting closely together. They were leaning over one side of Birrell's table, which had become an illuminated display of central London that pinpointed the locations and timings of his shady operation.

'Let's go through this then, one more time,' demanded Birrell, 'we're not having any loose ends left waving in the wind when our *Legion* brings the storm.'

The two men with him then finalised the treacherous heist.

'Our unit will attack first, from the west,' said the first spectacled and wiry accomplice; the man from the Burlington Arcade.

He had been responsible for the *Tear's* destruction and now was planning even greater devastation. His haggard features cast a ghoulish image from the glow of the table.

'Two drones, carrying high explosives, will target this point of the Jewel House. As they strike, the impact should expose an entry way through which the second wave will go to work.' He spoke with gritty assurance.

The map was focused in on the various structures of the Tower of London. Target areas were highlighted, as were the approach strategies of each drone. Birrell and his organized criminal outfit were about to launch an attack on the Jewel House. The degree of detail in the Tower's blueprints, from every conceivable depth and position, left little to chance or guess.

The third member at the table was shorter and had a precise tone that matched his sharp-lined beard and stiff features. He ended the discussion with his specific exit strategy.

'We will join the assault from the south. As you both know, my unit is responsible for acquiring and transporting the jewels. Each drone will fly in formation, timed to arrive and sweep the rooms one after the other. They'll leave with as much as they can collect in the time window presented to them. They have each an assigned, pre-set location to make their drops.'

The screen showed many wooded and watery positions across London. The assumption was that each drone would make a separate escape, dropping its share of the stolen royal wear in a remote location. The "rob and drop" method had been used on many occasions, with pick-ups made safely later, using tracking devices. Never, however, had it been attempted on such an audacious scale.

Birrell looked at his scheming partners and gave his verdict.

'No one will see us coming and you know the best thing? No one will see us leaving either!'

The room bellowed with smug and cocksure laughter.

'Now, all we have to do is wait for good old Felix to arrive with the bait and then it's time for some real Christmas illuminations.'

The confidence of the men, like their anonymity, power and influence in the world of technological crime, was immense.

Eddie jumped up from his restless thoughts at the approaching sound of brisk footsteps. He had stared at the handle for hours it seemed, longing for it to turn. As the bolts were unlocked, Eddie took a small step back and waited. The door swung wide.

'Ah, you're still here…good!' the *Suit* joked and offered a polite smile. 'Come on then…' he beckoned Eddie, '…unless this place has grown on you?' he added, confused at Eddie's lack of response.

'No, I don't want to stay,' Eddie said, quickly following the *Suit* out.

They paced along the hall and through a door leading downstairs. After minutes of walking along a pitch-black passage, they arrived at a wall ladder on one side.

'Up,' the Suit snapped.

Eddie climbed but instead of a hatch at the top, there was a platform, just big enough for him to stand on. Then, he noticed a small door opposite, framed in the brickwork. Taking no time to explain, the *Suit* climbed past and after taking a moment to look through what seemed like a spyhole in the wall, slipped through the small opening. It emptied into a wet, murky backstreet. Though Eddie had to move sharply to keep up, he couldn't resist looking back. A shoddy brick wall covered in the scars of old adverts and posters gave no clue to what it hid. The heavy mist in the air gripped Eddie as he reached for a snack, beckoning from an outstretched arm. The *Suit* always seemed to provide solutions, even if the problems were also of his making.

'Thanks,' he said. No look or word came back. They continued at pace, towards the entrance of a busy tube station.

At the Freeman family home, there was a loud thump and the sound of carol singers. Opening the front door, Eddie's mum and was greeted by the sight and sound of fast-fading music. The parting festive melody followed the line of a softly whirring drone that swept away, above the misty lampposts. Ally stepped out from the porch to follow its path but immediately lost sight of it behind the nearby trees. Turning back to the house, her eyes met with something left on the front door:

To find him, they must stop looking and wait…S.A.S.

The message gave Eddie's mum the warmth of renewed hope but also a sickening chill that lingered from this unknowable foe. The small symbol printed next to the words, however, left Ally in no doubt as to what to do.

Talking in quick rhythm with his feet, the *Suit* spoke for the first time since leaving Eddie's makeshift cell. 'He's gathered a mob of dark drones and deadbeats. It's a robbery, Eddie, the like of which London hasn't seen in centuries. They need free air and that's why you're here with me. If they get their way, they'll destroy half of London and after they've plundered it, they'll escape untouched… lost to that darkness above us.'

His briefing came with short, sharp hand gestures that shaped imaginary features in the air. They were of no help to Eddie. The words were sinister but confusing. Regardless, the *Suit* was already flying down the stairs into Green Park tube station and Eddie had to hurry just to stay close. They waded and worked through the rushing stream of commuters that had flooded the ticket lobby and made for a southbound train. Neither of them spoke again until back at street level, as they headed west out of Vauxhall station, when Eddie decided it was time.

'Where are we going? Dragging me around London won't stop them. It doesn't matter where you take me, the Patrol will never give up.'

'That's what I'm relying on. I'll be telling them how they can find you just before we launch. You're going to be a rather helpful decoy for us.'

As they turned onto a quieter street, Eddie swung round at the sound of a whining engine and squealing tyres.

'Trust is all we have, Eddie,' said the Suit, lifting a dark piece of cloth from inside his coat.

A scratched and battered old van mounted the curb and jammed to a halt recklessly close to them on the pavement.

'You know the drill... just a few minutes!' The *Suit*, with comparative composure, covered Eddie's head and stepped him up through the side door of the van.

The journey was short to Birrell's hideout. Eddie felt like he could easily have got away at any time so far. It was his choice to go with the *Suit*. His trust had been won... what had he to lose?

'Let's see him then,' Birrell scoffed.

The *Suit* stood Eddie in position and lifted away the cover on his head. The flashy villain's face turned from a cocky grin to a searing scowl. His overcooked pancake of a forehead curled around his eyes.

'Is this it? This is their big stick? Their great weapon? All this fuss for a puny stump of a boy...pah!'

He walked towards Eddie and snarled, 'What d'ya think *you* could do to stop us? You're just a boy!... pretending to be something you're not. Stick him downstairs, Jenkins.'

Birrell acted in angry haste. Not understanding consight, he dismissively turned back to his table of schemes.

The *Suit* eased his way out of the room calmly behind Birrell's henchman. Eddie questioned himself. Had his trust been misplaced? The henchman's heavy hand throttling the back of his neck made him start to think, maybe!

Back at control, in the Commander's room, Gibson and Freeman fought angrily over the message that Eddie's mum had passed on.

'Sitting on our backsides won't help at all. It doesn't make any sense, Michael! We're just giving them time to do whatever they want with my son, why are you even listening to him? Don't you remember? He deserted us.'

'I share your emotions, Peter, but part of me is compelled to take him seriously. Yes, he has betrayed us, he did walk away and of course he's deceived us but…'

'But what?' badgered Freeman.

Gibson paused, seeing the man he once knew beckoning from his memory.

'I remember a man whose loyalty was beyond question. A man whose trust could never be lost and whose actions were always for good. Let's wait…not all night… but at least for now. Ally received the message at eight; it's nine-thirty now. The message said tonight, so please Peter, let's prepare for tomorrow.'

Mr. Freeman shook his head, not in disagreement but as if his suffering was too much to take. Throwing his hands behind his head, anguish replaced his breath and filled the room. The two friends looked hard into each other's eyes and were each reminded of all that they had been through together. Peter's hands dropped, and he retreated.

'Ok, but if nothing comes, then we go out with everything!' he demanded from the doorway.

With one firm nod, Gibson gave his guarantee. Every second that passed for Eddie's dad was like a slow turning vice, crushing him into an excruciating state of helplessness. Eddie had been taken downstairs and found himself, once again, locked in a small room with a steel door. Some of the building's floors were ramshackle and unlit, others showed signs of a previous life with lines of trailing wires leading to cubicles that now sat bare.

'Tell him I'll be back up in a few moments,' the *Suit* said to Birrell's stooge.

Jenkins shrugged his shoulders and shook on the locked door as if to remind him who held the keys. Much like his boss's, his feeling of power acted like a drug. He finally left the *Suit* who leant up against a small, shoulder-height, access hatch.

'I'll return, Eddie. When I do, be ready. You'll have full charge of your consignt. You'll be able to control it.'

'To do what?' Eddie called back.

'I can give you all the power you need but this time you'll have to stretch your thoughts, employ your magnificent mind like never before and find what we all need.'

Eddie had no choice at this stage and nodded in agreement.

'But what am I looking for?' he asked.

'Family, Eddie...family.'

As the *Suit* walked away, he seemed conflicted; unsure, or maybe undecided, about how the evening would play out. Dishonesty rarely serves a good purpose but the conflict between the D.E.E.P., the Overland Legion and the captive Mrs. Andrews meant that, for now, he could only be true to one. He returned upstairs, preparing for one final act of deception.

Entering Birrell's room with more authority than he left, he turned all attention on Eddie.

'How far do you want this goose chase to go? They need to believe you have him somewhere hard to find. We need to be sure that they'll send every machine they have. If not, I can't guarantee the sky will offer the easy escape you're expecting.'

'Like we agreed, Felix, just before midnight, you're gonna tell them… Cliffe Pools is a pretty place, that's where we'll have 'em go. Searching down there in the dark should keep them busy long enough for us to complete our evening's business. Who knows; maybe we *will* hand him back at the end of it. He seems about as dangerous as a dandelion.'

The *Suit* went along with the laughter of taunting disdain that filled the room, showing nothing in his face but scorn.

The D.E.E.P. was quiet and poised. Peter, however, sat alone in his room. In his anguish, he had shut himself off from every means of contact and thought of nothing but the avenging of his son. Then news came… Gibson flew out of the control room.

Seconds later he was hurtling down the curved hallway and bursting in to Room 3.

'Peter, it's him!' he proclaimed. 'We've got a location, east. He's in an open area so we're sending everything to pinpoint him fast. Let's go!'

Peter sprang from his chair then for a split second froze. 'And if he's not there?' he said doubtingly.

The thoughts of the night so far, had not left him encouraged.

'If he's not, then you have my word. I'll pass total control of the Patrol over to you. You can lead any response you deem fit…I still trust him, Peter, you know that.'

'Yes, Sir…I do,' Freeman replied in reluctant obedience.

Cliffe Pools, a remote and desolate nature reserve a few miles east down the Thames, was messaged as the handover point. The *Suit* had timed his transmission to coincide with the raid. It was convincing enough for the desperate and out of options patrol to instantly prepare a full rescue attempt.

'It's done,' the *Suit* said solemnly.

'Good! Now gentlemen, let's get this party started. Felix, I suggest you make yourself scarce for a while.'

'What about our agreement?

'We'll talk after Christmas…I'll need time to play with all my presents!' The sarcastic outburst made obvious Birrell's dislike for the *Suit*.

He saw him only as easily bought and weak; an unwelcome downer who frankly, despite his invaluable service, was spoiling the villainous vibe.

'Time to move gentlemen. Our great day of destruction is about to begin!'

The legion's leaders scuttled passed a motionless *Suit*. With a smirk and a grunt, Jenkins forcefully dropped his shoulder into the *Suit's* side, thumping him off balance and sending him stumbling awkwardly across the room.

'Who are ya? You're nothing to no one and that's exactly who you have now…no one.' Birrell's minder sniggered with scorn and swaggered off, not yet knowing that his unprovoked assault had given the *Suit* the jolt and conveniently the means, to carry out a plan of his own.

He had *betrayed* the Patrol for one reason and it wasn't for the wealth and power that Gibson and the D.E.E.P. assumed. The risks had always been high, his methods unconventional but the *Suit* knew himself better than anyone. Redemption could be his if the bleak circumstances in front of him could be transformed. He glanced down with amusement at his quivering and colourless fingers. They were holding a black digital key tag, pulled from a pocket in Jenkins' oversized jacket. The *Suit* wrestled to clear his mind. As he battled, just one thought fought through; something his conscience was unable to fend off.

He had only a few minutes to act. Leaping from the floor, the *Suit* vanished out of the room.

From the Patrol, I.M.P.s, M.E.R.M.A.s and every UAV at their disposal were all sent to help with the rescue. As quickly as they could be launched, one after another, they left in frantic search for Eddie Freeman.

'Please let us help!' begged Howie as she chased her anxious uncle around the control room.

'Wait in your action bay, Avery. We have a few more units than runners so your time may yet come. We need our most experienced flyers out first. The Commander and Mr. Freeman will call the orders from the field.'

Howie was impatient for action. Climbing up the ladders and onto the gantry, she stopped by Simon's action bay. 'They say we're not experienced enough…that we have to wait. I just want him back!'

'We all do, Howie. They're doing everything they can, so we have to as well.'

Looking down, they both could see the control room humming at full capacity. Every seat, every position, every machine and every member of the D.E.E.P. was being tested to the limit. From the action bays around them to the engineer's room, below the platforms, the entire Patrol had scrambled and now laboured relentlessly together.

'We need to be ready to help them, so strap in and *be* ready, ok?' Simon demanded, trying and failing to disguise the loss of his own patience.

He, more than anyone, was desperate to fly to his friend's rescue. Their distress deepened as the last runner raced their drone out of the exit vent. The drifting echo left Simon and Howie even more restless to join the fight.

The *Suit* jumped the final few steps of each flight, drumming down to the deserted level. Making for the room where Eddie had been imprisoned, he pulled out a device that quickly span to locate the *Suit's* face. Sliding his eyes in precise movements, he started feverishly messaging.

Eddie had exhausted himself, once again, attempting to escape his confinement. His efforts carried more anger than anticipation now, starting to believe that he was some kind of unnatural machine. Was there something inside of him that could be programmed to operate his body more powerfully? Had he been a failure to his family in his natural form? Were his thoughts even his own? He thrashed around, belting, whacking and lashing out at the walls; confused, unhinged and derailing. He did not even notice the sound of the automatic lock releasing. It was only the appearance of the *Suit*, standing in the open space where the steel door had been, that broke his rage.

'It could be worse, Eddie,' said the *Suit*, before slowly lifting his eyes from his device, 'if that troll who put you in here finds us, we'll both be flatter than that table you've taken care of.'

'You're back!' shouted Eddie, his face transforming.

'No time for a gushy reunion I'm afraid, listen very carefully, my *deep-thinking* friend.'

Miles across town and hundreds of feet below it, a message was being received in the Patrol control room.

'Jonathan!' called Dr. Walsh.

'What is it?' Mr. Bird leant over her shoulder.

'It's a series of coordinates, pointing to three different locations.'

'What about the other text above it?' puzzled Mr. Bird.

'It's the same code we received earlier, it's from *him* again,' said Dr. Walsh.

'If it is the same encryption, the translation should be up in a few seconds,' said Mr. Bird.

The data on display faded and letter by letter the interpretation (provided by Chips and Soda) replaced it. As both Dr. Walsh and Mr. Bird read the text, the blood drained from their faces.

'We've got to get them back,' they grimly echoed.

The announcement was made to those on the rescue mission that there was no rendezvous, that there was no collection point and to worsen it all, they were powerless to prevent the attack that was about to happen right under their noses.

'They're going to destroy the Tower!' panicked Mr. Bird.

'Not if I have anything to do with it,' replied the steely Doctor.

'Practically the entire fleet is down there, Eleanor. If this information is reliable, they won't be able to get back in time!'

'You're right, Jonathan…that's why we're taking matters into our own hands,' she responded and turned assuredly towards two expectant figures who stood ready, burning with impatience, by their bays.

All runners on the gantry frantically redirected their drones to the scene but they were still miles away. Birrell's deceiving tricks and dark drones had created havoc. Mr. Bird sensed the hopelessness of the situation. Then, looking up into the willing determination shining from Simon and Howie's eyes, hope flickered and tears welled in his own.

The stroke of midnight rang from the bell tower of Big Ben, ushering in Christmas morning. Eddie and the *Suit* found themselves between floors, in a stairwell of the uninhabited building. The *Suit* began to work on his device again. Tilting it towards Eddie before sliding it up and down between them, he prepared what Eddie thought was an activation of consight.

'Remember what I've told you, Eddie, I can give you the power, but you have to reach deeper into your mind to see her and that's how we'll find her.'

'Find who?' asked Eddie.

'Our reason for all this, Eddie. I'm trapped because they have her. Only you can set me free. Mrs. Andrews is looking for you…now close…shut your eyes and find her.'

The *Suits* eyes, ice cool but alive with the force of an ocean, were Eddie's last sight of the world around him. Something about the *Suit's* actions and his own eyes closing had sparked flashes of his consight memories. As if playing back in scenes; every moment he had experienced under its influence, repeated itself, quickly and in sequence. From his recent flights in the *Tear*, all the way back, into the underground room, Eddie sensed a link. Finally, seeing the *Suit* in the underground room, snatching the tiepin from his dad before cunningly planting it as he turned back to face the onrushing Mrs. Andrews. The sight of her fateful and cheated face from the *Suit's* view, brought Eddie's own eyes back to life.

'She's here…upstairs!' he blurted, then calmed before agreeing, 'you were right, she's been looking for us.'

As he did, he noticed that the tiepin he had managed to keep with him, even after his kidnapping, was shining from his hand, involuntarily held up in front of him.

'No time for an antiques roadshow, Eddie…' replied the *Suit*, curling Eddie's bewildered fingers back around it. 'Come on my boy, we've got some real jewels to save,' his voice lifted as he sprang away, 'let's fly!'

They both seemed to glide up the stairs, without effort, picking up speed as they climbed. Eddie had found the ability to locate Mrs. Andrews and speeding through the empty hallways, sensed her near.

The assault on the Tower of London, meanwhile, had already begun. With a low hum, high above the neatly lit Christmas tree on Trafalgar Square, two heavily laden machines led the attack. Over the rooftops of the hotels, restaurants and theatres of Northumberland Avenue and turning away from the London Eye, the two flying felons growled and prepared to strike heartlessly into the same walls that had held captive the traitors from days gone by.

'Simon...Howie... your displays should be coming up?' came Mr. Bird in their bays.

'I see mine,' replied Simon.

'Mine's good too,' followed Howie.

'You're active...the hatch is open...quickly, GO!'

No sooner had Dr. Walsh spoke than the two units were out of sight.

'You'll have speed, but the old equipment attached will affect your turns. Your visuals are also limited. Keep your camera set forward, you have less than four minutes,' she continued.

The two of them already were up to full power and now cut a straight line towards their mark.

Somewhere, out of the limelight and a long way from danger, Birrell sat forward in his seat, laughing in anticipation of the havoc he was about to create. His twisted pleasure grew at the sight of his preprogrammed drones making their steady descent towards their target. His loyal and witless protector, standing by the door, had started whistling *Silent Night* in a mocking and flat tone. Birrell chuckled and appeared to start drooling with excitement.

'Oh, this is gonna be good, Jenkins...this is gonna be very good,' cooed the classless governor as another screen showed a second wave of drones.

They seeped from the opening in a viaduct, below railway lines, south of the river then rose like a constellation of lawless stars filling the sky.

Eddie sensed a change in his consight and instead of closing in on Mrs. Andrews' position, he was now actually being pulled towards it. His feet still felt light as he reached what looked like the end of the stairs. Standing at the top of the landing, Eddie span round in confusion. 'I don't get it. She's here…she's right here!'

'But there's no door,' stated the *Suit*.

Realising he had made a startlingly obvious point he looked up, drew in deeply, then blew out as he leant himself, arms behind back, against the landing wall. Suddenly, to Eddie's astonishment, part of the wall moved. The *Suit* smiled and coolly spun round as the wall behind him began to separate and slide apart. Behind this opening, stood a door, identical to that which had held Eddie a prisoner, hours earlier. The *Suit*, with Jenkins' key tag still in his pocket, had managed to unlock the entrance to the sealed-off cell. They made short work of the inner door and thrust it open.

'MRS. ANDREWS!' screamed Eddie.

'Oh, hello. I thought I heard something,' she softly replied, standing upright and calmly collecting her jacket. She draped it elegantly over her arm and made her way to the door.

'Did you bring my sweater by any chance, Felix?' she quipped then caught the *Suit* with a telling wink.

After easing her way gracefully past them, she turned back in a fashion more like her old self.

'Well, let's not waste time. I've had quite enough of this place.'

Eddie, shocked by her unusual air of unruffled poise, looked up at the *Suit*.

'It's a family thing,' he said and clipped after her, back down the stairs.

AN
HOUR
FROM
REDEMPTION

They sped recklessly along the empty streets of East London. The report had come through that Eddie was nowhere to be seen at Cliffe Pools and the smokescreen collection point had sent Mr. Freeman wild with rage. He turned his fury on Gibson.

'You've trusted his empty words one time too many, Michael. He's made fools of us all and now he's doing it with my own son.'

'I know this could be another ploy, it could be a ruse or even some kind of trap but what else is there? If we don't take the Patrol back towards the new positions, where else do we go?' replied Gibson.

'The Tower of London, a viaduct off Vauxhall Bridge and the outfield of The Oval cricket ground...really Michael? They're just more false trails. Can't you see? Let's get back at him! We've sourced the location of his message this time, let's target that.'

It was Gibson this time, who took on the regretful acceptance. 'I gave you my word that you could take control of the Patrol if this rescue failed...do what you will.'

The orders were relayed. The entire fleet, led by Mr. Jacobs, now followed Mr. Freeman's instruction and charged towards the *Suit's* originating signal. All that is, except for two drones. They were past the point of return and frankly, Dr. Walsh had no intention in calling them off anyway. Simon and Howie began their short descent and prepared for whatever they were about to meet over the Tower.

'Do you see that?' asked Howie.

Their displays showed two moving objects, airborne at a slightly higher altitude but descending directly towards the intended target.

'Yeah, this is it Howie…,' Simon replied. 'Oh, badgers in bomber jackets.'

'Engage as high and as quickly as you can,' instructed Walsh, 'and do try and stay in one piece up there.'

'I'll take the one in front,' said Simon, seizing his controls firmly and engaging his tracking system on the approaching enemy.

Howie swept down and around, trying to give Simon space and remain undetected. The Tower was now in clear view and there were only seconds to act. Simon instinctively put his machine in direct line with the lead drone. He sensed, by its size and speed, that he could get between it and the Tower in time, but then what? He was just metres away and had few options. Knowing he had to stop it, he remained locked on course, lowering at the same height as the diving drone that was now passing over the Tower's perimeter wall.

In an attempt to save his machine, Simon shot out the only weapon available the old craft had; a trapping net. It burst out in front of him with surprising power and accuracy, wrapping itself around part of the attacking drone and causing it to lose height immediately. It fell under and out of Simon's view. He couldn't turn in time to see the result of his last-ditch effort. The impact of the collision was gigantic. The drone, with blades snared in the twine of the net, pummelled into the ground just short of its target and disintegrated in a huge fireball. It lit up and shook the whole area around the Tower, as well as the cold, dark sky above it.

'Great work, Simon!' screamed Dr. Walsh.

'NO!' shouted a disbelieving Birrell, watching to his horror, from his room. 'The filthy turncoat…He's fixed us up!'

'Simon!' shouted Mr. Bird from the control room.

His son sat motionless in his bay for a short while, trying to comprehend his actions. The displays around him showed only what was in front of his still turning drone. Slowly, his mouth gaped open, seeing the fiery remains of his foe. His eyes then doubled in size realising that no harm had been inflicted on the ancient structure. His face transformed into a beaming smile of amazement.

'Woah!' exclaimed Howie sharply.

Her unit had been shaken violently by the explosion and she was fighting to see, let alone maintain its line towards the underside of the second drone.

Using split second speed and timing she tilted her unit, catching the large, lumbering machine and sending it off course. Howie's second pass allowed her to latch a line to the wavering craft, pulling it off course. With it awkwardly trying to regain control, she sealed its fate in one move. Releasing the attached line from her drone, she was able to whip the loose end around a lamppost. The large moaning motors strained as it swung around. The pull of the wire snapped off one of the drone's props, sending the main body of the machine into a fatal spin. Another gigantic explosion engulfed the riverside as the drone smashed into a pier just south of the Tower.

'AGHH!' Birrell roared his disapproval and turned in fierce anger towards Jenkins. 'He's made his last mistake. Go and fetch the old woman.'

As Jenkins left, he went to grab his key tags but stopped in his tracks as he discovered them gone.

'I don't understand…How?'

Both men looked at each other and paused, waiting for the others' response.

'FELIX!' they exclaimed together in fury.

The *Suit* himself had already taken Eddie and Mrs. Andrews out of the building and stood in a nearby street, readying an escape plan.

'Getting inside the ground should be easy enough. You should be safe there until help arrives.' He then turned in the opposite direction before calling out his last words. 'Just wait on the grass and keep looking up.'

'Where are you going?' quizzed Eddie.

'I have a few loose ends to tie up. You'll see me soon enough... Now GO!' The *Suit* slipped away.

Mrs. Andrews looked at Eddie with expectancy.

'Shall we?' she invited.

They both chased towards the cricket ground a few streets away.

The other waves of drones were now wildly scrambling in the crisp clear darkness. Their heist and whole operation were in ruins. At the same time, some of the faster members of the Patrol's fleet were closing in. After Simon and Howie's encounter, control had picked up more dark drones at one of the other transmitted locations.

'Commander, I can't do this,' Mr. Freeman conceded, recognising his pride had overtaken his intuition. 'You were right, I should have trusted you,' said Mr. Freeman.

'Please...just find my son.'

'Find him we will, Peter. You see, layered between the coordinates and locations, we found a strange additional message. There is no drone activity over the cricket ground, yet he has called for a specific type of air support there; the *Tear* drone... and he wants it unmanned'

'That's impossible, it's destroyed,' stated Mr. Freeman in dismay.

'Mr. Ackerman is reprogramming the original prototype unit. If anyone can get it to fly and land without an onboard pilot, he can. Meanwhile, you have my permission to get us back as quickly as possible.' Mr. Freeman's distracted thoughts had allowed the car to slow.

He smashed his foot down and screamed back to the D.E.E.P.

The midnight sky had become a battlefield. Enemy drones, with laser cutters, heavy drills, circular saws and other tools of demolition, flew without order or purpose. The Patrol's skilled pilots started to circle into position to intercept the dangerous enemy. In the conflict, the Patrol's jamming and disabling equipment was predictably hampered by the Legion's remote forces. Some dark drones continued their assault on the Jewel Tower which forced the sacrifice of some Patrol drones. The ancient structure had to be preserved at all costs.

'We've lost three now!' called Mr. Bird, his face twisting in agony.

Precious time ticked by and Mr. Jacobs, struggling to fly as well as lead the attack, called the Patrol's drones into retreat.

'Where is the Commander? The H.U.M.M.E.R.S. are almost here as well. We can't carry on like this!'

A great wave of enemy drones regrouped and formed above the Tower. They seemed poised to strike. With the Commander and Mr. Freeman still not back in the control room and Mr. Jacobs searching for ideas, once again, the situation looked dire. However, an unexpected event, witnessed in disbelief by every pilot, engineer and officer of the D.E.E.P. then occurred.

Dr. Walsh read out the message in the control room. 'It's open season…No need to thank me.'

'What does that mean?' puzzled Mr. Bird.

'I'm not sure, but if what I'm seeing is anything to go by I'd say things have just turned in our favour.' She gazed in amazement at the view in front of her.

Mr. Bird looked with her, as did the entire Patrol, to take in the image from the battle scene. The dark drones surrounding the Tower had started to make their move but not in the way the D.E.E.P. were fearing. Instead, they were tilting back and forth like one giant hypnotic, mid-air display. The entire cavalcade, every single sky bug gathered against the Patrol, was suddenly crippled by the same wavering motion.

At the same time, the *Suit* stood up from the table display in Birrell's office and inhaled in his customary deep way. His hands grasped the back of his head. The satisfaction of his efforts illuminated his face.

'Well, don't just watch them…TAKE THEM DOWN, BOYS!' he cried.

In his action bay, Jacobs looked around disbelievingly.

'Is everyone seeing what I'm seeing?' he called.

'That's confirmed, Patch 4. All dark drones have been…disabled.' replied Mr. Bird. 'May I suggest one last run at them, before the law arrives.'

'Agreed,' snapped Jacobs. 'I don't know which good king did this but I'm looking at the feast of Stephen!' he rallied.

During the next moments, Birrell's dark drone army capitulated to the might of the Patrol. Such was the disarray, some of the stricken machines even turned on themselves; sawing, drilling and hammering into their own bodies like sky bugs possessed. Those that remained airborne were dealt with by the superior and now fully effective powers of the Patrol.

With the burning wrecks and smashed machinery left decimated on the ground below, Jacobs backed his group away.

'We've done enough. Runners…let's run!'

In an instant, they scattered and made separately for the D.E.E.P. Disappearing behind buildings, across water and high into the darkness, they flew as the fortuitous heroes of the hour. The Patrol had vanished out of sight and away, leaving the law to arrive on a scene of unexplained carnage. A firm thud on the door marked Birrell and Jenkins' angry return. Though not unexpected, it ripped the *Suit* from his triumphant moment.

'Felix, you piece of scum, I'm going to…' Birrell's rant was interrupted by the sound of police sirens.

The *Suit* backed towards the other door behind the desk.

'You know what they say, you can't serve two masters. If you love one, you'll hate the other.' His words left Birrell's face boiling.

'Don't expect to see that beloved old lady of yours again, Felix,' warned the foiled fugitive.

The *Suit* turned. 'I'll see her before you see Felix again… whoever he was. It's surprising what people will believe…if you know what they want to hear.'

Jenkins had heard enough and with an angry yell, charged at the *Suit*. Skilfully kicking a chair across the room to block Birrell's tough guy, the *Suit* tripped his attacker and slipped away. By the time Birrell had barged over the chair and his fallen thug of an assistant, the hallway beyond the door was empty. The *Suit* had vanished.

Nearly all the drones had returned to the D.E.E.P. through the many hidden and disguised foxholes that led to the tunnel into the control room. Runners had started to exit their action bays as Peter Freeman and Commander Michael Gibson returned to a scene, mixed with emotion. Mr. Bird rose from his chair and turned towards them.

'The Tower is safe, Sir. Law enforcement is cleaning up the mess and they've just made quite a find at the other location we gave them.'

'Great work, Jonathan. What did they find?' asked the Commander.

'Well, it appears that a criminal drone network had been established in those viaducts and the police have managed to seize the majority of the operators and their equipment from their base under the railway line, west of Vauxhall Station. Quite a few big players apparently. Anyway, they have enough to go on to make our lives a little easier for a little while.'

'And what about our lost drones?' continued Gibson.

'It's interesting,' replied Mr. Bird, 'there hasn't been a report about any of our machines being recovered. Certainly not from the positions where they were lost. If I didn't know better, I'd say that...'

'...Let's just focus on what we know!' barked an agitated Mr. Freeman. 'What's happening with the *Tear*?'

'It's almost at its location, Peter,' reported Mr. Bird, 'but you can see from the display, the cricket ground seems desolate.'

The area outside the Oval was dark and the streets quiet. Standing by a high brick wall, Eddie and Mrs. Andrews worked on scaling over it. They had escaped their captors and followed the *Suit's* instructions. As he fled, Eddie had tried to remember the streets that would lead back to the old concrete tower.

'You first,' said Mrs. Andrews and backed herself against the wall.

Swiftly, Eddie took a couple steps towards her and lifted one foot into Mrs. Andrews clasped hands. In one movement, he was sent high into the air and found himself perching on top of the wall.

'Nice landing,' came the voice below. Looking down on the even tinier looking lady who had just chucked him up there, Eddie smiled and lowered his hand.

'Ready when you are,' he called.

'You'd better be!' came the firm response.

Mrs. Andrews sprang up from the path outside the ground. With more than natural agility, she joined Eddie on the wall with barely any assistance.

'There…now, let's hope Santa's disabled the security,' she joked as they slipped down the other side and headed for the field to wait in the silence for whatever next.

A faint wind ruffled Eddie's hair and then the unmistakable whisper of the rushing fan blades came from above.

'What now?' asked Eddie.

'We fly, Eddie…we fly,' came the response.

'But how…?' he said.

Mrs. Andrews had already opened the side hatch and begun fastening herself in. The memory of the shadowy limb appearing from the *Tear*, on his first visit to the F.I.Z. came shining back.

'…There were a few of us who could help test this thing. For obvious reasons, I was one.'

As she spoke, two small stirrup-shaped metal grips dropped like silky landing gear.

'You found me, Eddie, now find the strength to stay with me.'

'But it's not up to me. I need help. He said…' Eddie had believed every word the *Suit* had told him. As a result, he felt that holding on to the rails under the *Tear* would be impossible now, without his help.

As she started to close the hatch and wind up the blades to full power, Mrs. Andrews stopped Eddie and opened his mind to the *Suit's* world, as *she* knew it.

'…He uses words to help achieve an objective. The words are what we need to hear but the power is in us. It's always been in us. He only speaks to make up for our doubt.'

The hatch closed and Eddie clutched the handles as the *Tear* hovered above him. The enormous force of air alone was enough to throw him off but he gripped hard and in seconds, found himself high up over the stadium. The more he travelled up into the darkness, the brighter his view.

The London landscape was one of crisp colours and beautiful bright lights. Christmas morning had come to the capital. It could not have come in an unimaginably more thrilling way.

Straight ahead of him, the glimmer of lights lining the Thames seemed to act like the lines of navigation he had viewed when piloting the *Tear*. In the distance, Piccadilly Circus, Oxford Street and other London images radiated their festive blaze. The fires from the fallen enemy near the Tower came into view and with it, two drones either side of him. They gave off such an intensity, he felt he could let go and still be flying.

The three machines soared together with Eddie under them like a hanging ornament. Simon and Howie sat smiling, consumed in the moment; flying home with their friend and the Patrol's champion. Eddie sensed the affection and smiled towards one unit before turning and winking at the other.

The wind and every other force had no effect on Eddie as he hung easily from the *Tear*. It lowered and dropped him behind a clump of trees on the roundabout where he had first met Hackman. Mrs. Andrews, Simon and Howie sped their machines away. Eddie looked up and breathed deeply.

'See ya soon,' he whispered and leapt towards the grass-covered hatch.

It was already open. His dad stood by it, looking relaxed (though in reality, he could barely contain himself).

'Merry Christmas, Elf,' he said softly.

'Merry Christmas, dad,' Eddie replied. They collided and sunk into each other's arms.

Breaking away, Eddie reached into his pocket. 'I don't suppose I can keep this now?' he asked, holding up his dad's tiepin.

'I think you've earned it now son, don't you?' came the reply.

Moments later, the two were gliding along the curved and ever lowering tunnels back towards the Patrol. Their speed made short work of the passages and the shining light of the Patrol came quickly on them, from the end of the last of the tunnels.

'I thought she might have had betrayed us too, Eddie. When *he* got into the school, I blamed her for compromising our underground action bays,' explained his dad.

'So, you moved me to Westlake with Simon?' Eddie said.

'Things moved more quickly than they should. Your mum and I tried to protect you as long as we could but we had no choice. Only now, are we sure whose side they're on,' explained his dad.

'They were… all along,' suggested Eddie.

'He left us. Then Hazel… Mrs. Andrews to you, disappeared and things looked bleak. If he was with us, he certainly didn't act like it,' said Mr. Freeman, 'but now we know differently and now we know *you* were *his* last desperate hope of salvation before *he* was *ours*.'

Behind the double doors that led into the F.I.Z., dull murmuring could be heard; the kind of which you hear before a curtain goes up at a theatre or before a team runs out from a stadium.

Peter stepped ahead of Eddie, opened one of the doors and invited him through. A huge riot of celebration erupted as the entire Patrol welcomed Eddie home. Even the drones saluted him, high up in the hangar, with festive flashing lights and lasers. He stood, just a few feet in from the entrance, and stared around. Simon and Howie ran forward and squeezed Eddie from each side. Eddie, in turn gave them the same bashful smile to one and assuring wink to the other.

'How did you know it was us?!' his friends said together.

'Don't know what you mean,' Eddie playfully replied.

As fun as the moment was, Eddie began to heat with guilt. After all, it was the *Suit* who had inspired him, guided him and ultimately drawn out the belief in his power. A belief that found and freed Mrs. Andrews and perhaps even swayed the *Suit* into sabotaging Birrell's criminal ambitions.

As he dwelt on his feelings, a wavering picture shone up above on the main F.I.Z. display. It was from the Christmas tree in Trafalgar Square. The shot lowered and focused on the presents beneath. The Patrol's three lost drones lay there, wrecked but salvaged. A small message was tied to one of the units.

Sorry for the drastic measures. Forgive me.

The screen faded with the F.I.Z. in stunned silence.

'GET SOMEONE ON THOSE UNITS!' called Commander Gibson.

'Already on their way, Sir,' replied Dr. White.

What had happened was clear now to Gibson and he could not wait to celebrate it.

'To our fearless, nameless and indisputably loyal, friend of the D.E.E.P.' Huge cheers went up in honour of the brave and now redeemed kindred of the Patrol.

Eddie felt better for the *Suit's* recognition and turned through the waving arms and sea of jubilation, looking for Mrs. Andrews. She was standing alone to one side of the hangar, still looking up at where the image had been.

Silently, she lipped, 'Thank you, my son.'

CHAPTER 20

AN
OLD
SCORE

Ally threw herself around Eddie before he could stand up out of the car. The lingering darkness of the night had made the actual time anyone's guess. It wasn't important anyway. Being home was all that mattered. With the door closed and the world asleep, Eddie rested in his parents' arms, drained and overwhelmed. They sat for a while in the kitchen with warm drinks. Eddie knew by the silence that much would be said after he'd gone to bed. He had grown up knowing when to leave his parents alone together. For a couple who suffered a tragedy like they had, though many years ago, it was always obvious. The hours they'd spent without Eddie brought back long unspoken pain.

On his way to bed, Eddie lingered at the bottom of the stairs. Through the open door of the lounge, he noticed the family tree; it was still lit. His eyes reflected a grateful glow from its old lights, baubles and ornaments. The familiarity soaked over him like warm water. He trudged upstairs, thankful for his bed but even more so for his family. The waiting presents seemed insignificant. Perhaps they would mean more after some sleep.

Simon shared a similar moment but also discovered, for the first time, that his mum knew as much as his dad ever did. I suppose it shouldn't have surprised him. Her reaction to every form of stress was to bake which sort of explained Mr. Bird's recent increase in stoutness.

'Do you want to open a couple of presents, Simon?' Mrs. Bird asked. 'Reindeers in ripped jeans, mum, don't you think I've had enough excitement for one day?' he replied, 'plus, I'd never hear the last of it from Sarah if I started before her.'

Laughing, they all went upstairs. Within seconds of falling into bed, Simon was out.

Before he'd left the D.E.E.P, Eddie had done his best to identify the building where Mrs. Andrews had been held hostage. After the Patrol passed on the information, the decaying concrete building was searched and scoured. Pieces of furniture and miles of cables were found by investigators but Birrell's antiques and high-tech emporium was long gone. The place had been stripped and showed the hallmarks of a hasty exit. Birrell himself and his conspirers had become ghosts. Since the day the *Suit* thwarted them, many attempts had been made to trace their whereabouts. However, all trails had run cold before they had even started.

The whole of the holidays went as if stuck in one long Christmas Day afternoon. London's skies returned to their wintery grey, the Patrol was relieved to enjoy the quiet and Eddie, Howie and Simon rested; thinking of what *normal* would be like when they all started school again. Thoughts of the new year back together at Westlake dominated their minds.

The *Suit,* having regained Mr. Freeman's trust and understanding was the subject of a late-night conversation between Eddie and his dad: 'You see, Eddie; he was caught in two worlds. The actions he took weren't just to convince you of your skills but also to persuade Birrell he was as crooked as him. Taking you down was a show of loyalty to him. Money had tempted the *Suit* to turn but losing his mother and the Patrol proved too costly a price. Turns out, fortunately for us, family is the only thing he truly values. Though I think you are the first and only guest he's *shared* his hideout with!' They both laughed.

'So, do you know his *real* name, dad?' Eddie pressed.

'Patch 2 is the closest I've ever got,' replied his dad, '…for my own good. The truth is behind the deception of his identity, Eddie. Birrell, like many before him, underestimated the depth and strength of our roots. When you think about that kind of love; invisible and unspoken, it makes consight seem not so difficult to believe and its honour more valuable than the world's greatest treasures.'

'So, when did he decide…you know…to sort himself out?' Eddie quizzed. 'Who knows, son? He has always been a law unto himself. His consight, much like yours, has extended the power in a new direction. I can tell you this though…I've learned that there's no such thing as a black sheep; just family.'

Unusually, it was Eddie who stood waiting on the corner, the day school started back up. As he chatted to himself, blowing warm air against the Westlake scarf wrapped over his face, he enjoyed the muffled cackle from beneath, left over from the lingering cold in his throat. The grating and stifled sound stole his imagination and sent him undercover. Using coded language, over popping radio waves, he aired the details from the operation underway in front of him. He took pleasure from each daydreaming second, spinning his head up and down the street as the transmissions became more intense. 'Hey, hello in there!' Simon shouted, standing within reach of Eddie's misting breath. 'AGHH! You scared me,' exclaimed Eddie with a start.

'Was it these?' laughed Simon, throwing up his oversized hands that were holding what looked like at least three pairs of gloves on them.

'What you doin' with all those on?' chuckled Eddie.

'You forgotten? It's the regionals this weekend, it's going to be freezing,' Simon said, continuing his obsession with the weather, 'I've got to make sure Westlake's most valuable possession is in prime condition!'

'Yeah, alright,' Eddie tried to interject but Simon was rolling. 'Hey, it's going to be pretty tense. Eight teams, one trophy and...,'

Eddie seized his chance, '...One top scoring match-winner!' he screamed, wildly dancing in mock celebration.

'You know who's going to be there, don't you?' Simon asked. 'Oh yeah, like I'd forget,' Eddie replied. The prospect of playing against their old school kept them excitedly walking along the few remaining roads to school. They played *Crow* for the first time in a while and rattled on about everything from paybacks to penalty shoot-outs, their train of thought on a non-stop journey for winning glory.

During the week, apart from the knowing glances that he would share with Simon and Howie, Eddie also seemed to be drawing someone else's attention too. A frowning and angry looking Jonny Wilson seemed to be constantly scowling his way. After the team met with Mr. Jacobs during lunch break, a very suspicious Eddie took his chance.

'Hey Jonny, what's all the staring about? Got a guilty conscience?' challenged Eddie.

'Not really, just confused if I'm honest,' he replied.

'What are you talking about?' Eddie snapped.

'Ever since you came to Westlake, I've been doing a little job for someone. Now, I kept up my end of the bargain, did as I was told...'

'...Snooping around where you shouldn't, you mean,' Eddie sternly interrupted.

'What makes you so important?' Wilson carried on, 'photos of weird stuff in your bag, trying to remember things you've said, I've taken all kinds of orders. And now, he's said he doesn't need me anymore. He's vanished like he was never here. So who was he?'

Eddie paused for a moment. 'How would I know? In fact, how do I know you're making *him* up? You should stick to what you're good at mate. Your snooping is even worse than your tackling!'

Jonny gave up with a huff, moping off, brooding and apparently none the wiser about Eddie, the *Suit* or the D.E.E.P.

The weekend arrived along with Simon's worst fears. A convoy of players and their families arrived at St. Joseph's, the tournament venue, on a toe-numbing January morning. The team shared mixed feelings as they squeezed around a board by a large marquee where the teams and fixtures were listed.

'Brockton aren't even in our group,' moaned Bobby.

'Neither are Mildham,' added Simon.

'That's ok,' chimed Max, 'we'll get to smash 'em in the knockout stages.'

The draw was made up of two leagues of four teams. Each team played three games in their league with the top two teams, from each pool, heading to the semi-finals. Westlake took advantage of the kind draw and made short work of their opponents including beating the host team 3-0. By the end of their three games, they had yet to concede a goal and had banged in seven on their way to topping their table. Eddie and Howie already had two goals each. George, Bobby and David had also scored. In the other group, both Brockton and Mildham had beaten the other teams and scrapped out an ugly draw between them in their last game of the group stages.

'So, who have we got in the semis?' asked Joe, looking back cluelessly from the results board. Numbers were not his strong point.

'It looks like Brockton,' Bobby said, 'they scored less goals than Mildham so ended up second in their group. We were obviously first in our group.' Joe remained bemused, as well as white with cold.

Mrs. Bird tried to warm the boys; handing out her hot chocolate and a bite to go with it.

'What do you think you are doing, Joseph Mackenzie?!' scolded Mrs. Bird, catching Joe pouring his drink purposely over his boots. 'Sorry Mrs. B, it's just that I can't feel my feet,' he replied, immediately regretting his decision to try and warm his feet.

Steam billowed off his boots as he leapt about.

'Joe, we've got heat packs if your feet are cold,' shouted Max. 'Hang on, I'm trying to get those moves down!' George cracked, mimicking Joe's manic footwork.

The rest of the team made disbelieving remarks and laughed their way to the coach's huddle. Once there, Mr. Jacobs was eager to get their focus back on the football.

'Right lads, this is it!' he asserted, 'We know this lot well enough, just remember to keep pressure on them. If we give them too much room, they can hurt us. It starts with you two.' He was looking at Howie and Eddie. 'You score the goals but I want you to make their defenders' lives miserable. Chase everything and everyone, ok?'

They both nodded from behind the foggy mist surrounding their cups. 'The rest of you…this could be our last game of the tournament…how you play will dictate that. Now let's do what we're best at…and let's do it the Westlake way!'

Pumped up and encouraging shouts accompanied the back-smacking and the team blazed onto the pitch.

George was inspired and purring with confidence. He cleverly cut through three players on his way to setting up the first goal; an easy tap in for Howie.

The second half saw two more goals and total domination by Westlake. Whitey scored after a neat one-two with Max and then Bobby hit a cannon from way out. It seemed to speed up off the slick turf and left the Brockton keeper rooted. The parents were ecstatic and heaped praise on the whole team as they came off the field as one triumphant pack.

'Ok, well played lads. Let's get some air back in and see who we'll play in the final.' Mr. Jacobs was not about to let them get carried away with themselves. 'Over here please, let's stay together, let's stay focused.' He managed to sit the team away from their families so they could watch the other semi-final in his earshot.

'Come to watch some real football, have ya?' called Sam Stratton, bold as brass as he jogged past them onto the pitch.

'He's such an idiot,' said a blood-boiling Howie.

'Your words will never get through to a player like that, but your football can,' said Mr. Jacobs turning to his niece, 'leave him to his weak and empty words. If we stay together, we have something that is far, far stronger.' His message sunk deep and the team fell silent with renewed purpose.

'Now not another word. Our game is about us as much as it is about football. Champions don't need revenge or retaliation…they just need resilience.'

Mildham cheapened themselves at every opportunity. Shots that flew wide were met with painful and distressed expressions, as if the goalposts had been moved. Each player overreacted to any tiny contact or tackle, crying out like wounded fawns. It seemed that Wernham had been coaching gamesmanship and giving acting lessons rather than imparting the skills and strategies of real football. Nonetheless, their pitiful tactics saw them though.

Predictably, the Stratton twins both scored, and their arrogant boasting lingered long after the game had finished.

Jacobs did his best to calm his seething team who in turn channelled their emotions toward the final.

The other teams played off for the minor positions in the tournament. During this time and all the way up to the final, butterflies had really started to kick in. Eddie tried to settle himself by hitting some warm-up shots at Simon.

'I know I shouldn't even think it,' he said, 'but you know what would take these nerves away?'

'You're right, you shouldn't think it,' replied Simon, 'we're going to be on our own out there, win or lose. You know that's how it should be.'

'Yeah, I know,' Eddie conceded.

There was a long whistle and the captains were called. Bobby paced forward and met Ben Stratton on the halfway line. Mildham won the coin flip. 'We'll have kick-off,' demanded Stratton. 'Ok, wish each other well then, gents, and let's have a great final,' said the referee. Bobby caught Ben's eye and leant forward. 'Good luck,' he said, offering his hand out. 'You're the ones who need the luck, mate,' sneered Ben.

He slapped at Bobby's hand and turned back to yell his orders to the rest of his team. His aggression continued into the game. Ben tapped the ball to him from the kick-off and Sam charged up field with the ball seemingly on a string tied to his foot. Before any player could get close enough to put in a challenge, he'd smashed in a long-range shot. Simon was quick but could only get a finger to the shot. It was the tiniest of touches and barely enough to change the ball's direction. It clanged off the inside of one post and flew across the goal, skimming off the other. From the stodgy sidelines, the parents all gave out a moan and sighed with relief.

'LET'S GO!' shouted Simon, as Bobby picked up the loose ball and fired it out to George who was out wide on the right.

'Take 'em on, Digger!' urged the captain.

As he did, Ben Stratton instantly upended him with a savage tackle. Mildham had seen the damage George did in the semi-final and obviously had it in for him. Hobbling to his feet, he left the free kick to Charlie.

'If that's the only way they can deal with you, we've got 'em beat already,' David said, trying to keep George's confidence up. Charlie drilled the free kick at Howie's feet. She touched it one side of the defender's lunge and twisted the other way, meeting the ball behind the lumbering thug. Her curling shot just missed the target, as did the Mildham defender's late tackle on her, much to his dismay.

'Great move, Howie!' yelled Max.

'Next one's going in!' called Whitey.

The rest of the Westlake players weren't so quick or fortunate to avoid the terrible tackles and taunts. They were hacked and mocked relentlessly during the first half. It was almost impossible for them to make any sort of play without being whacked or whined at. The referee seemed keen to stay out of most of it and turned a blind eye as well as a deaf ear to the bitter scorn being dished out. Painful though it was to the players, Jacobs and the spectators suffered more, as they watched on, powerless to stop the madness.

'I've had enough of this,' Bobby said to himself, picking up the loose ball from another traumatising challenge.

He'd seen that the Mildham defence were pushed up a long way from goal and struck a clever diagonal ball over them towards his strikers. 'You're in, Eddie!' he called as Freeman's quick feet broke clear towards goal.

Every player and spectator held their breath. Eddie took control of the ball with a deft touch and ran in, one-on-one with the keeper. The fast-closing defenders were helpless to stop Eddie sliding the ball low to the left of the onrushing goalie. It was an instinctive finish and Eddie's arm was already in the air ready to celebrate, as he skipped over the diving keeper's legs. The ball nestled firmly in the corner of the net and the deadlock was broken. Eddie began to smile but a searing pain exchanged it for a hard wince. His foot had been twisted and caught between the legs of the chasing defender. His ankle cracked violently as he was scythed from behind.

The tackle was so late and blocked from sight by the keeper's sprawling frame that many onlookers including the referee did not see the horrific assault. The sound of cheers drowned out Eddie's cry and it was not until his teammates joined him that anyone knew what had happened.

'Great goal, mate! Up you get,' shouted Max, leaning down to pick Eddie up.

'AGHH! STOP! I CAN'T MOVE IT!' howled Eddie. Willis waved to the touchline, cutting short his team's celebrations.

'Stand back lads! Give him some room!' ordered Jacobs. He and Eddie's dad quickly lifted Eddie up and carried him off, making sure no one was aware of the full extent of the injury.

As if that was not enough, the shell-shocked players were caught out by the very next attack. A quick run down the right by Sam Stratton ended with a deep cross. From behind the defence, his brother had appeared from nowhere. He thumped the ball into the top corner of the goal and ran off into the arms of his brother. Sam joyfully sang his own praises. 'You ok, Eddie?' asked Howie.

Eddie nodded but Jacobs was already pulling his niece and the rest of the team away. Consight was absorbing the pain that Eddie's natural body was going through. His leg was well covered, giving the impression that he was cold as much as hurt. Mr. Freeman was right by him. He and Ally knew that Eddie's ankle was badly broken. Still, they could not convince him to leave for hospital so helped the only way they could.

From the restart, the match was really turned on its head. Somehow, from the kick-off, both Jonny, who'd come on for Eddie and Howie left the ball for each other. Ben Stratton preyed on their hesitation and ran in smashing the ball with huge force. It flew way up. Simon was on the edge of his area, way out of position and certainly not expecting the ball to be coming his way. The ball ripped as hard into the net as agony did through Simon's heart.

It was the sucker punch of a bruising first half. The long shrill sound of the half-time whistle was more like the bell of a boxing ring for Westlake. They looked dazed, in a total mess.

They were brought together and sat miserably in front of a fierce but composed coach.

'Now, you've got one more reason to give your best…' started Jacobs, surrounded by shocked and dejected faces.

'…another team might look for revenge, maybe they'd give up or even turn on each other but you have got more in you than that. One thing will get you through this… unity. What does the shirt you're wearing mean to you? Take a look at the badge on your teammate's chest, who else is going to defend it? It's all there inside of you. No tackle, shove or loudmouth can stop you if you're together in this.'

The fury from the first half left each player, replaced by eyes burning with desire and bodies fired up with passion.

'Now, say nothing, get on that field and let every move, every run and every action roar Westlake!' They were ready…

Jonny Wilson, who had endured a humiliating start, stopped in front of Eddie briefly before going on to the pitch. The thoughtful glance that they exchanged eased the tension between them. 'Get one for me!' quipped Eddie.

'I intend to,' Jonny replied and jogged to the centre spot.

'Don't forget to pass!' added Eddie.

Jonny smiled back almost in recognition though perhaps it was more in sympathy of his injured teammate. Westlake kicked off with total focus and took control. Each run, move and pass was as precise as it was slick. Try as they might,

Mildham could not get anywhere near the ball, or their opposition and their frustrations grew. Jonny and George used their heads instead of their feet and played quick one-touch football with their teammates.

'Get a tackle in! You're chasing shadows! Wake up and get'em…or you're off!' Mr. Wernham had forgotten coaching and turned to aggressive threats.

Despite their entertaining domination, Westlake were still one down and time was ticking. 'Hey Bobby, we need a goal!' called Simon 'remember last time?' The other players were out of earshot and seeing the lack of urgency, the captain took control. Firstly, he put Sam Stratton on his backside with a superbly timed sliding tackle. Getting up with the ball at his feet, he charged up the pitch, swapping passes with Whitey and Max on his way forward. Finding himself deep in the Mildham half, he looked up to see Howie bursting through a gap in their defence. 'Yes, Bobby!' she yelled.

Moore timed his pass beautifully. Howie took the ball silkily in her stride and cut away from a defender's desperate lunge. With a superb drop of the shoulder and sidestep she slipped past the tied-up legs of the last man.

'Hit it!' screamed every blue shirt on the field.

They need not have bothered, Howie had already wound up her lethal left foot. The goalkeeper's hands were left flapping in mid-air as the ball blistered in to the net.

'YYYES!!' The whole team went bananas and chased after Howie to celebrate.

'Westlake! Keep your heads… stay focused!' Mr. Jacobs demanded calm, knowing it was only 2-2.

He caught Howie's eye to share a quiet, joy-filled moment before the game restarted. Mildham looked wretched and had nothing left. It was then that Jonny saw his chance and stole the ball away from Ben Stratton, who was still trying to take on the world.

The directness of his run showed signs of a character change and he took his own team, as well as Mildham, by surprise. His goal would always be remembered for one reason. Not for being the winning tally but for scoring the Westlake way. He passed, ran and finished the move using teammates rather than selfish ambition; using the collective power of the team over his own self-interested efforts.

Having scored the vital goal, Jonny unexpectedly ran away from his joyous friends and headed for the touchline. He stopped at the side of the pitch, directly in front of Eddie. Transformed and finally seeing the light, Jonny saluted, dropped his head and gave a theatrical bow in front of everyone gathered. Eddie started to chuckle then burst into laughter as Jonny was wiped out by a crashing wave of ecstatic players. The sodden grass became covered in a blanket of bodies, all revelling in the victory.

From behind the overgrowth and hedgerows of the adjoining field, two ordinarily dressed country ramblers were standing, taking in the scene. 'Such a strange thing; football. Don't you think?' the *Suit* said.

'Everyone needs a platform for their passion, Matthew. You of all people should know that,' replied the Commander.

Sitting high on Simon and Howie's shoulders, throwing the cup above his head, Eddie came to realise the undeniable truth. No one can achieve anything good, by themselves.

For those I've visited or taught in schools, you have been my inspiration. Each classroom character has, in some way, made this happen!

Thank you, all of you.

To review the book or learn more about G. B. Strong and his work –

elfbooksltd.com

For school visits and an experience from the future –

info@elfbooksltd.com

Special thanks –

To Rich and Lyds for the late nights you sacrificed.
To Mark and Laura for always being prepared.
                    ...And to Megan, but not as much as tomorrow.